ARROW'S HELL

D0661124

ALSO BY CHANTAL FERNANDO

Dragon's Lair

ARROW'S HELL

CHANTAL FERNANDO

4181 2799

East Baton Rouge Parish Library
Baton Rouge, Louisiana

G

GALLERY BOOKS

New York   London   Toronto   Sydney   New Delhi

Gallery Books
A Division of Simon & Schuster, Inc.
1230 Avenue of the Americas
New York, NY 10020

This book is a work of fiction. Any references to historical events, real people, or real places are used fictitiously. Other names, characters, places, and events are products of the author's imagination, and any resemblance to actual events or places or persons, living or dead, is entirely coincidental.

Copyright © 2015 by Chantal Fernando

All rights reserved, including the right to reproduce this book or portions thereof in any form whatsoever. For information address Gallery Books Subsidiary Rights Department, 1230 Avenue of the Americas, New York, NY 10020

First Gallery Books trade paperback edition June 2015

GALLERY BOOKS and colophon are registered trademarks of
Simon & Schuster, Inc.

For information about special discounts for bulk purchases, please contact Simon & Schuster Special Sales at 1-866-506-1949 or business@simonandschuster.com.

The Simon & Schuster Speakers Bureau can bring authors to your live event. For more information or to book an event, contact the Simon & Schuster Speakers Bureau at 1-866-248-3049 or visit our website at www.simonspeakers.com.

Manufactured in the United States of America

10 9 8 7 6 5 4 3 2 1

Library of Congress Cataloging-in-Publication Data

Fernando, Chantal.
  Arrow's hell / Chantal Fernando. — First Gallery Books trade paperback edition.
  pages ; cm. — (Wind Dragons Motorcycle Club ; 2)
  1. Motorcycle clubs—Fiction. 2. Motorcycle gangs—Fiction. 3. Brothers and sisters—Fiction. I. Title.
  PR9619.4.F465A89 2015
  823'.92—dc23
                  2014046244

ISBN 978-1-5011-0619-4
ISBN 978-1-5011-0622-4 (ebook)

To you.
The one who helped save me.
You will find love again, for you may hate deep,
but you love even deeper.
No matter how much you try to deny it.
You're beautiful, inside and out.

"Your joy can fill you only as deeply as your sorrow has carved you."

—*Kahlil Gibran*

PROLOGUE

ARROW

I STARE down into my Scotch, twirling the amber liquid around in the glass. The clubhouse moves around me, people talking, laughing, and carrying on, but I feel like I'm frozen. Like the world is moving around me, but I'm stuck in place. I know I'm held back by my own demons, my own guilt, but I don't deserve any redemption. My neck strains as I tilt my head back, memories playing in my mind like an old movie.

Mary gathers her clothes and dresses slowly.

I take in her every move.

Everything about her is gentle.

Beautiful.

What the hell am I doing? Why do I keep her at a distance?

Faye is right—Mary is one of a kind and I shouldn't be fucking around on her. Even if she knows about it. Mary has never once tried to change me. She's taken me as I am—my many faults and all.

How many women would do the same?

"Have a safe run, Arrow," she says softly, lifting her dark hair off her back and tying it up.

"Come here," I demand softly.

She instantly complies.

She's good like that, always wanting to make me happy, but at the same time—she's not weak. She's intelligent, sharp, and knows what she wants in life.

I'm just lucky enough to be one of those things.

I want to tell her that I only want to be with her and that I'm going to do right by her.

I want to tell her I want her as my old lady.

But I don't.

"We need to talk when I get back," I say, needing time to gather the right words.

She nibbles on her bottom lip. "Is everything okay?"

"It will be," I tell her, kissing her heart-shaped lips.

It will be okay the moment I tell her how much I love her.

My eyes snap open, and I shake my head, laughing without humor.

I never did tell her that I loved her.

She was dead because of me, and she died thinking . . . What would she have been thinking? That I didn't care for her? That I should have been there to protect her? To save her? Maybe before her life faded away she wished that she'd never met me, never wasted her time on me.

She might have been right.

I lift the glass to my lips and drink, the warm liquid sliding down my throat with ease. Since getting out of prison, I've been spending some of my time at local strip clubs, and I know everyone thinks I am getting laid, but I'm not. I let them think that. The truth is, I go there to torture myself. I drink; I watch; I keep my mind busy. What I didn't do was fuck anyone. I haven't been with anyone since Mary. It has been years—five, to be exact. She doesn't get to move on and live her life, so why should I? I like the fact that she is the last woman I was with. What I couldn't give to her in life I am giving her in death.

Rake walks in, a blond woman by his side. I know exactly who she is, because Rake's been bragging about her ever since the day I fuckin' met him. I've seen a picture of her, but it seems to have not done her any justice.

Anna.

Just the temptation I don't need.

Her eyes dart to me as she offers me a small smile.

I don't return it.

I peruse her body slowly, tempting myself with something I could never have.

When I feel myself harden, I know I need to get the fuck out of here. Standing up, I down the rest of my drink and place it on the table. Rake is introducing Anna to everyone, and I need to leave before it's my turn, but my feet don't seem to want to move.

What is it about this woman? I can't remember the last time I studied one so carefully. To me, they are all the same, some just come in better packaging. Maybe it is all the things Rake has told me about her over the years? I almost feel as if I know her. She's even more fuckin' beautiful up close and personal. I hear the stories about her. Everything from their childhood antics to what she's been studying in school. Rake thinks the world of her, and either he's blinded by her, or the woman truly has a heart of gold. She's apparently intelligent and sweet, but she also has a wild streak in her. And she has a fiery, tough side, from what I hear. An interesting mix for a man like me. Mary was all sweetness, but that didn't exactly work in her favor—she was just too good for me. With my lifestyle, I need a woman who can handle everything that comes with it, the good, the bad, and, most important, the ugly.

What the fuck was I thinking?

I don't need a woman right now. At least not anything long-term. I need a drink and some willing pussy, not an old lady. Anna is completely off-fuckin'-limits. I got the last woman I cared for killed. I'm not going to put anyone in that position again. Being with me isn't safe, and I don't deserve some poor woman caring about me anyway. Mary got death, but I got a sentence. Not just to prison, but to be alone. That's my penance.

The smell of a fresh vanilla scent pulls me from my thoughts. Something that doesn't help with my boner. Great, I was standing here, fuckin' daydreaming like a kid, and didn't make a getaway.

"Arrow, this is Anna," Rake says, smiling proudly. "Anna, meet Arrow."

"Nice to meet you, Arrow," she says, her plump lips curving around each word.

I nod my head. "You too."

Fuck, she's beautiful.

I look to Rake and slap him on the shoulder. "I'm going out. I'll see you later, brother."

I have no right to be attracted to Rake's sister.

So what if the moment I saw her, the world around me unfroze?

I don't deserve sweetness like that.

Rake frowns. "You can't stay a bit?" He steps closer to me so only I can hear. "I want Anna to feel welcome."

He doesn't want her to run scared, I can see it in his eyes. He's afraid she won't want anything to do with us, him, or this lifestyle.

A valid concern.

I lick my bottom lip, not wanting to hurt Rake but needing to get away right now.

He saves me. "Don't worry, you go on ahead."

"Thanks, brother," I tell him, flashing him a grateful look. I can't help myself—my eyes dart to the woman before me, to see her already watching me, a thoughtful expression on her face.

Yeah, that's not good.

"See you around, Anna," I manage to get out.

She arches a delicate brow. "You can count on it."

I leave the clubhouse feeling like something just changed, even though I know it is impossible.

Mary is six feet under, where I should be.

It should have been me. I lead this life. She was just a veterinarian who hooked up with the wrong man. A man who couldn't offer her anything other than a good fuck. Not even monogamy.

I don't need to drag anyone else down with me; what I need to do is to stay away from Anna, the first woman who's stirred any interest in me in a long time.

I get on my bike and ride away, pushing thoughts of a perky little blonde out of my head.

ONE

ANNA

D O you have any plans now?" Damien asks as we walk out of the lecture.

I turn to him. "My ride will be here soon. I'm just going home. I have a lot to do."

"Oh, okay. How about this weekend?"

Damien's a nice guy, but I don't feel anything when I look at him. He is just a friend; not even that, more of an acquaintance.

"I'm going out with my best friend, Lana, this weekend," I reply, forcing a smile. I don't want to lead him on, but I don't want to hurt him either. I am horrible in these kinds of situations.

"Maybe I could take you—"

I roll my eyes as I hear the rumble of a motorcycle, stopping Damien midsentence. Sliding my phone into my bag for safekeeping, I say, "Gotta go, Damien. I'll see you tomorrow, okay?"

"'Bye, Anna."

Right on time—like clockwork.

I glance around the courtyard, then walk toward the parking

lot. You would think at my age I could catch a bus home to my apartment without any drama, but that isn't the case. I don't have a car, but I'm saving up for one. However, my brother makes sure I have a lift home after class, especially if I finish in the late afternoon. I'm still not sure how I feel about it. It does feel good to have someone, my brother in particular, looking out for me, but at the same time, after doing my own thing for so long, I feel a little claustrophobic.

My brother is one of my favorite people in the world, and after not having seen him for some time, I am happy to be getting to know him again. I just moved back to the city, and am finding the move easier than I had anticipated, mainly because my best friend, Lana, is here. We'd stayed in touch ever since I moved away, so I'm psyched to be so close to her now. My brother has changed, but I know that he still loves and cares about me. I'm the only family he has, after all. His overprotectiveness, however, needs to change. I know he means well and is trying to make up for lost time, but the constant escorts are beginning to drive me batshit crazy. He keeps an eye on my every move and sometimes tries to dictate them. I feel like I'm in a damn prison. I love my brother and I'm trying to make this work for the both of us, but we're both still on shaky ground, not 100 percent comfortable with each other yet. We're feeling each other out, seeing how we've both changed and how we've stayed the same.

I don't miss the curious stares from the other students on campus, but I ignore them. I can just imagine how it looks, my getting picked up every day by a different man on a motorcycle, each one of them sporting a Wind Dragons Motorcycle Club cut. Luckily for me, I'm not a young, insecure girl anymore and there's only a handful of people in the world whose opinion I actually care about. Likely they think I'm a biker groupie, or something along those lines. In reality, I'm just a twenty-five-year-old PhD student and a girl who happens to be the younger sister of a Wind Dragons MC member. If people want to judge me, that's their prerogative, and I couldn't care less.

I'm proud of my brother. He is who he is. He means well and I know he loves me. Yes, he's a biker, belonging to a motorcycle club that is well-known in these parts, but he's also a good man.

Adam's always been a good man.

He also happens to be a huge pain in my ass, a total man-whore, and overprotective to the point of stupidity. Ever since I was a little girl, he'd taken his role of big brother very seriously. It probably had to do with the fact that we didn't know who our father was, and our mother was . . . absent. That was putting it nicely—in fact, our mother was a junkie who left us to fend for ourselves ever since I could remember.

My brother also made it his business to scare off any potential dates, and that hasn't changed. If anything, it's gotten worse. It seems when most men around here find out who my brother is, they decide I'm not worth the ass kicking they'll get—but in a way it's almost like a screening test. I don't want a man who's a pussy and afraid of my brother. I want a strong man who'll tell my brother to fuck off and smile while he's doing it. The thought makes me grin to myself.

I wonder who my babysitter will be today.

Seeing the sexy beard and the wide shoulders encased in tight black fabric, I smile broadly, pleased with my escort for today. I walk straight up to his idling bike, sashaying my hips with each step.

"Good afternoon, Arrow," I say, grinning cheekily.

He narrows his eyes on me. "You gonna give me trouble today, Anna?"

Probably.

But only because he needs it. The man hardly smiles, so I find myself being more playful around him than I am around anyone else, just to get a reaction out of him.

"Anna?" he repeats, staring at me weirdly when I don't reply, continuing to study him, lost in my own thoughts.

Fuck, but I love the way he says my name. Arrow must have a good ten years on me, but he doesn't look it. Not to me. He has a better body than most of the men my age and a beard that looks badass on him.

I do love a good beard.

You can tell that under the beard is a strong, square jaw. I wonder if he has a dimple in his chin.

He also has soulful brown eyes that you just know have seen the world at its worst, but he's still survived. He has faint crinkles on either side of his eyes, letting me know he once used to laugh a lot. His mouth is full, firm, and entirely lickable.

"I have no idea what you're talking about," I tell him with a shrug. I push my blond hair off my face and flash him an innocent look. I have the same green eyes as my brother, and while his incite lust from the opposite sex, mine don't seem to be doing the same. Arrow's face turns grumpier, if that's even possible. What the hell is he so moody about all the time? Yes, I heard he did time in jail, but most bikers do at some point, don't they? At least the ones I've heard of. Okay, I guess I shouldn't stereotype like that. But Arrow did do time, although I don't know what for. I overheard my brother talking with Tracker, another member of the MC. I've been around these bikers for a month or so now, and out of all of them, Arrow is the one who keeps both his distance *and* his guard up.

He's also the one I can't stop thinking about.

Quite a conundrum.

Well, for me anyway.

Have you ever seen someone for the first time and just *wanted* them? Something about them attracts you, like a moth to a flame, without rhyme or reason. Every time I look at Arrow I feel that pull. That want, that need. There is something about him, something that draws me to him. Sure, he is gruff and rough around the edges. He is also temperamental, broody, and usually pretty damn grumpy. He is a man of few words—the strong, silent type. The more time he is forced to spend as my babysitter, the more I've gotten him to open up. Slowly, little by little, he's started speaking to me. It is progress, but still, I know I am stupid to hope for anything more. Sure, my heart races whenever he is near, but I try to ignore that little factor as best as I can. It doesn't change anything. Arrow is my guilty pleasure, something I know I shouldn't want but want anyway. The thing is, I've seen little glimpses of him that make me believe he is more than he shows the world. I've seen him playing with Clover, the MC president's daughter, and sneaking her strawberry candy. I've seen him tickling her, her loud giggles echoing throughout the room. I then overheard him telling her that if any boy messes with her, to let him know and he would take care of it because no one hurts the princess.

She's five.

No one can tell me the man doesn't have a heart.

"Get on the bike and hold on," he demands, turning away

from me. It frustrates me that he never looks at me for longer than he has to. Is he not attracted to me at all? I'm not vain, but I know that I'm not completely unfortunate in the looks department. Adam has even said I'm too beautiful for my own good, but as my brother, I guess he's a little biased.

Maybe Arrow sees me as nothing more than Adam's baby sister. But that doesn't explain why he always seems so eager to leave my presence. I like to think I'm easy to be around, and sometimes even a little fun.

"Where are we going?" I ask as he hands me my helmet.

"Rake wants to see you at the clubhouse," he replies distract-edly.

"Then why didn't he pick me up himself?" I ask. Not that I'm complaining, since I secretly covet being around Arrow, but still.

"I was closer to campus, so it just made more sense. Now are you getting on the bike or are we gonna sit around while all these stuck-up assholes stare at us?"

I look around.

Yeah, people are still staring. If he didn't want the attention, maybe he shouldn't have worn his cut today. Who am I kidding? People would stare either way. Arrow is imposing. It is in his build, the breadth of his shoulders, the way he carries himself. The sharpness of his gaze. He just commands attention around him, and there is nothing he can do about it. He couldn't fade into the background if he tried. I slide onto the back of his bike. Wrapping my arms around his waist, I grip the leather in my hands and lean into him. He smells like leather and . . . straw-berry candy? I want to ask, but before I can he starts the engine and pulls out of the lot. I hold tight, enjoying both the ride and the feel of my body pressed against his.

I'd never been on a motorcycle until I moved back here. It was a new experience, and one I found that I loved. Nothing felt more freeing, and I found myself wanting to get my own motorcycle license. If being on the back feels this way, I can only imagine how good it feels to be in front, in control of the bike.

I wonder what my brother would think about that idea.

Adam and I didn't have the best childhood growing up. Neither of us talks about it much, to each other or to anyone else—at least that's how it used to be before I left. After I turned eighteen, I moved to the other side of the country for college. That was the year Adam—or should I say Rake—joined the Wind Dragons MC. We kept in touch here and there, messages, phone calls on birthdays and holidays, but for the most part we grew apart. He was busy, I was busy, and we were too far away to be of any real use to each other. I know he's proud of me. He used to tell me every time we spoke on the phone. He was happy I was making something of myself—starting from scratch to become someone statistics prove I shouldn't be. I also know he wants the best for me, he always has, but it almost feels like he doesn't know how to act around me anymore, how to be himself. He's changed over the years, I guess being in a motorcycle club will do that, but underneath he's still my Adam. A mix of protective, sweet, and goofy and usually found with a grin on his face or a woman on his arm.

That definitely hasn't changed. My brother has always been, and will always be, a ladies' man. However, he's gotten even more protective of me than he was before I left the city, which makes no sense, because I'm not a girl anymore, I'm a grown woman. I'm his baby sister, by a year, but he's acting like I'm seventeen and trying to keep tabs on my every move. It was cute at first—but now it's getting damn annoying and he and I are in need of a good chat. I can't imagine he's any better at compromising than he was growing up, but maybe I can use my puppy-dog eyes to let him loosen the reins a little. The truth of the matter is I love being around Rake and his MC. I just don't like being controlled. I want to be there on my terms, not his. I want to be given choices and know that I'm being heard. Being around a group full of alpha males isn't easy.

I sigh against Arrow's back, enjoying the sensation of being pressed up against a man I should be glad wouldn't give me the time of day. He's dangerous, I know it and so would anyone who saw him. It is more than his physical appearance. You can almost feel the menace radiating from him, the raw power. It also doesn't take a genius to see that he has an extralarge chip on his shoulder, weighing down on his muscular build. My breasts rub against his back and I feel him tense, so I move away slightly, my fingers gripping him with more pressure than before.

The ride is quick, and Arrow's bike soon skids to a stop. I climb off, handing him back his helmet.

"Thanks, Arrow," I tell him quietly.

He grunts in response and takes the helmet from my hands, but doesn't bother to look me in the eyes.

"How's your day been?" I ask, tilting my head to the side and studying him as he gets off his bike.

He glances up at me, finally, and rubs the back of his neck. "It was okay. You gonna ask about the fuckin' weather next?"

"If I have to," I mutter, rolling my eyes. "In case you were wondering, my day was kind of awesome."

He grins then, his eyes softening on me slightly. "Good to hear, Anna, good to hear. Now get your ass inside."

He is trying to get rid of me. How predictable.

"Arrow," I say, taking advantage of his attention. "Do you think Rake will tone down the whole escort thing?"

He licks his top lip, then follows through with his teeth. I stare at his mouth, mesmerized by the action.

He clears his throat. "Don't look at me like that, Anna."

"Like what?" I ask, still staring.

"Anna," he snaps. I lift my gaze, my cheeks heating. "Go and ask Rake, but I don't think so. He just wants you safe. Bad shit has happened before, and he's going to make sure that nothing bad touches you. And I agree with him. Now get your ass inside before he calls me asking where the hell you are."

"Okay," I reply, puffing out a breath.

He steps to me and touches my cheek in an almost-there caress. Okay, this is new. He's never shown this type of affection to me before.

Our eyes lock.

I swallow hard.

He pulls away and turns his back to me. Looks like I've been dismissed.

"Nice chatting with you as always," I call out as I walk into the clubhouse. The scene before me is a familiar one. Rake is sitting there with a woman on his lap, blissfully unaware of the rest of the world. Faye, the president's wife and queen bee of the clubhouse, is talking with Tracker, another MC member and a friend of mine. Sin, the club president, is nowhere to be seen. Faye turns when she notices me, her auburn hair framing her pretty face. I nod my head at her, giving her the respect she's due as Sin's old lady.

I know Faye is a badass chick, I've heard all the stories about her. I tend to stay out of her way—we don't really interact, even though she's close with Rake, Tracker, and the rest of the guys. I think in any other situation, we'd probably really get along well. I've heard nothing but good things about her, but I still have no plans to befriend her anytime soon. I'll never admit this to anyone, but I envy her. She has all the men wrapped around her finger, but more important, they treat her like an equal. No one tells her what to do or orders her around. They listen to her and respect her. And it pisses me off that while I'm treated like a child, she can do as she pleases.

I know the men keep a close eye on me only because of Rake's commands, and I hope that will ease up when my brother realizes that I'm a woman who can take care of herself. I think he needs to figure out that he never let me down when we were younger, and he has nothing to make up for. He's a great brother, even though he can be a tad excessive when it comes to me. I know it's because of how much he cares about me, but I don't think he knows what to do about it. Or me.

Tracker walks over to me when he sees me, a smile playing on his lips, and wraps an arm around my shoulders. "Anna Bell!"

"Don't call me that," I reply, raising an eyebrow at him. Tracker is friendly, easy to get along with, drop-dead gorgeous, and completely fuckable. Shoulder-length blond hair frames a handsome face with bright blue eyes and full lips. His body is impressive, lithe and toned, and covered in tattoos. Why he's with Allie, I have no idea. I think it's one of those things—like how good girls always finish last, because the bitch definitely won when she got her paws on a man like Tracker. The first time I came to the clubhouse, he approached me and made a comment about breaking in the fresh meat. I replied with a joke about how I was harder to get than Rake, and we both found that amusing. We've kind of become friends since then. Tracker is very easy to be around, and he's a good listener. I just bonded with him from the very start.

"It's a very cute name, for a cute lady," he says, squeezing my cheeks, shaking my head left and right.

"Fuck off," I tell him with a smile, slapping away his hands.

"How was class?" he asks, pulling on a lock of my blond hair. Could he be more annoying? He treats me like the sister he never had yet didn't want, so I make sure to return the favor.

"It was okay," I reply. "Still thinking about quitting and becoming a club whore though. It seems to hold a certain appeal."

He laughs, a deep rumble. "Don't let Rake even hear you joke about that."

"What would he do? Treat me like a kid and have people escort me everywhere?" I ask, voice full of sarcasm.

"And that," he says, smirking, "is the reason you will never be a club whore."

"What?" I ask, confused.

He chuckles. "Your sharp tongue. We like the club women to be pliable and—"

"Stupid? Easy? Flexible?" I offer, waggling my eyebrows sleazily.

He laughs harder. "I was going to say accessible."

My lip twitches and I shake my head. "I can't believe we're having this conversation right now."

"It's a normal conversation for me," he adds.

"I'll bet."

"Where's that sidekick of yours?"

I narrow my eyes on him and purse my lips. "Why do you want to know?"

I saw the way my best friend, Lana, stared at Tracker when she met him. Like he was fucking Superman or something. I caught Tracker studying her too, but didn't think much of it until now.

I know that Lana would never be someone's side chick, but Tracker has this way about him . . . I hope he just leaves her alone. Lana is smart, bookish, and doesn't have much experience with men. If Tracker shows interest in her, that's not a good thing. Allie is his woman and is so crazy—legit crazy, not just crazy in love—she'd probably claw Lana's eyes out. I don't miss the looks she gives me when I talk to Tracker, and I'm just a friend.

Of course, Allie might have to watch her back. Lana can be quiet and unassuming most of the time, but she has a serious temper on her. Trust me, I've seen it firsthand. It hardly ever comes out, but when it does, everyone is in trouble.

He shrugs like it doesn't matter to him either way. "Just making conversation. Put those claws away, Anna Bell."

Rake walks over to me like he's only just realized I've been standing here. Which he probably did.

"Hey, sis," he says as he rubs his scruffy jaw. Blond hair and green eyes the same shade as mine, my brother has an eyebrow piercing and lip ring that suit him. He's good-looking and knows it.

Yes—he's one of *those* men. He uses his good genes to his advantage and no woman is safe in his presence. I wonder when he'll settle down, and the type of woman it would take to make him do it. I'm thinking she would have to be pretty freaking phenomenal, because Rake seems to like a lot of variety and never stays with one woman long enough for me to even get to know her. Okay, that's not exactly true. Rake started acting this way only after he broke up with Bailey in high school. She was the only woman I've ever seen Rake pay any real interest in. I wonder what Bailey's up to these days.

"Hey. Why did you want me to come here?" I ask him, getting straight to the point.

He looks confused. "I thought we could hang out; I haven't seen you in a couple of days."

I blink slowly.

"Okay. Will she be joining us?" I ask, pointing to the woman who is now standing behind him wearing a pouty expression.

"Fuck, no," he replies, turning back and telling his tag-along something.

"Cut him some slack," Tracker tells me softly so no one else can hear.

My mouth drops open. "But . . . but . . ."

He grins. "I know, but he's trying."

I know he's trying; I do. He isn't used to me in his space, I'm not used to being in his space, but I'm getting there. It is a lot to take on, being thrown headfirst into the MC lifestyle. I am adapting though, and know it means a lot to Rake that I try to fit in here.

When I see Rake walk past Faye and kiss her on the top of her head, my throat burns. How can he be so loving and affectionate with her but not his own sister?

I pretend his casual affection with her doesn't hurt.

Rake says something to Faye, and she throws back her head and laughs. "What have you done now?"

Rake grins boyishly. "Nothing . . . yet. Just need some legal advice on something. Make some time for me, woman."

Faye looks amused. "Come see me tomorrow."

My brother nods and says something to her in a low tone that I can no longer hear.

"He doesn't wanna fuck things up with you, so he's being careful," Tracker muses from beside me.

Thank you, Dr. Phil.

I sigh and lean my head on Tracker's arm. "I know he cares about me. I just wish he wasn't so . . ."

"Slutty?" Tracker adds with a wolfish grin.

I laugh, shaking my head. "No. It's almost like he's scared to be himself around me."

"I think he just wants you to be proud of him and not scare you off with his bikerish ways."

"I am proud of him," I say, cringing when he slaps the woman's ass as she leaves. "Okay, he can be a pig sometimes."

Tracker's loud laugh gets us looks from everyone in the room.

"What's so funny?" Rake asks as he walks over and moves me away from Tracker. He sends Tracker a look that says *She's my sister, asshole.*

I roll my eyes. Rake has the protective big-brother thing down pat, that's for sure. He's always looking out for me, always has.

Tracker raises his hands, proclaiming his innocence. "We're just friends, man, you know I wouldn't go there."

"And why not?" I ask him in a sweet tone. "Is there something wrong with me?"

I put my hand on my hip, cocking it to the side, and give him a look that dares him to say anything other than how I'm one of the most beautiful women he's ever seen. I try and keep my face serious, not wanting to break out in the smile that's threatening my lips.

Tracker tilts his head to the side, taking me in from top to bottom. "You kind of look like Rake if you squint your eyes, so yeah, no, thanks."

He doesn't expect the punch in the gut. "Ow! You're strong for someone so little."

Rake grunts. "Come on, Anna, stop bullying my brothers."

Tracker laughs and rubs his rock-hard stomach. Like that even hurt him.

Arrow chooses that moment to walk in, and as always, he garners my full attention. I watch as he storms into the kitchen and comes out with a bottle of Scotch in one hand, a cigarette in the other.

He plops down on the couch and starts to drink straight from the bottle.

He doesn't look up, or pay attention to anyone around him, until Faye walks over and starts to talk to him in a hushed tone. I follow behind Rake as he leads me toward a long hall, forcing myself not to look back at Arrow. We stop at a door, and he grins boyishly at me as he opens it.

"This is your room. So, you know, you always have somewhere to stay, no matter what," he says, gesturing for me to enter. The room is bare except for a stunning black leather bed.

"It's new," he explains as I turn to stare at him.

"I have my own place," I tell him, feeling confused. Growing up, we didn't really have a house. We moved around and stayed wherever we could, couch surfing or living with our mother's latest boyfriend. We didn't have a stable life, or many other things that most people took for granted. We didn't come first to our mother; the drugs did. Maybe that's why he wants me to feel as though I have a home here? That no matter what, I'll always have a place to go? A place where I will be welcome?

My heart warms at the sentiment, but it isn't necessary. I am no longer that scared little girl; I am now a woman who knows how to take care of herself.

"I know you do, but you also have a place here. With me. You will never have to worry again."

Looks like I was right.

"Rake—"

"You don't have to call me that," he says, not for the first time.

"I know, but it's weird when I'm the only one calling you Adam and no one knows who the hell I'm talking about. Although I still call you Adam in my head," I try and explain.

His laugh makes me smile. I like seeing him laugh. "It's weird having my baby sister calling me Rake."

I raise an eyebrow. "So you're nicknamed after a man who lives in an immoral way and sleeps around a lot."

I used the dictionary for that one. It says a rake is another name for a womanizer, or a libertine.

The flush that works up his neck lets me know he isn't exactly pleased to be having this conversation with me. "Maybe I just like to . . ."

He searches fruitlessly for another reason to be called Rake.

". . . get rid of leaves?" I suggest in a dry tone.

"You always were a smart-ass," he says with good nature. "Fine, I like women. Sue me. I'm the perfect example of a man you shouldn't date. Learn from it."

"Surely there are some good men around this clubhouse . . . ?" I say casually, pretending to look around.

Like Arrow.

That's what I really mean.

Rake's laughter isn't what I was expecting in response. "No one will go near you, Anna. They know you're off-limits."

"How would they know that?" I ask him suspiciously, my hackles rising.

"Because I told them," he replies, unable to keep the smugness out of his tone.

My mouth drops open. "Why would you do that?"

"Because you're my sister," he says, crossing his arms over his chest.

"Yes, but I'm not asexual," I reply dryly, walking farther into the room and sitting on my new bed.

"To me you are," I hear him mutter. "Look, Anna, now that you're back here . . . I want to be here for you, like I haven't always been in the past."

Ahh, the infamous Jacob incident.

"That wasn't your fault," I say for the hundredth time.

He ignores me.

"Do you wanna get a drink?" he asks, the conversation clearly over. "You can tell me how your week has been."

"Sure, I could use a drink."

I wonder if Arrow will share his bottle.

TWO

I SIT at the clubhouse bar sipping on my screwdriver, sandwiched between Rake and Tracker.

"Where's Allie?" I ask the man on my right.

Not that I like her, I ask just to make conversation.

Tracker's reply is a non-amused grunt.

I grin into my drink. "Trouble in paradise?"

"Anna Bell, you are too young to understand the concept of—"

"I'm the same age as you," I cut in in a bored tone.

We both turn to look at each other. "You're twenty-five? You look nineteen."

"I'm choosing to take that as a compliment," I mutter, lifting the glass and tipping its contents into my mouth.

"As you should," he replies.

I chew on an ice cube and say, "Your woman doesn't like me very much."

"She doesn't like anyone."

I don't miss the way he downs his Scotch, drinking every drop in his glass.

"Except you," I add with a grin.

He smirks. "Who doesn't like me?"

I go to raise my hand, but he grabs my wrist and holds it down playfully. "Bully."

"How's school, Anna?" Rake asks, pulling my attention to him. His knuckles are bruised and red, and I can't help but wonder what exactly he's been up to.

Maybe I don't want to know.

"Great, actually. I ran into a friend of yours . . . Andrea?"

His brows furrow in confusion. "Who's that?"

Seriously? How many women does he sleep with?

"Model-looking redhead. She has a tattoo on her right boob. A cherry, I believe," I explain, ignoring Tracker's amused chuckle.

My brother's eyes widen with realization. "Oh, Andrea."

"Yes, *Andrea.*"

"What did she tell you?" he asks as he pours himself another drink.

I shrug. "Nothing much, just how great a lover you are and how you have a kinky side because you like to—"

He puts his hand over my mouth, cringing. "That bitch told you that?"

"That and more," I reply, my voice muffled under his hand. I cringe at the details she thought to share with me. How Rake likes to tie women up, their hands bound behind their back as he takes them from behind. Why? Just why would I want to know these things? I ended up walking away because she wouldn't shut the hell up. It was that or punch her in the face. The angel on my shoulder won, and I retreated to pretend I'd never heard anything about my big brother's sex life.

"Bitch goes to college?" Tracker asks, laughing hard now. He slams his palm down on the countertop, his wide shoulders shaking.

Rake pulls his hand away, so I turn to him. "No, she was picking up her stepson."

Silence, then more laughter.

Assholes.

Arrow walks by the bar, and my attention immediately turns to him. He doesn't look up as he slams down his half-finished bottle, licking a last drop from his lips.

"Arrow, you good?" Tracker asks, studying him.

He lifts his face.

Short brown hair, just long enough to run my fingers through.

Light brown eyes framed in thick dark lashes. Firm, perfectly kissable lips, and that beard that I have fantasies about tugging on.

"I'm good. You wanna head to Toxic?" he asks, eyes darting to me for a second before returning to Rake.

"I'm with my sister," Rake replies, in an *Are you fucking serious?* tone.

Arrow looks directly at me. "I'm sure Anna won't mind."

Toxic is a popular strip club, and from what I'd heard, a place Arrow likes to frequent on occasion. He is trying to unnerve me, to make me squirm and shy away. He is challenging me.

I shrug. "Who doesn't like boobs?"

Was that a twitch of his lip I saw? I feel proud at making this stoic man almost smile.

Almost.

Rake turns to me with a *Why me?* look on his face he wears a lot since I've come home. I shrug at him. "What's the real difference between a strip club and here?"

Tracker starts laughing, and even Arrow looks amused.

Rake, however, doesn't. "I'm not going to a fucking strip club with my baby sister."

I roll my eyes. "Then drop me home on the way; I have to study tonight anyway."

He sighs and plays with his lip ring with his teeth. "Why don't we hang out here a bit first? Or do you want to go out for dinner?"

I smile gently—he really is trying. "Okay, dinner sounds good."

Tracker nods his head and gives me a look of approval. I really don't get these men. They're always giving one another shit, but at the same time always looking out for one another. I grew up around men who looked like them—rough, covered with tattoos and leather. But the men my mom dated didn't *act* like them. Growing up without a father was hard. It sucked. Having a shit mom didn't help, of course, but I always wondered what my life would be like if I'd had a good dad and not the men my mom brought home to try and fill her void. The sad truth is, besides Rake, I haven't known many good men in my life. Maybe that's why every relationship I've ever had has failed miserably.

The Wind Dragons MC members *are* good men. I could tell that as soon as I met them, by the way they welcomed me into the family just because I was Rake's sister. There were no questions asked—Rake was a brother, and by extension I was their family too. That was the moment I understood why Rake had turned to an MC lifestyle—it offered him the family we never really had growing up. I know the Wind Dragons aren't saints by any means. They're badass men, and I can only imagine the shit they get into, but they don't mix me up in it and I get to come here and enjoy the perks of sexy men and good food. I simply feel safe here. I can't explain it, I just do. Home is wherever Rake is. I missed him while I was away, some days wishing I'd never left. I know they probably do illegal shit, but to me they've been nothing but amazing. As long as I don't see any women or children being hurt, I don't really care what they get up to. I know that my brother wouldn't get involved in anything too bad; he has a heart of gold.

I turn my head to see Arrow watching me over the rim of his glass. Nice to see he decided to use one. "Who was the *boy* talking to you today after class?"

I narrow my eyes. I feel my brother's gaze on me, now curious.

"A friend," I reply. "Am I allowed to have those?"

Tracker smirks. "You've got those." He points to himself, and I can't help but grin.

"You don't count."

He puts his hand over his heart in mock distress, then gives up the pretense and picks up his glass again.

"If you're going to date anyone," Rake says, "I want to meet him before things get serious."

I purse my lips and stare at my brother with defiance in my eyes. "And why would I do that?"

"Because I will let you know if he's worthy of you or not," he says in a casual tone, shrugging his broad shoulders.

"And if he's not . . ." Arrow adds, his brown eyes gleaming. "We will handle it."

We?

We?

Arrow wants to protect me when he spends most of his time ignoring me every time I'm around him? I don't even know what to say right now, so for once, I shut my mouth.

"No comment?" Rake asks, eyebrows raising.

"I'm not dating anyone right now, so there's nothing to discuss," I reply as my eyes scan the room before landing on Arrow.

I don't miss the way his gaze darts to my breasts and then quickly away before he downs the rest of the gold liquid in his glass. He slams the glass down on the table with more force than necessary, then walks out of the room without another word.

Okaaaaaay then.

"How's he doing?" Rake asks Tracker quietly.

I lean closer to hear what they're saying.

"He's angry. And still feeling guilty, I think. I hope he'll come around," Tracker tells my brother.

Guilty? About what?

Rake looks down. "Fuckin' hope so. All he seems to be doing is drinking and fucking."

I grit my teeth at that, apparently not liking the thought of him with other women.

He isn't mine, I remind myself, yet it doesn't soften the blow.

"Sounds like an average Friday night," Tracker adds with a smirk.

They both laugh.

I don't.

Rake finishes his drink, then looks over at me. "What do you wanna eat? I know this place close by that Faye always likes to go to."

Yeah, no, thanks.

I raise an eyebrow that says *You know exactly what I want to eat.* Rake cringes and turns to Tracker. "Coming to grab a bite with us?"

Tracker chuckles. "I just saw that look. What is she making you eat?"

"Sushi. It's always fuckin' sushi," he grumbles, scrubbing a hand down his jaw.

I smile, loving that he remembers. "Don't pretend you don't love it."

He gives me a gentle look, then looks down into his empty glass.

"All right then, let's go and get you fed."

I slide off my stool and sling my handbag over my shoulder. Rake and Tracker start talking quietly, so I walk out front and stand next to Rake's bike. When I hear steps behind me, I turn around, expecting to see my brother, but instead I stare into Arrow's handsome face. He doesn't say anything for a few seconds, just studies me with a penetrating gaze. I start to shuffle my feet, feeling uncomfortable under his scrutiny.

"Do I have something on my face or what?" I blurt out.

He doesn't look amused. "You with that guy I saw you with?"

Not this again.

"No, I told you I wasn't."

He shrugs. "If you like him, you'll stay away from him."

I scowl. "I don't get you. You can't tell me what to do, Arrow."

"Just stay out of trouble, Anna," he says suddenly, narrowing his gaze a little.

"Why do you care?" I ask, raising an eyebrow. He's being downright chatty today. At least by his standards.

He makes a soft scoffing sound and shakes his head. "I don't. I'm just looking out for Rake. Last thing he needs is to worry about your spoiled ass."

Spoiled?

I'm a lot of things—some of them not good—but none of them are spoiled.

"Don't pretend you know me," I reply while staring him down. "I love my brother. I don't know why you have a problem with me, but I don't think it's justified."

I don't like the gleam that enters his eyes. "I've had grown men too scared to talk back to me."

I stand straighter. "I know you won't hurt me. Rake wouldn't allow it."

Arrow leans forward, his gaze lowering to my mouth. "You like talking to me. Why?"

My eyebrows furrow. "What do you mean?"

"Every time I'm around you. You don't ignore me. You keep yapping away like I'm your fuckin' friend or something."

I purse my lips. "You are my friend."

Kind of.

Sort of.

Okay, not really.

His lips quirk. "Don't wanna be your friend, Anna, that's the whole problem here."

Well. Okay. The man is honest. Wait, did he mean he just didn't want to be my friend, or he wanted to be *more* than friends?

My eyes widen at the possibility.

"Whatever you're thinking right now, you need to stop."

"Why do you go to Toxic so much?" I blurt out, wanting to

know. There are always available women in the clubhouse, and it's not like he couldn't get anyone he wanted.

"Women there know what to expect," he replies, looking away from me.

"To expect?"

He nods sharply. "They get what they want, and I get what I want. Problem solved. I'm not looking for anything, Anna."

"Oh," I reply, feeling stupid.

His finger reaches out and runs down my cheek. I suck in a breath as our eyes connect, confused by what I see there.

Desire.

"You're beautiful, do you know that? If I was another man, I would be all over you."

So many questions flash through my mind. Why only if he was another man? Why not now?

I open my mouth, trying to think of a reply, when Rake walks out. Arrow instantly drops his hand from my face and steps away. Rake slaps Arrow on the back in a friendly gesture, then walks over to me.

"Let's do this," he says, handing me a helmet. "But next time I get to choose the place."

I smile, forgetting about Arrow and enjoying Rake's playful mood. "Deal."

THREE

WHISTLE. "Lana, you look smoking hot!"

My best friend turns in a circle, shaking her ass a little as she faces away from me, causing me to break out in giggles. At five foot two, Lana is tiny but curvy in all the right places. She runs her blue-tipped fingernails through her thick dark hair, courtesy of her Greek heritage.

"Thank you," she replies in her sweet voice, pulling up her strapless black dress. "I'll start on my makeup while you get in the shower."

By makeup, she means mascara and eyeliner. It's the only thing she puts on her face—not that she needs it.

I force myself to get off my soft leather couch. "I can't believe it's *you* dragging *me* out tonight."

What a change of events.

Lana grins. "You've made me go out every weekend since you got back, and now I find myself enjoying it."

"Good," I tell her, my lips twitching. "I better get my ass ready then."

"Yes, you better," Lana replies, fiddling with her dark locks once more. "I thought we could check out a couple of bars, broaden our horizons."

I blink. "Okay, who are you and what have you done with my best friend?"

Lana hates change. She always has.

We've been friends since kindergarten. I have a picture of us together on my bedside table, wearing hideous dresses and hugging each other at the tender age of four. We stayed friends even when I left town, keeping in touch via e-mail and phone. She's the best friend any girl could ask for. She's honest, loyal, and sweet and has always been there for me when I've needed her. She has a kindness about her that people seem to gravitate toward, and I was no exception. Growing up, I needed that kindness, that softness. My mother's addiction meant that more often than not, Adam and I were left to fend for ourselves. Sometimes my mother would forget to pack us lunch and we were left to go hungry. I would meet Lana at school, and she would share her food with me, without comment or judgment. She really is a shining star.

"I just need a distraction right now," she mutters so quietly I almost don't hear it.

My head snaps to her. "From what? What's wrong?"

She sighs and pins me with her dark eyes. "Nothing is wrong, it's just . . ."

"What?"

She bites her bottom lip, hesitating. "Promise you will never repeat this."

"You know I won't."

"I can't stop thinking about Tracker," she blurts out, then covers her face with her hands.

My eyes widen. Lana has met Tracker twice now, both at times when my brother has sent him to keep an eye on me.

"I knew it!" I yell, doing my victory dance, which consists of jumping up and down and shaking my booty.

Lana winces at my loudness and sighs. "Tell me how stupid I am."

"You're not—"

"He's taken," she says, counting one finger. "He's a biker." Another finger.

"Hey! So is my brother," I add, smirking.

"Anna! He's the sexiest man I've ever seen, and I'm sick of thinking about him. Time to move on. Out with the old and in with the new," she says animatedly, smoothing down her dress.

"So that's why you're wearing the smallest piece of clothing I've ever seen you in and want to go out and party?" I ask, blinking slowly a few times. "Lana, you're gorgeous. If Tracker wants to stay with someone like Allie, then that's his loss. There are plenty of men out there who would love to call you their own."

Coming from someone who only wants a man who barely looks at me.

I'm such a hypocrite.

Lana laughs, and I wait for her to call me out on that comment, but she doesn't. She just smiles at me and says, "You're right. There are plenty of men out there."

Lana knows about my crush on Arrow, she has to know, but she doesn't tease me about it. Knowing Lana, she's waiting for me to bring it up, waiting until I'm ready to talk about it. She's good that way, very patient, but I haven't missed the knowing looks she flashes me when I talk about him.

I take a quick shower and stand in front of the mirror, naked, to put on my makeup. A brown smoky eye makes my green eyes pop, and matched with a nude lip it doesn't look like too much. I flat-iron my hair so it's dead straight, then add some hair spray for a little volume on top. Deciding to go with a pair of black skintight skinny jeans and a black backless top, I slide my feet into my red pumps and spray a little perfume.

"You look amazing," Lana says as I walk out into the living room. She's put some music on and is pouring us drinks.

"Thanks," I reply, taking the seat opposite her. I pick up the glass. "To a good night!"

"To a good night," she repeats, and the glasses chime as we clink them together. I take a sip of the vodka and blackberry juice, then smile at my best friend.

"Why do I have a feeling we're going to get into some trouble tonight?" I ask with a raised brow.

"Because you're you."

"Hey! I'm a well-respected, educated woman—"

She cuts me off with her laughter. "Yes, I know. Biological science specializing in zoology, you're a huge nerd."

"Like you can speak," I reply, grinning. Lana is even smarter than me. I smile when she puts on her glasses, turning her sexy look cute. She's practically blind without her glasses, and I'm glad she's bringing them.

"I'll call a cab," I announce.

"Way ahead of you, Anna Bell, I already called one."

"Oh, come on, not you too," I complain.

She lifts her shoulder in a shrug. "It's catchy."

"Yeah, because it came out of Tracker's mouth," I reply, smirking at her.

She gasps and pushes her glasses farther up on her nose. "That is so not why!"

"Is too."

"Is not."

A horn beeps, interrupting our argument, the same childish words we've been using since we were four. We grab our purses, everything else forgotten, lock the front door, and slide into the back of the cab.

"What's the first stop on our pub crawl?" I ask her.

"Knox's Tavern," she replies, glancing down at her phone. I tell the cab driver where to go and relax back on the seat, enjoying the slight buzz from the vodka. When we arrive, the bouncer asks for our IDs, which, at twenty-five, is a compliment. A song I've never heard before is playing, and I move to the beat as we walk up to the bar. I sigh as I realize we will be waiting here for some time, the line to get drinks is that long.

"This place is packed," Lana says, looking around. "It's pretty awesome though."

I nod. "It is."

Fifteen minutes later I'm giving our drinks order to one of the hottest men I've ever seen in my life. He has a scar on his face, but it doesn't take away his masculine appeal.

"Two vodkas with blackberry juice, please."

"We don't have blackberry juice," he replies, leaning forward and flashing me an odd look. Does no one order that here?

"Orange juice?"

He nods.

"Please."

I hand Lana her drink and turn back to the bartender. "You wouldn't happen to be hiring, would you?"

I need a job to make some of my own money. Rake keeps putting money into my account, telling me it's no problem and that he has a lot saved, but I don't want to use it. It's just sitting there in my account and I plan to return every cent to him.

Mr. Sexy tilts his head and studies me. "You ever worked in a bar before?"

"Well, no—"

"Then, no, we're not hiring," he replies, cutting me off.

Jerk.

Lana speaks up. "She's a scientist, I'm sure she can mix a few drinks."

He doesn't look impressed, even though I'm totally overqualified for this job.

A beautiful woman walks up behind the man, looking flustered. "Reid, we need to hire someone else; this is insane."

Reid? Hot name for a hot man. Shame he's kind of rude. His eyes soften when they land on her, his whole expression changing.

That's love, right there. I wonder if I'll ever see a look like that pointed in my direction.

"I know, babe," he says in a gentler tone than he used with me.

She glances at me, and I grin widely. "I'm looking for a job."

"I'm so old," I mutter as I look at the time on my phone. One a.m. and I'm ready to go home. It's kind of sad really. I look for Lana, who is currently on the dance floor with some guy. I don't know who was more shocked when she said yes to his invitation, me or her. I'm assuming the many drinks she's consumed have something to do with it. I, on the other hand, stopped drinking at bar two and am now ridiculously sober. I guess one of us had to be the responsible one. Who knew it was gonna be me? I sit back on the barstool and look around, my eyes widening when I see a familiar face. Everyone around him gives him a wide berth, and with good reason. Behind him trails Tracker and my brother.

Fuck.

"What are you doing here?" I ignore Arrow and ask Rake, who is staring at me through narrowed eyes.

Rake's lips tighten. "You didn't tell me you were going out tonight."

"And I shouldn't have to."

Rake glances around the bar. "You know who owns this place, right?"

I shake my head. "Nope."

Arrow grins, all teeth. "We do."

I try to act like I'm not surprised. The bar is called Rift and, according to Lana, only just opened last week. We'd been here for about an hour, our third stop for the night. "So? Am I not allowed to be here? Last I checked, it is a free country."

"What the fuck?" Tracker growls. I look at him to see him staring out at the dance floor. Guess he spotted Lana, and I don't like the way he's looking at her.

Not one bit.

"Leave her alone, she deserves some fun," I tell him, my tone letting him know I am serious.

"Anna, if you're going out, let us know. I don't want to have to be worrying about where you are every weekend," Rake tells me, running a hand through his hair in frustration.

I grit my teeth. "Rake, I've been on my own for a long time. You don't have to treat me like a fucking baby."

I get that he cares, but seriously? I'm not a kid anymore, I can take care of my damn self. Do I want my brother's attention? Yes. Do I want to be a part of his life? Of course. What I don't want is to be under his thumb. I know he is looking after me the only way he knows how, to protect me and make sure no harm comes my way, but I don't want to be told where to go, or to have to check in with him to let him know my every move.

Or even more ridiculous—ask for approval.

I watch as Rake's face turns to stone. "You're going home. Now."

"The fuck I am!" I yell, even though I was planning on leaving anyway.

Rake gives Arrow and Tracker a look.

They both grin, evil glints in their eyes.

Tracker heads to the dance floor while Arrow lifts me in the air and throws me over his shoulder.

My mouth drops open in shock, while my body reacts to being pressed against his.

Okay, maybe it's time to go.

 **FOUR**

PUT me down, you rat bastard!" I yell, pummeling my fists on his ass. It's a very nice ass, but still, that's beside the point.

This is ridiculous.

And embarrassing.

Tracker puts Lana in the car. Unlike me, she never resisted when she was escorted out. However, I know that if I give in now, they will think they can do shit like this all the time. They will try to control my life. I can't let that happen.

I won't.

"Arrow, seriously! My jeans are falling down!"

I can feel a cold breeze on my ass.

He puts me down, grabs my nape, and steers me toward the car. "Maybe next time you should wear jeans that don't show your ass."

I wisely ignore his comment. "Where's Rake?"

"He's inside talking to the manager," he replies, his warm breath on my neck giving me thoughts I shouldn't be having.

I'm pissed at him!

Control yourself, Anna.

"Is that how you found out we were here?" I ask, straightening my posture as he removes his warm hand from my neck.

"Yep," he replies, sounding almost cheerful about that fact. "We told them to keep an eye out. The second you entered, we got a text."

"If any of you brutes so much as look at Lana the wrong way—"

"Lana is fine," Arrow replies calmly. "Retract your claws."

"I'm serious! She's not used to your overbearing, assholish ways."

"And you are?" he asks as he opens the backseat door.

I give him a pointed look. "Rake is my brother. I've been dealing with him my whole life."

"That's a nice way to put it," he muses, lip twitching.

I fume. "You guys need a life. Find something better to do on a Saturday night."

He sighs, and then his signature scowl returns. "Trust me, I was busy. Had a fine-looking woman on her knees, my cock deep in her throat, when Rake called me, telling me we had to go find his little sister. So don't push me right now."

My mouth drops open.

"Well, don't let me keep you. I'm sure she's a real catch," I manage to get out. Like I needed that image. Bastard.

And screw the whore too, whoever she is.

I look away from him and am about to get in the car, wanting to leave his presence, when I see someone I never wanted to see again, in my life.

Ever.

I quickly look around for Rake, hoping he doesn't remember what he looks like.

Jacob.

Fuckity fuck.

Jacob was the guy I dated in high school. I was fifteen and just entering the dating world. Rake pretty much scared off most of the boys who looked my way, but Jacob was different. He was two years older than me, and a year older than Rake. He was good-looking, with blond hair, hazel eyes, and he had a six-pack. Now, back in those days, a boy having a six-pack at that age was a *big* thing. It was like winning the lottery. So when Jacob asked me out, I was thrilled. He was a popular boy, liked by all the girls, and into sports. When Rake found out about the date, however, he wasn't so happy. In fact, he told me I wouldn't be going.

I begged.

He said no.

I cried.

He gave in and said yes.

But there were conditions.

He told me he would be meeting Jacob before the date and waiting up for me to come home, and if I was home even a second later than ten, he was beating the shit out of my date.

His words, not mine.

I agreed. Deep down inside I liked that Rake was looking out for me, so I never argued when he placed rules on me. I was a young girl with no father and a mother who didn't give a shit, so when Rake cared, I needed that.

He met with Jacob before my date, and I could tell he didn't like him. But me, being young, idealistic, and naïve, thought he was a great guy. We went to dinner and the movies, and then he dropped me back at my house. The problem was, we came home early. Rake was expecting us at ten, and we were home at nine. What I didn't know was, Rake was seeing a girl of his own and was planning on coming home by nine thirty to make sure he was here to see that I was home safely. So when Jacob walked me to the door and asked to come in for a drink, I didn't think anything of it. I'd called for Rake when we'd walked through the house but soon realized we were alone. I got him his drink and we sat on the couch, where he kissed me. I was okay with the kissing. It was when his hands went wandering that I told him no, I wasn't ready. But the bastard didn't listen. Rake came home just in time to stop something that could have been a hell of a lot worse than it was. Still, he blamed himself for not being there earlier. I remember just being happy I still had my virginity.

As if sensing someone watching him, Jacob turns and looks in my direction.

At me.

He studies me for a few tense moments, grins slowly. Not a friendly grin. No, more like a leer.

Yep—he saw me.

Fuck.

Creepy bastard.

"Who's that guy you're staring at?" Arrow rumbles from behind me.

I turn around, putting my back to Jacob. "No idea."

"Then why you fuckin' watching him?" he asks, narrowing his eyes.

"Maybe I think he's good-looking," I manage to get out, the words tasting like acid on my tongue.

Arrow stares at Jacob, but I don't turn around to see if Jacob is staring back. If he was smart he wouldn't, but he's not. At least, he never used to be.

"Will Rake know who he is?" he finally asks. "I don't like the way he's looking at you right now."

Shit.

I start to feel panicked. "Please, don't tell him, Arrow. Rake will kill him! Do you want my brother to go to jail?"

Arrow crosses his arms over his chest and leans down. "Who you really protecting here, Anna? Your brother or that preppy-looking dickhead?"

I huff. "Definitely not the dickhead. Trust me on that."

"Well, then you better get talking," Arrow says, waiting patiently.

I sigh, knowing he isn't going to let this go. "Did Rake tell you about Jacob? The guy who didn't know no was no . . ." Arrow takes a few steps in Jacob's direction. I put my hand on his chest, my eyes pleading with him. "Don't, Arrow. It was years ago. Like ten years. He's probably still pissed Rake kicked his ass."

My voice sounds doubtful to even my own ears.

"How far did it go, Anna?" Arrow asks through clenched teeth. His chest is heaving slightly, and I can tell he wants to go over there.

I lick my lips. "He didn't rape me. He put his hand . . ."

Arrow cups my face. "He touched you with his fingers?"

I nod, looking down, but Arrow lifts my face up. "Don't be embarrassed, darlin', you did nothing wrong. That fucker clearly doesn't know how to treat a girl, and that no means fuckin' no under any fuckin' circumstance."

"It was a long time ago, but I don't want to face him and I don't want to make a scene, so can we please just go?"

Arrow stares behind me. "He's the one making a scene. He should have fled the moment he recognized you."

He didn't want to let it go.

I grab ahold of his bicep. "Please, Arrow."

He sighs and scrubs a hand down his face. "Get in the car, okay?"

I slide in. When he closes the door behind me, I know.

He isn't letting it go.

I watch from the window nervously as he walks right up to Jacob and punches him.

Right in the nose.

Jacob holds his face in his hands, blood spurting everywhere. The men Jacob is with don't step in. They take one look at Arrow and take a step backward.

Arrow says something to him, then walks back toward the car.

Jacob lifts his head and looks through the window, right at me. He can't see me, because of the darkness and the tinted windows, but I feel like he can. My body shivers, and I watch him as his friends help him up and they leave the parking lot.

Good fucking riddance.

Arrow leans back on the car and lights a cigarette.

I open my mouth and then close it again. How can he act so casual after that?

"Who's the guy Arrow hit?" Tracker asks, making me jump. I didn't even realize he was in the car. I turn my head to see Lana, who has fallen asleep against Tracker—who is staring at me with an amused raised eyebrow. It pisses me off; he does not get to be amused right now.

"Some dickhead that Rake doesn't need to know about," I murmur.

Tracker chuckles. "Rake will find out; we don't keep shit from each other."

I grit my teeth, then turn the tables on him.

"Allie know you're out saving other women?" I ask sweetly.

"Arrow know you want him?" he fires back.

I shut up.

He grins but does the same.

I get out of the car, closing the door behind me, and stand next to Arrow.

"How's your fist?" I ask him, glancing down at his hands.

He blows out a breath of smoke. "Fine."

"I wish you hadn't done that, but . . ."

"But what?"

"But thanks," I whisper.

I exhale deeply and look up at the night sky. "How fucking ironic is it that if you guys hadn't dragged me out he would have come in there and I would have had to face him alone?"

I feel like a stupid fifteen-year-old girl again.

"And then you could have just called me and I would have been here in five minutes. Same outcome. My fist in his face. Him whimpering like a little bitch."

My lip twitches as I look back at him. "How can you make me smile at a time like this?"

He pushes some errant hair back behind my ear, then leans forward, making it seem like he is going to kiss me. I forget to breathe as he places a kiss just outside the corner of my mouth. "'Cause you know you're safe with me, darlin'."

Our gazes lock, and for a moment we're both tongue-tied. But then he clears his throat. "With any of us, I mean."

I swallow hard, pretending I didn't notice his slip. "Right."

"But you know you can always call me if you need something. Anything. If you're ever in any trouble, or need help."

"I thought you didn't like me much," I mumble. "You said I was spoiled."

He glances around before looking back at me. "You're not spoiled. You are a pain in the ass though."

"Why?" I grumble. "Because I interrupted your stellar blow job?"

His mouth twitches. "No, Anna, because I was fuckin' thinking about you when her mouth was on me."

Holy fuck.

Did he just say that?

"Did you just say that?" I ask, eyes widening.

The way he looks away and doesn't reply makes me feel like he regretted the words the second they left his lips.

Rake walks out of the club and Arrow pushes off the car, stepping away from me and getting into the driver's seat. I get back into the car the same time that Rake gets into the front seat.

No one brings up what happened, and I for one am grateful.

I look out the window, just wanting to get home. I sit there for about ten minutes before the silence is broken.

"What did you learn today, Anna Bell?" Tracker asks me in a cheerful, condescending tone.

My hands turn to fists. "To find out what businesses you guys own and avoid them at all costs."

Laughter from everyone except Arrow and a sleeping Lana.

"Where are we dropping them off?" Arrow asks Rake.

"Clubhouse," he replies curtly. "They can both sleep in Anna's room."

"Take me home," I demand, crossing my arms over my chest. "I don't want to go to the clubhouse."

I'm ignored.

I turn to Tracker. "Lana's never been to the clubhouse, don't make her go."

Tracker sighs. "It's not a big deal. She should get used to us."

I watch as he smiles down at Lana.

"You gonna sic Allie on her then? Lana's too sweet to even be in the same vicinity as that bitch," I grit out, losing my temper.

"Anna," Rake warns. "Stay out of it."

I can feel Tracker staring at me, but I don't look at him.

"No one is going to hurt Lana," he finally says.

I scoff and shake my head. He already is, and he doesn't even know it.

"Anna, I promise you no one will hurt Lana. Allie included," my brother interjects, his voice losing its steel. "Besides, I know what you're capable of."

"What the fuck does that mean?" Arrow asks, deciding to speak.

Rake shrugs. "My baby sis is badass."

The men chuckle.

Once again, I don't.

Growing up in a neighborhood so bad you had to learn to defend yourself isn't something to be proud of, at least in my eyes. I became even more badass after Jacob, I guess you could say. I refused to be a victim again. I *am* proud of being a fighter, a survivor, but sometimes it gets exhausting being your own hero. Rake was there for me but he couldn't always be with me, so I had to watch my own back.

When the car comes to a stop, Tracker carries out Lana, and I walk behind them, ignoring Arrow and Rake. I can feel their eyes on me as I walk in front of them, but we all remain quiet. Loud music blasts through the clubhouse, but I ignore everyone and everything. As we enter my room, Tracker pulls the blanket down and tucks Lana in, then turns to me with a *Don't start* look on his face.

I shrug. I don't need to say anything. It's obvious he has some kind of fascination with Lana, but he also has a crazy girlfriend he's apparently been with for years now. When he leaves the room, I lock the door behind him, strip down to my panties, and climb in next to Lana.

I will deal with all this shit tomorrow.

Tomorrow comes sooner than I would have hoped. Lana is still asleep when I wake up to take a shower but then realize that I don't have any clothes here. I know I should have left some, but to be honest, I didn't ever plan on crashing here. With a towel wrapped around me, I peek my head outside, hoping to see Rake. Of course, my luck isn't that good, and instead of finding my brother I find Arrow.

"Where's Rake?" I ask him, the ends of my damp hair dripping down my back.

"Why?" he asks, tilting his head and staring at my body. At least what he could see of it.

"I need to borrow something to wear," I explain, pointing to my towel-clad body.

Arrow stands, and it's then I realize he's wearing nothing except a pair of shorts, sitting low on his lean hips. I blink slowly as I take him in, ripped abs, broad shoulders, muscular arms and pecs that I wouldn't mind sinking my teeth into. Don't get me started on that beard again. It's fucking sexy.

"You done?" he asks in a low tone I've never heard him use before.

I clear my throat. "I need clothes."

"I got that," he says, scratching his chest lazily. "I was waiting for you to finish eye-fucking me."

"I wasn't—"

He walks away. Rude.

So rude.

But then he comes back, holding a white T-shirt and a pair of shorts.

"Thank you," I say softly, taking the items from his hand. His fingers touch mine, and something passes between us. I know he feels it too, because he pulls his hand back like it's on fire.

"I mean it, Arrow," I rasp. "Thank you, for last night with Jacob."

He bobs his head. "Don't thank me, Anna. Rake isn't the only one who wanted to kill him."

"But you didn't," I say. "And thanks for not saying anything or making it a big deal."

He sighs. "Your brother knows what happened, but I told him you didn't want to talk about it and that I handled it."

Which is why I appreciated it so much.

"I owe you one."

"You don't owe me anything, Anna," he says quietly.

I swallow. "Okay then. Maybe we could—"

He cuts me off. What was I going to say anyway? Maybe we could hang out sometime?

Christ.

"Don't open the door in your towel again, Anna," he rasps. "Some of the men might take it as an invitation."

"But not you?" I ask, unable to stop myself.

"Trust me, darlin', you don't want my brand of fucked-up," he says before he walks away. I stare at his retreating back until he's out of sight.

He thinks he's fucked-up?

Well, who isn't?

I close and lock the door and dress in the T-shirt and shorts. I put on last night's bra but go without panties, then head to the kitchen in search of food. There's a bald guy in the kitchen—Vinnie, I remember his name is.

"Hey, Vinnie," I say, taking the milk out of the fridge.

"Hey," he replies, and slides over the box of cereal in front of him. "Hungry?"

"Starving," I reply, grabbing a bowl and spoon and sitting down opposite him. I tip out the cereal, smother it in milk, then scoop up a huge mouthful.

"When's the last time you ate?" he asks with a grin.

"Very funny," I reply with an eye roll.

Two women walk into the kitchen wearing nothing but makeup piled on their faces. Vinnie looks at my expression and laughs.

"They can take the time to put on more makeup than any woman should be wearing, but they can't put on clothes?"

He laughs harder.

"I'm serious! This is why I don't like coming here."

Poor Lana will walk out and get the shock of her life.

"Rake wanted me to stay naked," one of them says to me. She speaks in a fake baby voice that makes me cringe. Why do women do that? It's not cute.

"Well, then you better do exactly as he says," I tell her in a sarcastic tone.

"Oh, we do," the other one replies, either ignoring or misunderstanding my condescending tone.

"Plus we know how amazing we look, so why not show it off?"

I'm all for women feeling comfortable in their skins, no matter what shape or size, but walking around naked in a house filled with people? I don't know what to say.

"I can actually feel my IQ dropping, just being in their presence," I mutter to Vinnie, who chuckles. Was one of these women with Arrow? Maybe she was the one he was with last night. I dig my nails into my palms.

Don't let it get to you. He isn't yours.

Tell my stupid heart that.

Speaking of the devil, Arrow walks in, now freshly showered and dressed in jeans and a tight black T-shirt, molded to his impressive physique.

"Arrow!" the brunette squeals, walking over to him and rubbing her breasts against his chest. He glances at me for a sec, then turns to her, his hand going to her shoulder.

I look down into my cereal, grab the spoon, and shovel in a few more mouthfuls, wanting to get the hell out of here as soon as possible. My day gets even worse when Allie walks in, her nose in the air like always.

"Anna," she purrs. "Still here, I see. What a fuckin' shame."

"I can see why you would see it that way," I reply, playing on her known weakness of insecurity. "Since I'm so close with Tracker and all."

She gives me a dirty look and flips her hair over her shoulder. "Like he'd even look in your direction."

I sigh exaggeratedly. "You'd be surprised."

"Anna," Arrow says, his voice filled with warning.

What? She started it.

I chance a look at him. He's now standing away from the brunette, watching me. I glance around the room.

"Well, this has been interesting," I say as I stand up, walk to the sink, and wash my bowl and spoon.

"Because of you, Tracker had to leave me last night. Next time can you just do as you're told so my man doesn't have to babysit you?" Allie sneers.

"Actually, Tracker volunteered to go with us, so stop running your mouth, Allie," Arrow adds, then looks to me. "You want a ride home?"

"We'll take a cab," I tell him. I turn around just before I walk out of the room. "Oh, and Allie . . . go fuck yourself."

Lana wakes up and takes a quick shower while I go in search of Rake. I knock on his door, hoping that he's alone.

"Yeah?" he calls out.

"It's me!"

"Come in, Anna," he says, so I turn the doorknob and enter his room.

"Please tell me you're alone," I say with my eyes closed.

He laughs and throws a pillow at me, which hits me in the face. "Think I'd invite you inside if I wasn't?"

I open my eyes, pick up the pillow from the floor, and throw it back at him. "I never know with you."

I sit down on his bed. "Did Arrow tell you what happened last night?"

"He told me. What I want to know is why you didn't."

"I didn't want to make a big deal over it. You taught him a lesson back then, Rake. You beat the shit out of him, and Arrow decked him last night. While I hated to do it, I'm glad you made me file that report on him, because I didn't want him to do the same to another woman."

"I'm glad Arrow handled it," Rake replies. "My brothers will always take care of you if I'm not there."

"I know," I say. "I'm glad Arrow was there too."

"Next time you're going out like that, give me a heads-up."

"Going out like what?" I ask, watching him as he puts his hands behind his head.

"Dressed up like . . . that."

I bite my lip to stop my grin. "Dressed like what, Rake?"

"Christ, Anna," he growls. "All the men in that place were watching you. We were lucky we made it out of there with only one guy getting hit."

My lip twitches. "Aren't you happy I came back home?"

His eyes soften at that. I'd said it as a joke, but I could see he didn't take it that way. "I'm beyond happy, Anna; trust me on that."

He puts his palm over his heart. "Everything feels right, you know? I was unsettled when you were gone."

And this is why I love my brother.

I clear my throat. "Can I ask you something?"

"Sure, go ahead."

I look away, staring at his door. "What happened to Bailey?"

He's silent.

I look back at him to see a weird expression on his face. "That was years ago, Anna."

"I know," I say. "I was just wondering."

"I don't know where she is," he says. "After high school finished we went our separate ways."

"Did you love anyone after her?" I ask him.

"I've loved a lot of women, Anna," he says with a cheeky grin.

I roll my eyes. "Not like that. I mean *love*."

He shakes his head. "Why all the questions?"

"Just something I've been wanting to ask you for a while," I say, shrugging sheepishly.

"It's in the past, Anna," he says, his voice barely a whisper. "Doesn't matter anymore."

I thought it did, but I didn't want to push any further.

"Lana's in the shower and we're going to catch a cab home."

"I'm taking you both home," he says, his tone final.

"Bossy."

"I thought we could grab some lunch or something on the way," he says.

"Sushi?" I ask, perking up.

"No," he replies, laughing. "Definitely not. How about we grab some sushi for you, then go to another restaurant where I can get a decent meal."

I gasp. "Was that you compromising? I can't believe it."

"Don't get used to it, baby sis," he says, picking up another pillow and throwing it at me—this time I catch it in my hand.

"Mature, Rake!"

I hear Lana call my name and I stand up.

"Oh, shit," I mutter. "The reason I came here in the first place was to get some clothes for Lana to borrow."

Poor thing must be waiting in a towel like I'd been doing earlier this morning. Rake gets out of bed and pulls out a T-shirt and boxer shorts. "Looks like we're taking you to your house first to get dressed before we can go out for lunch."

"Or," I say, "we can get drive-through and go to my apartment and stuff our faces."

"I like how you think, Anna."

"Glad you approve," I say, taking the clothes and walking toward the door.

"Thanks, bro."

"Anytime, sis."

 **FIVE**

WHEN I get a call from Summer a few days later, I'd forgotten that I'd given her my number in hopes of a job at the bar. She tells me to come in for a trial. I'm sitting in the kitchen with Lana, about to get ready to go, when she speaks.

"Have you ever been spanked?"

I choke on my piece of toast. Lana taps me on the back until I turn and look at her. "Why the hell would you ask me that?"

She grins and pushes her glasses up on her nose. She's a picture of innocence until she opens her mouth. "I was just reading a book." She points to the trashy romance novel she's left next to the toaster. "And I was curious."

I blink slowly a few times. "No, I can't say I've ever been spanked. Why? Does it tickle your fancy?"

Her face turns red, the heat creeping up from her neck. "I didn't say that!"

I start laughing. "Never mind Tracker, you should hook up with my brother instead! Apparently he's into that stuff."

She punches me in the arm.

"Ow!"

"Shut up," she mumbles.

I try and keep a straight face. "I've heard it's enjoyable though."

"What's enjoyable?" my brother asks as he walks in.

I look behind him. "How the hell did you get in?"

He's wearing all black, jeans and a T-shirt and his cut. He holds up a key. "I got a key made when you moved in."

I bite the inside of my cheek.

"Five, four, three, two, one," Lana mutters under her breath.

"You're psychotic, do you know that?" I yell. He has a key to my house? He needs to learn the word *boundaries*.

He just grins at my outburst. "It's just in case of emergencies."

"And what emergency is it today?" I ask, sitting back down and picking up my other piece of toast.

Rake gives me a shy smile. "Breakfast?"

Charming bastard.

"I'll make you something," Lana says softly, and gestures for him to take a seat. Rake sits next to me and gently bumps his shoulder against mine.

"You still angry about the other night?" he asks me in a gentle tone.

"You mean when you got Arrow to pick me up and drag me out of the club like I was fourteen?"

He nods, and shrugs sheepishly. "I worry about you."

I sigh, the anger leaving me. "I know you do, Adam, but how about some freedom? I've been without you for years now, and it's kind of hard playing my old role now."

"Old role?" he asks.

I nod. "Baby sister to dominant bossy man."

He's quiet for a few seconds. "I'll try to loosen the reins."

"I'd appreciate that," I reply in an extremely dry tone. "Don't get me wrong, I really want you to pay attention to me and for us to spend time together, but maybe ease up on the controlling part?"

He nods and clears his throat, looking down at his hands on the table. "I can try. But it's hard, Anna—I just got you back. I didn't want you to go, you know that, right? But I know I've changed and . . ."

"And what?" I ask quietly.

"And I don't want you to leave because you feel like you can't handle who I am," he admits, still staring down at his hands. "And at the same time I want to protect you more than anyone. You're always my baby sister, Anna. Always."

I swallow hard, not expecting him to be so honest. I speak softly so only he can hear. "I love you, Adam, no matter what. I won't run. I would never turn my back on you. Never. I miss how we used to be. I know we've both changed, but I want you to be yourself around me. I miss how close we used to be, and I want us to get that back."

He glances up at me, looking a little surprised. "That's really how you feel?"

I nod. "It is."

He rubs the back of his neck and bites out a curse. "I didn't want you to hate the club, Anna. I was fuckin' scared, if I'm being honest. I didn't want you to see us like Mom's boyfriends, useless thugs."

"I'd never think that of you, Rake," I reply honestly. "I'm proud of you, you know that, right?"

I can see my words matter to him by the way he beams at me.

"You're the only person whose opinion I care about, Anna, so it means a lot to hear you say that. I always wanted to set a good example for you, and I know I haven't done that," he says, looking sheepish. "But you turned out amazing, so I'm taking credit for that anyway."

We both laugh at that, lightening the moment.

"Would the two of you like to come over for dinner tomorrow night?" he asks, raising his voice so Lana can hear. "The women are cooking."

Of course they are.

"We'd love to come," Lana replies, shooting me a smirk.

We would?

"Actually—"

"We don't have anything going on, Anna, don't worry," she adds, eyes alight with mischief.

"Traitor," I mouth to her, and she laughs. A dinner where all the club women cook and I'll probably have to watch Arrow with one of them? No, thank you very much.

I turn to my brother. "Lana wants to know about spanking."

Lana's eyes turn to slits, and her face returns to tomato red.

"Spanking?" Rake asks, sounding strained and looking anywhere but at me.

"Yes," I say. "I heard you like spanking women, so maybe you could explain the pros and cons to it. What are the benefits?"

He stands. "I'll pick up breakfast on the way home."

He walks toward the door.

I burst out laughing. "Rake, stay. I'll shut up, I promise."

He shakes his head and bolts for the door. "I'll take a rain check; see you later!"

I sigh, grin still wide on my face.

Lana, on the other hand, isn't so amused. "I hate you."

"You love me."

She covers her face with her hands. "He's going to tell Tracker, isn't he?"

That's what she's worried about?

"Screw Tracker." I glance at her. "And not literally either. Besides, he looks the type to give a good spanking himself."

"And Arrow doesn't?" she asks, raising a dark, perfectly arched brow.

Okay, maybe all the bikers do.

"I was waiting to see if you'd bring Arrow up."

She tightens her lips. "Normally I wouldn't, but turnabout is fair play and you've been giving me shit about Tracker."

Her words are true.

"I don't think there's any chance of Arrow and me happening, so there's nothing to say really," I reply on a sigh. I don't know why I was upset over it. He was a criminal and a biker. I had enough crazy in my life; I didn't need to invite more in. I should be happy nothing was going to happen.

"How do you feel about dating someone in an MC?" I ask.

She tilts her head to the side. "I don't know. I guess I've only ever seen the nice side of the guys. I've never even seen them do anything crazy or violent. I know they have another side, but it's kind of hot that they're badasses."

I giggle at that. "I guess I know my brother would never harm us, and these are his family. So they're mine now. Rake will always have my back and never let anything happen to me. I'm just drawn to Arrow. I can't even explain it."

She puts her hand on her hip. "At least Arrow is single. Tracker has a woman. There's no chance there either, so you're not alone."

"Unrequited lust," I blurt out, causing us to giggle, although nothing was really funny.

"We have the weirdest conversations," I muse, my lip twitching. "It's good to be back in town with you."

Lana bobs her head in agreement. "It sucked big-time when you left; but you're here now, and we get to make the most of it."

"We do," I say, standing up and putting my plate in the sink. "What are we doing today anyway?"

Lana smiles widely. "I'm going to the library to study, and you have your work trial."

Right.

"We're so fun," I grumble. "I'm going to jump in the shower."

Lana picks up her book. "I'm going to read a little while I wait."

I bite my bottom lip, trying not to smirk. "Maybe next time just ask Tracker anything you want to know. Or your sluttiest friend."

Maybe just ask Rake, the man-whore of the century. I think the only reason he got awkward about it was because I was there. I have a feeling if I wasn't, it might even be his favorite subject.

"You are my sluttiest friend," Lana replies in a dry tone, causing me to laugh. In Lana's twenty-five years of life, she's slept only with two men. According to her, those two men didn't really know what they were doing. I offered to give them a map with a woman's clit marked on it. I know she's curious as hell and wants to try out everything she reads in those books. Whoever lands her and brings her out of her shell is going to be a lucky man indeed.

"You need to find more friends," I call out to her as I enter the bathroom, closing the door behind me.

"You're more than I can handle, thank you very much!" she calls out. I can't help but wonder where all her friends are, the ones she would have hung out with when I left the city. She hasn't mentioned anyone else, and I'm a little curious as to why. Reminding myself to ask her about that, I undress and step into the shower, enjoying the feeling of the warm water cascading down my body. When the water starts to turn cold, I hop out and dry myself, then choose what to wear for my first day at work.

If I get the job.

I settle on black pants and a loose black shirt, since I remembered Summer wearing something similar. I put on my black boots, a little bit of makeup, tie my hair up in a ponytail, and I'm good to go. When I walk out, Lana lifts her head from her book. "You look very nice."

"Thanks," I tell her. "I want to look neither too slutty nor too professional."

She laughs at that. "Well, you nailed it. Want to grab a coffee before you start?"

I nod. "Sounds good."

She stands up and slides her book into her handbag, then smiles up at me. "I know just the place."

I look up and we leave the house, getting into her car that has seen better days.

"I need a new car," she grumbles, like she always does.

"Hey, Ronald is a classic," I reply, lifting my hand to fiddle with the stereo.

"Ronald needs to be replaced," she says. "We've had some good times, don't get me wrong, but I think he's going to fall apart at any moment."

She isn't wrong. Ronald's time is nearing. I also know she doesn't have the money to replace him. Lana's mother worked her ass off as a nurse at the hospital, and Lana was a full-time student. She started her degree later than she could have, because her mom was ill for a little while and Lana worked as a waitress full-time to help pay the bills. She deserved everything, had nothing, but never complained.

"I have money in the bank that Rake gave me—we could get you a new car with that," I offer, but already know what her reply will be. Lana is also very proud, and stubborn as hell.

"Anna, thanks, but you know I couldn't accept that," she replies quietly. "I have some money saved away, you don't need to worry about me anymore."

"I know." I sigh. "But I'm always here, no matter what you need."

Considering Rake's money was sitting in my bank because *I* was too stubborn to use someone else's money, I could see where she was coming from. However, my circumstances were a little different than hers; I had only myself to worry about and a brother who would give me the world.

The music chooses that moment to turn on, Sam Smith playing through the car.

"See, Ronald is good to us sometimes," I say, making her smile.

"He has his moments."

*　　*　　*

After my second smashed glass, I hear Reid mutter something about a "clumsy scientist." His twin Ryan, on the other hand, laughs and tells me not to worry about it. Ryan is easy to be around, and extremely laid-back. Reid is kind of grumpy, and a little scary. I was told that he's a badass MMA fighter, which is why no one messes with him.

Summer arrives and takes over my training, thank God. Reid was getting on my last nerve.

"It gets pretty busy on the weekends," Summer is saying. "Will you be able to work Saturday nights?"

"Yeah, no problem," I tell her. "What other days will you need me?"

She tilts her head to the side, thinking. "Wednesdays, Thursdays, and Saturdays would be perfect. We have a girl who does Friday nights now, so that's covered."

"Those days work fine for me," I reply.

She nods, then smiles. "I think we're going to get along just fine, Anna."

"Thanks for giving me the job, I know he isn't so thrilled," I say, nodding my head toward Reid, who is scowling in my direction.

Summer laughs. "Actually the reason he didn't want to hire you was . . ."

She glances at Reid, then back at me, and lowers her voice.

"Summer," Reid calls, walking over and kissing her on her brow. "I'm sure Anna has work to do."

I cross my arms over my chest and stare him in the eye, not backing down. "Why didn't you want to hire me? Tell me the truth."

He raises an eyebrow. "A bit bold for a woman who just got hired thirty seconds ago."

He is right, but I still want to know what the hell is going on. I decide to goad him. "Fine, I guess you're scared."

"Of what?" he growls.

I shrug nonchalantly. "Of whatever you won't tell me."

He grits his teeth. "You don't know who I am, do you?"

Is he famous or something? I have no idea who he is except for extremely hot and even more rude.

I bite my bottom lip. "No, but if I had a woman as hot as Summer in my bed I'd be a lot less grumpy."

Summer bursts out laughing.

Reid, on the other hand, sighs and rubs his chin. "I know who you are, that's why. You're trouble."

"And who am I?" I ask, confused. "I'm not trouble. I'm an upstanding citizen and a well-educated woman."

I hear Summer's laughter but ignore it.

"You belong to the Wind Dragons; don't play dumb," Reid replies, crossing his arms over his impressive chest.

My mouth drops open. "I don't *belong* to anyone, thank you very fucking much."

He studies me, looking amused. "Babe, you may as well have 'Property of Wind Dragons MC' tattooed on your forehead. Anyway, I wanted to ask them if they were cool with you working here, but they haven't been in in a while."

"You know them?" I ask, my eyes widening.

Fucking hell.

This city is too small.

"'Course I do," he says without smugness, just pure fact. Reid obviously knows a lot of people.

"It's a job, why would they have a problem with it? They don't own me."

Assholes.

Reid chuckles deeply. "You don't know how the club works, do you? It's a bar. You're a beautiful woman. Do the math."

I narrow my eyes, ignoring his compliment. "Summer works here; she's hot."

His lip twitches. "No one will touch Summer."

I roll my eyes and look at Summer, who is grinning. "And no one will touch me either, even if I don't have a scary fighter for a boyfriend. Let me worry about me."

I've been doing it for so long anyway.

"They're a possessive bunch, Anna; you know it and I know it. To be honest, I didn't want the drama, but Summer said she wanted you to work here, which is why you're standing here right now."

"But this isn't fair. I need a job, and just because my brother is a Wind Dragons member doesn't mean I should be discriminated against."

Reid shrugs. "Just being honest with you like you asked."

I sigh. "Yeah, you're right."

"Once word gets out who you belong to, I think the men will stay away anyway. I just don't want anyone trying to get at you to make the club angry."

"What do you mean?" I ask, frowning.

"Let's say someone wants to start shit with the club; they know that if they go near you it would accomplish just that," he explains. "I didn't want that drama in my bar, because then it becomes my problem."

I rub my temple, a headache starting to appear. "I'm just

going to serve drinks and not worry about things I have nothing to do with."

Reid smirks. "If you think so."

"It'll be fine," Summer adds, stroking Reid's impressively muscular arm.

Reid gives me a look and says, "It better be."

SIX

WHEN I see Arrow waiting for me after class, I try to hide my smile.

My day is suddenly looking up.

"Pull the short straw again?" I ask as I walk up to him, grinning.

The look he gives me lets me know he's not impressed. "Rake's on a run, wanted me to pick you up."

"Where did he go?" I ask, wondering why he hadn't said anything.

"Club business," Arrow grunts back, then rubs his beard.

Fuck, he's hot.

His eyes snap to mine and narrow. It's then I realize that I said that out loud.

Holy shit.

"I mean, fuck, it's hot," I blurt, clearing my throat.

It isn't really that hot, so I sound even more stupid.

I look down so he doesn't see my flushed cheeks. The last thing I need is for him to know the extent of my attraction to him, so divulging shit like that is not something I need to be doing.

"You're pretty hot yourself, Anna," he replies. Was that amusement I can hear in his tone?

I look up and, yes, his eyes are dancing with it. I decide to play it off with a shrug. "What? You're a good-looking man. Is it a crime to admire the wrapping?"

"Fuck," he whispers quietly.

"What?"

"Be easier if you weren't attracted to me."

My eyebrows raise. "Why is that?"

A muscle tics in his jaw. "I think you're really something, Anna. But people I care about get hurt. If you're smart, you will hide what I can so easily see in your eyes because it makes me tempted to take what you're offering."

I look down.

I do want him.

I don't know what he saw in my eyes, but I can only imagine. I wish my eyes weren't so expressive.

My phone vibrates, so I pull it out of my pocket, glad for something to do.

"Who's messaging you?" he asks.

My head snaps up. "A friend."

It was Damien, wanting to meet up to study.

"This friend have a cock? 'Cause then we got a problem," he rasps, grinning and showing off his straight white teeth.

"So what, I'm not allowed any male friends? Never mind, don't even answer that because I don't want to hear what you have to say," I snap, shaking my head in astonishment. "Give you men an inch, I tell you what."

"You done?" he asks, obviously sick of me rambling on. "Besides, pretty sure it's meant to be the man giving *you* inch by inch."

Did he just make a sexual innuendo?

"For now," I say, wanting to have the last word. "And I wouldn't know about any inches because I've been having a dry spell for quite a while now."

"How long?" he asks, watching me intently.

"Long enough."

"Hmmmm," he replies, then clears his throat.

"I'll be picking you up tonight as well, after your shift," he says when I don't speak.

He reaches out his big hand and I pass him my bag. "I don't remember telling anyone about my job."

His brown eyes search mine. "Rake is fuckin' confused as to why you got yourself a job when he gave you a shitload of money that should last you all fuckin' year."

"I don't want his money, I want to make my own money."

It was as simple as that.

"Stubborn."

My lips tighten. "I'm not lazy. I can work to support myself. Only a lazy woman is impressed with wealth, while hardworking women can go out there and get money themselves."

Arrow shakes his head. "Your brother wants to help you; cut him some slack. Christ, you're a pain in the ass."

"Don't get me wrong, I'm grateful to him, and it's nice knowing the money is there if I ever get in a bad spot."

"Did you tell Rake that?"

"Of course I did," I reply, frowning. "It was a generous thing to do."

"It was very generous. Rake is a good man."

I nod. "I know; trust me, I know. I'd do anything for him too. I'm just hoping he will give me a little more freedom."

He shrugs, like it doesn't bother him either way. "Take it up with him. Let's get moving."

I don't move a muscle.

"What?" he barks.

"You don't have to be so rude. A *please* wouldn't go astray, you know," I grumble, stepping toward his bike.

"Anna, just get your little ass on my bike. I have to make a stop on the way and I'm already late, so stop fucking around," he says quietly, then turns his back to me.

"I want to make a stop too," I say.

"We don't have time."

"We do," I say. "It will only take an hour max."

He tilts his head to the side. "Better be fuckin' important."

"What the hell is your problem exactly? I think I prefer your silence and your grunts to your being an asshole," I snap.

I grab my bag from his hand and hitch it over my shoulder. "Go where you need to go; I'll take the bus home."

Without another look at him, I turn and head toward the bus stop. It's no big deal to me, I have no problem taking the bus. I take three steps before his hand clamps down on my bicep and pulls me to a stop. "Rake wanted me to take you home, so I'm taking you home."

"Don't bother."

"No arguing."

"I'll just tell Rake you took me home, so consider yourself absolved from babysitting duty."

He grits his teeth. "We could have been halfway by now. Stop wasting time and stop being so stubborn. Remember, I'm picking you up tonight."

"Reid can drop me home."

"I said I'll be there to pick you up, Anna. Stop arguing for the sake of it," he grits out.

"I just don't see the point—"

"Anna," he says in warning.

"Fine," I snap, pulling my arm out of his hold and stepping to his bike. He hands me a helmet in silence, puts his own on, and gets on the bike. He has my messenger bag across his back, holding it for me, which I think is kind of cute. Too bad he's being a jerk right now. I slide on behind him, my hands finding the bottom of his cut and holding on. I lean forward against his warm body, until I realize what I'm doing and purposely lean back. The last thing I need is to get close to this man. When we come to a stop at a house, Arrow gets off the bike and I do the same.

"Wait here," he tells me, then walks to the front door. I look around the middle-class neighborhood, trying and failing not to be curious about what Arrow is doing here. When a pretty brunette opens the front door and welcomes him inside, I get my answer. I don't expect it to hurt so much, but it does. He brought me with him to see his fucking girlfriend? Am I meant to just stand here while he does whatever with her? I grit my teeth and look away from the house. Pulling out my phone, I'm about to call Lana to come pick me up when I hear him behind me.

"Let's go," he says, nodding toward his bike.

That was . . . quick.

I avoid his gaze and get on his bike once more.

"Where to now, Anna?"

"The zoo."

He turns his body to look at me. "The fuck?"

"I need to go to the zoo. It's important."

He sighs. "Right."

He turns around, and I hide my grin. I don't actually have to go to the zoo today. I just want to share something that's a part of me with Arrow.

When we arrive, we walk side by side to the entrance. Arrow looks menacing in all black, his leather cut garnering more than a few stares. He ignores everyone, instead looking down at me.

"This is what you want to do with your life?"

My lips twitch. "Something like that."

"Hi, Anna," Beth calls out. She's working as cashier, collecting tickets.

"Hey, Beth, how are you?" I say as we walk by.

Her eyes go to Arrow and widen. "Um. G-good. You here for more observations?"

I nod. She lets me and Arrow through.

Pulling Arrow by his T-shirt, I lead him to my favorite enclosure.

"You brought me here to see a giant turtle?" he asks, staring down at Dave.

"He's a Galápagos tortoise," I say. "They can live to be over a hundred years old. I don't know why, but this is my favorite spot in the zoo."

I look at Arrow to see him studying me, grinning. "Christ,

you should see the way your face lights up talking about a damn turtle."

"Tortoise," I correct.

He chuckles. "Tortoise. Right. What else can you tell me about him?"

I beam.

He is going to be here for longer than an hour.

I wish I could say I was surprised when they walked into Knox's Tavern at midnight, but I wasn't. Even though I'd argued, saying I could get a ride home, Arrow, Irish, Tracker, and Vinnie take a seat at the bar and stare at me expectantly. I glance at Reid, who raises an eyebrow at me. *I told you so.* Arrow doesn't miss our exchange, and his eyes narrow on me, then dart from me to Reid. After spending two hours with me at the zoo, I thought Arrow might let his guard down around me permanently, but by the look of his shuttered gaze, I can almost feel the wall he's put up since our outing. He'd been funny, attentive, and curious today. I found him to be a good listener too. We'd had fun and enjoyed each other's company. At least I'd enjoyed his.

When I look at Reid, I find him still watching me. I glance at Arrow, and I can almost see the moment when he comes to the conclusion that I must be fucking Reid. I look away from him and scan the faces of the other men.

"There's a million other bars you could be in right now," I say to them, wiping my hands on a tea towel.

Tracker smiles widely, blue eyes sparkling. "And miss this

great customer service? Hell, no. I'll have a beer, Anna Bell."

He has his blond hair tied back in a way that I can't help but find attractive. "Loving the man bun by the way," I tell him.

He smirks. "I thought you would."

I'd been going on about a certain sexy model who rocks a beard and a man bun. And tattoos.

Hot!

"What would the rest of you like?" I ask, feeling Arrow's eyes on me.

"Whiskey," Arrow says as he turns from me and glances around the bar. Irish and Vinnie order beers as well. I've met Irish once or twice, but I've never really had a conversation with him. He's a good-looking man, with dark hair and eyes and scars that only add to his appeal. I get the beers first, then pour Arrow his whiskey and slide the glass over to him.

"Put it on our tab," Arrow says, then clears his throat. "Please."

My eyes flare. Did he just say please? Because of our conversation this afternoon? I nod and flash him a small smile before heading to the opposite side of the bar to serve other customers. I see Reid chatting with Arrow, the two of them laughing about something. When everyone is served, I walk to the tables and collect the glasses, piling as many as I can without dropping them. I carry them to the back, almost running into Tag, another guy who works here.

"Need some help?" he asks, eyeing the huge stack.

"No, I've got this. But thanks," I reply, smiling up at him. "You can man the bar though."

He smiles crookedly. "Already giving out orders, hmmmm?"

"What? Trust me, you haven't seen me take control yet." I smirk, giving him a wink for good measure.

He laughs loudly, shakes his head, and walks to the bar. I stack the glasses next to the sink, then tidy up the station before returning out front. I watch as Arrow sips his drink, his gaze never leaving me.

"Slow day at the office?" I ask, leaning my elbows down in the bar.

He shrugs his broad shoulders. "Have to babysit you, so thought I might as well have a drink while I do it."

My smile drops. "You don't have to babysit me, you only have to pick me up. Two hours from now, might I add. And where's Rake?"

"Out," he replies. "I told you he's on a run."

"On a run with who?" I ask, watching as Arrow licks some whiskey off his full, firm lips.

My mouth suddenly feels parched.

I turn to Tracker, much safer territory. "Want another beer?"

"Yes, please," he replies, sliding his empty bottle to me. "Where's Lana tonight?"

"On a date," I reply, not looking up.

"With who?" he asks quietly. "I didn't know she was seeing anyone."

I reach down to the fridge and pull out another beer before I answer. "She wasn't. Now she is."

She wasn't, not really. Some guy asked her out and she was forcing herself to go, determined to forget Tracker—but he didn't need to know that.

A group of women walk in, about six of them. Only two are beautiful, but I see the men around me staring at all of them.

Must be the cheerleader effect in action. Irish calls two women over—the good-looking ones, of course—and one instantly sits on his lap, the other on Vinnie's. I look to Arrow and raise a brow, wondering when he is going to get his man-whore on like the rest of them. When Tracker pulls a middling blonde onto his lap, I judge him.

Hard.

"Tracker—"

"Not your business, Anna," Arrow cuts in. I snap my mouth shut and glare at Arrow, but still can't ignore what Tracker's doing. I don't even like Allie—you could actually say I hated her—but if you don't want a woman, or a man, you end it with them. You don't cheat. There's no honor or loyalty in cheating. Just don't be with that person if you're not happy—it's as simple as that. I've been cheated on before, and it hurts. There's a moment, if only for an instant, when you wonder what you didn't have that the cheater felt the need to seek elsewhere. I had that moment. Then, when my self-respect kicked in seconds later, I realized it wasn't my fault but his. I wasn't the one being disloyal for whatever reason; I'm more honest than that.

I walk away from Tracker and his new friend, who is now straddling him, and stand at the opposite side of the bar. If Tracker ever mans up, dumps Allie, and goes after Lana, there is no way in hell I'm going to be on his side when I see him acting like this. I get drinks for a few rowdy women out for a divorce party, then grit my teeth as I watch the divorcée herself strut over to Arrow after a few shots of liquid courage. I lean back on the bar, cross my arms over my chest, and watch the show.

I need to remind myself that Arrow is not and never will be the man for me.

SEVEN

SHE runs her hand down his shoulder, and it's then I notice none of the men are wearing their cuts. I look away as Arrow whispers something into the woman's ear, unable to keep my eyes on him any longer. Why did I have to have these feelings for him? It would be so much easier if I didn't. If I could see him like I do Tracker, almost like family.

"You okay?" Reid asks as he stands next to me. I have to look up to see his eyes; the man is tall. Maybe even as tall as Arrow. "Why wouldn't I be?" I reply, wiping the bar top to keep my hands busy.

"Because I'm not stupid," he replies quietly, nodding in greeting at a customer who walks in.

I look up at Reid's handsome face. "It's just a little crush."

Maybe if I keep saying it, I will believe it myself.

I say it softly, so no one else can hear. "You repeat it and I'll deny it."

Reid chuckles, then sobers. "You're a smart girl."

"A scientist," I add, grinning. "But where are you going with this?"

"A scientist," he repeats with a nod. "I'm not good at giving advice or anything, but, Anna, as a man, I can tell he has it bad for you. The question is, what are you going to do with it?"

"With what?"

"With what I just told you," he says, looking agitated. "You sure you're a scientist?"

"About as positive as I am that you're a jerk," I shoot back.

He grins. "Pretty positive then, huh?"

"It seems that way."

"You talk to all your bosses like this?" he teases.

"No, Reid, I'm saving all my charm for you."

Reid sighs. "I thought you might say that. You remind me of my sister, Sephie, sometimes."

"Sephie?" What the fuck kind of name was that?

"Persephone," he explains.

"Oh, does she ever come in here? I'd like to meet her."

Reid touches the scar on his cheek absently. "Sometimes. She's on vacation right now in Scotland. But when she's back she's usually here harassing me and Ryan."

"She sounds great," I reply instantly.

"I think I have something that might cheer you up, by the way," he announces, grinning. I watch as he walks to the fridge and opens the door.

"What?" I ask, following him and peering into it.

All lined up in a row were four bottles of blackberry juice.

"For me?" I ask, smiling widely.

He nods. "For you."

"Reid," I say, wrapping my arms around him and giving him a quick hug. "Thank you. I can't believe you remembered!"

He starts to respond but stops when Arrow materializes in front of us.

"Summer know you're flirting with other women when she's not around?" Arrow asks, a muscle working in his jaw.

Reid scowls. "Summer knows I'd never do that, and I'm allowed to talk to my employees."

He gives me a look I can't interpret and walks off, leaving me with an angry-looking Arrow.

"What?" I ask.

"I don't like you working here," he grits out.

"So?"

"So? Men have been staring at your ass and tits all night, and I'm sick of it. I'm gonna have a talk with your brother because he sure as hell won't like it either."

"I can't help it if men stare at me!"

He looks down at my chest. "Maybe cover up a little more?"

I look down at my top, which is a V-neck but hardly revealing. "What do you want me to wear? A turtleneck?"

He nods. "I think that's a fuckin' fantastic idea."

He was insane.

Certifiably insane.

I tuck a loose lock of hair behind my ear and lean my face closer to his. "This is *my* life. You don't get to control it. Who are you to me, Arrow? My brother's friend and my babysitter. Nothing more and nothing less. How dare you tell me what to wear. I'm not even dressed slutty, and it's not illegal to show a tiny bit of cleavage!"

He stares at me for a moment, the air around us thick with tension. Finally he takes a step back and says, "You know what, you're absolutely right."

I watch as he walks up to Tracker, tells him something, and

then leaves the bar. But he doesn't leave alone. He grabs Miss Divorced on his way out, making sure to palm her ass so everyone can see. I make a sound deep in my throat, unable to mask the hurt, ignoring the curious stares from the other bikers. What did I expect? I pushed him and now he is going to fuck another woman. Maybe this was for the best? Maybe it would make it easier for me to forget him and move on, because I'm certainly not one to share.

I force a smile and continue serving drinks for the rest of the night, trying to push Arrow out of my mind.

And failing.

A million questions are running through my head, a million different scenarios.

Did he take her back to the clubhouse?

Is she staying the night?

Was he touching her right now?

Apparently I liked to torture myself.

When two a.m. hits it's time for me to go home.

"Let's go, Anna Bell," Tracker calls out. I look to Reid, who nods his head, so I clock out and grab my handbag, then walk up to Tracker.

"I'm ready," I tell him, biting the inside of my cheek as he pats his companion on the ass.

"You okay to ride?" I ask him, not wanting to get on the bike with him if he is drunk.

"I had two beers," he replies. "I'm fine."

I bite my bottom lip but nod my head.

"You got something to say to me?" he asks quietly, tilting his head to the side. "Come on, Anna Bell. Don't look at me like that."

"Like what?" I ask, brows furrowing.

"Like I just told you your dog is dead," he replies, pulling on my ponytail gently.

I shrug.

"Not like you to hold back," he murmurs, studying me.

"Okay," I start. "Out of all the men I know, I thought you were the good one. Yes, slightly stupid, but the best one. Now I'm not so sure. I need to reassess the situation."

He blinks. "Did you just call me slightly stupid?"

I smirk at him. "You're with Allie, aren't you?"

Tracker shakes his head. "You better not be talking like this to any of the other men—they won't take your shit. Lucky for you, I consider us friends."

He emphasizes the word *friends*, as in, I'm not acting like much of one right now. I step forward and lay my head on his chest. "I don't like cheaters."

"Not your business. You know the rules. And I didn't cheat. You didn't see my dick out, now did you?"

I slap at his arm. "No need to be so crude."

"Anna, you need to get used to this shit, I'm not gonna lie. This life isn't always pretty, but it is what it is, and we don't judge each other. So I don't need your judgment right now, all right? You don't even like Allie, why you giving me a hard time?"

"It doesn't matter what I think. You're right; it's not my place to judge," I reply, looking down.

He lifts my chin up. "I love you like a sister, Anna. Just don't give me any shit, all right? I shouldn't have to explain myself to you."

"Then why are you?" I find myself asking.

He smiles then, a small lift of his mouth. "Because you're one of my favorite women in my life."

I lift my gaze to his. "Okay, I'm backing off. It's just that . . ."

"What?"

"What if one day you and Lana get together, then . . ."

His eyes widen in realization. "That's why you're upset! Not because of what I was doing, but because one day you think I could be doing that to Lana."

I nod. "I guess so. I'm judging you on the standards I would use on someone who was dating my best friend. I shouldn't, I know, but that was why."

He leans down and kisses my forehead. "If I had a woman as good as Lana, sweetie, I wouldn't fuck it up. I promise you that much."

I smile. "Thank you for telling me that, Tracker."

"You want to tell me what's going on with you?" he whispers.

"What do you mean?" I ask.

"There's some tension between you and Arrow, what's that about?"

I purse my lips. "Nothing's happening there. Didn't you see him leave with that woman?"

"Yes," he replies. "I saw that. I also saw your face as he did it. You looked crushed."

I cover my face with my hands. "Was I that obvious? Great, now everyone knows."

He pulls my hands from my face. "No one knows shit; I was watching you closely."

"Don't say anything, Tracker," I plead.

"Hey, no judgment from me, Anna Bell. Just be careful, all right?"

"I'm taking Anna home," comes a rumbly voice from behind me. The hairs on the back of my neck rise.

I thought he left.

I sigh into Tracker's chest, then turn around and look at Arrow. "Back so soon? I thought you'd be spending the night with your guest."

His mouth tightens but he stays silent. Tracker touches my back, rubbing it gently.

I suddenly feel drained and just want to get home to my bed.

"Whoever is taking me, can we please go? I'm tired and I have to get up early to study," I say softly, rubbing my upper arms.

Arrow steps forward, pulling me closer to his body. He takes my arm and leads me to his bike as I say my good-bye to Tracker and wave to Vinnie and Irish—who aren't going home alone.

The ride home is a little tense, for a reason that I can't pinpoint. I shouldn't feel anything for Arrow, and he could bed whomever he wanted—I had no claim on him. I don't know why he came back; I guess he feels a sense of responsibility over me. I'm going to have a talk with Rake and tell him that as much as I appreciate his concern, this shit has to stop. I don't need a group of men keeping an eye on my every move. What if I wanted to go home with someone? I'm old enough to do as I please. I want them to see me as an equal, not someone they have to look after. If Rake won't give in to that, I'm going to ask for anyone except Arrow to pick me up.

That's going to be an awkward conversation.

As we pull up at my house I murmur a thank-you and get off the bike as quickly as it comes to a standstill, but Arrow doesn't let me get away that easily. To my surprise, he slides off his bike and pulls me to him. Taking the helmet from my hands, he leans down and stares into my eyes.

"Fuck," he whispers.

"What?"

"This is a bad idea."

"What is?" I ask, my eyebrows furrowing in confusion. I can't think straight with him being so close to me.

Then, catching me off guard, he grazes his lips against mine. Subtly at first, a chaste kiss. A sweet kiss. But then that kiss changes.

And I become lost.

Arrow is kissing me.

I can't count how many times I've dreamed of this moment.

How much I wanted it, and now it was mine.

Sucking on my upper lip and then my lower lip, his tongue begs entrance. I open my mouth to him, inviting him in, giving him everything he wants and more. His fingers grip my nape, and mine rest on his biceps. I knew it would be like this with him—passionate. Hungry. Greedy.

I knew it.

And now that I've tasted it, I want to keep it.

He pulls away much too soon for my liking, his gaze lowered onto my mouth.

I take a step back, shocked by what happened, but he reaches for me.

"Need to tell you something," he says, grabbing my wrist firmly yet gently.

"What?" I whisper, looking up at him. The moonlight shines on his face, and he seems to be searching for the right words to say.

"I'm not the man for you," he says quietly. "I'm not a good man, and I'm not saying that I'm bad, but . . . I'm bad for you."

"Then why did you just kiss me?" I ask.

I should feel embarrassed about his acknowledging that he knows I like him, but I'm grateful for his candor. This needs to be out in the open no matter what the outcome.

"I needed to kiss you, even if it was just once," he replies as he strokes my cheek. "I'm a selfish fuck."

"I know you did time," I blurt out. "Is that what this is about? You being in prison?"

He scrubs a hand down his face. "I did, but that's not all I'm referring to. I killed the president of the Wild Men MC. Did you know that? You want to be with someone like that? I have blood on my hands, Anna, and it never goes away."

I knew he killed someone. I also knew there had to be more to the story. Maybe it was a club war? Turf war? Something, I don't know what. I knew Arrow was loyal to his club. I couldn't hold it against him. Rake was the same.

"Arrow—"

"It's not just that. I don't have anything to give a good woman like you, Anna. And I don't like feeling guilty because I want to fuck someone, seeing those wide green eyes staring up at me with hurt in them."

I suddenly feel a mixture of anger and embarrassment. I can't believe he called me out on that—and to think I thought I was doing well schooling my expressions. "I didn't ask you for anything, Arrow."

He dips his head. "You didn't have to. You say it all in those eyes."

"What if I just wanted sex?" I whisper, my cheeks flushing.

"You want your brother to kill me?" he says in a low, husky tone. "No, you know what? You would be worth that. But you still deserve better, Anna, and I'm going to try and do the right thing here."

Ahhh, yes. My brother. I forgot about that.

"I won't see you hurt because of me. Violence and pain follow me. I don't want them to touch you, do you understand?"

"Fine," I say after a few seconds. "This conversation never happened. Don't let my wide green eyes stop you from whatever you want to do next time, okay?"

I walk away from him then, but before he starts his engine I'm almost sure I hear him say, "Trust me, I'm trying."

By November—two months later—I'd settled into a routine in my doctoral program and had done my best to put Arrow out of my mind. After spending a long day doing observations at the zoo, I take a hot shower and put on my pajamas. I told my brother I would cook him dinner tonight, the one meal our mother used to make us whenever she was sober, which wasn't very often. I'm glad to be able to spend some quality time with my big brother. He's slowly becoming more open with me, as if he now believes I'm not going to up and leave every time he does something I don't like.

I put on some music as I cook. First I marinate the chicken and put it in the oven, then steam the vegetables and make the mashed potatoes. I grin when Rake knocks at the door—apparently he's learned his lesson about using that damn key. Wiping my hands on a dish towel, I rush to the front door. I shouldn't be surprised when I open it and see not only Rake at the door but Tracker and Arrow as well, but I am.

Arrow has stayed away from me for the last month, avoiding me at every opportunity, and Rake never mentioned he was bringing anyone with him. Luckily I decided to cook a lot, thinking I'd enjoy the leftovers tomorrow. If I'd known they were coming over, I'd have invited Lana too.

I step aside so they can enter. Rake grins and kisses me on my forehead, and Tracker does the same. When Arrow steps through the door, I move away and follow behind Tracker. What the hell is he doing here?

"Smells good," my brother says, grabbing a chair and taking a seat. "Next time I'm bringing Faye. She'd love this."

Great, just what I need, watching the men fawn over her in my own house.

"Nice pj's," Tracker says, smirking at my baby-blue cotton tank top and pants. They have pink unicorns on them with sparkly manes.

"Thanks," I reply. "Dinner's still cooking."

Tracker and Arrow take a seat, and I ignore the heated feel of his gaze on me.

"I had no idea our Anna Bell could cook," Tracker says to my brother. I raise my eyebrow at "our Anna."

"I can't," I insert. "Not really. I mean, I've mastered a couple of dishes and that's the extent of my talent."

"Anna used to cook for us when we were kids," Rake says, glancing at me with a proud look on his face. "If it wasn't for her we would have eaten bread every day."

Arrow and Tracker don't react to his statement, and I wonder just how much they know about our childhood.

"You guys want a beer?" I ask, heading to the fridge before they can reply. I set three beers in front of them, then check on the food while they chat and joke around with one another.

When there's another knock at the door, I have no idea who it could be. Rake gets up to answer it, and when he walks back in with Dex, aka Sin, the MC president, my eyes widen and my mouth drops open. Sin and I don't really know each other. In fact, a head nod is the extent of our familiarity, which he gives me as he steps into my now extremely cramped kitchen and takes a seat at the table. I grab a beer and slide it over to him without a word. It's almost like I'm at the bar.

I scan the four men's faces. "Someone want to tell me what the fuck is going on?"

Rake is the one to reply. "We want you to move into the clubhouse."

"Why?" I demand. I look around my little apartment, my own place, my independence. I like it here, and I'm not going anywhere.

"Because it's safer," he says gently. "And I'll feel better knowing that you're there."

I clench my teeth together. "And you needed three other men to tell me this?"

His brows lower. "What? No, these guys were just hungry, and I'd been bragging about your cooking."

Some of my anger evaporates.

Some.

"Well, I'll happily feed all of you, but I'm not moving to the clubhouse," I tell the lot of them, then turn my back and check on the chicken in the oven. When I close the oven and turn around, I come face-to-face with Sin. He's a handsome man, nicely built with dark hair and eyes that see through you.

"You're staying with us for a couple of days, and that is that," he says, looking down at me. "We got some club business going on and I need Rake's head in the game, not worrying about where his mouthy little sister is, you got me?"

I open my mouth, but then snap it shut. Rake had warned me about this—I needed to respect his president. I didn't really respect him, because he'd done nothing to earn it from me, but I could fake it.

"A couple of days," I grit out in reply, swallowing my pride. If I hear the words *club business* again I am going to stab someone.

Sin's eyes soften. "Good. Faye will be there; she'll take care of you."

Faye and I don't even know each other.

This was going to be awkward.

 **EIGHT**

DINNER was a huge success, and the four of them cleaned their plates. Arrow was quiet throughout the meal, answering only when spoken to. I pretended he wasn't there and eventually relaxed and enjoyed myself. I start to clean up and surprisingly, they all help. Even Sin—looks like Faye trained him right.

"Thanks for dinner," Arrow says, coming to stand next to me.

"You're welcome," I reply, keeping my tone even.

"Even better than Mom's, sis," Rake tells me, coming behind me and wrapping his arms around me. I swallow hard at his casual affection, after wanting it for so long and finally getting it. The kisses on the forehead started a few weeks ago, and now this.

Progress.

"Thanks, Adam," I say quietly. "I'm glad you enjoyed it."

"I more than enjoyed it," he says, then looks next to me at Arrow. "We should get back. Jill must be waiting for you at the clubhouse."

Jill?

Who the hell is Jill?

I look at Arrow, who cringes slightly and rubs the back of his head. Oh, right, my woe-is-me eyes. I avert my gaze, not wanting him to feel guilty. He isn't mine, and he can be with whomever he wants, even this *Jill*. I hate that she has a name, and that I now know it, but it isn't his fault I'm stupid and can't seem to stop myself from wanting him. I don't even know him. I think I've been reading one too many romance novels.

"Jill does what she wants," Arrow mumbles. "She isn't mine."

Rake chuckles. "I heard you were keeping her busy."

"Is this what I'm going to have to listen to when I stay at the clubhouse? If so, I'd rather take my chances here," I say, regretting it as soon as I say it.

Great, let him see just how much it affects you.

"Calm down," Rake tells me. "It'll be fun, I promise."

"Define *fun*," I say. "You guys get to fuck and drink and screw around; I don't get to do any of those things."

Rake clears his throat, suddenly looking extremely uncomfortable. "You can drink."

I spin around and shoot him a glare. "Thank you for your permission."

He frowns. "What is this really about, Anna?"

I throw my hands in the air. I can't say what this is *really* about, which is the fact that I am angry and hurt over the fact I have just heard that Arrow has someone and that I am going to have to face this woman. I am jealous, and the thought of Arrow with another woman is killing me. Burning me from the inside out.

"I have no freedom," I tell him.

Which is also true, but I am overreacting and I know it.

Sin looks to Rake. "I went through this with Faye. Give her a little space, brother. I know you want to protect her, and we all will, but she's young and needs to live a little too."

I smile gratefully at my unlikely savior. "Thank you, Sin." He just earned my respect.

"You have freedom," Rake says, looking between Sin and me.

"Really?"

"Yeah," he replies. "You go to school and do your thing. I'm not with you all the time."

"College is my freedom?" I ask in a dry tone. "What about with men?"

Tension fills the room.

"Like I said, I'm not around you all the time. You have freedom."

"No, I don't. I can't even have a boyfriend who I don't have to hide."

Three voices come at me, speaking over one another. "Who the fuck are you seeing?"

"What boyfriend?"

"The fuck?"

"See?" I yell. "Do you see what I have to deal with?"

Rake sighs heavily and scrubs a hand down his face. I notice his knuckles are busted up again. "You're my sister, I can't even think about you—"

"Fucking?" I add dryly.

He grimaces. "Yes, that."

"Well, I'm your sister and I don't want to know about you being into bondage and shit, but I still hear it around, don't I? And I'm alive."

"No men are allowed in the clubhouse unless they're a brother," Sin says as he grabs another beer from the fridge.

"Maybe I'll just hook up with a brother, then," I say casually, ignoring the four pointed glares I instantly receive.

"That's not happening," Rake adds. "No fuckin' way."

"Why? Your own club brothers not good enough for me?" I ask, crossing my arms over my chest.

"No one is, Anna," Rake replies. "No one is good enough for you."

My eyes widen. He actually believes that.

"This is all about what happened with Jacob, isn't it? You need to let that go, Adam! He didn't get to hurt me! You saved me, and I'll always be thankful for that, but now you need to trust that I can protect myself."

I realize I call him Adam every time I get emotional.

I watch as his expression turns fierce, his eyes sparking with anger. "Don't even say that fucker's name to me! He's lucky to be breathing, and only it's thanks to you he is!"

Okay, bad idea bringing up Jacob. The atmosphere in the room is now even more tense, and filled with scowling pissed-off alpha males.

Note to self: never bring up Jacob again.

The men glance at one another but stay silent.

"What about Tracker?" I ask, choosing him because he's the safest. "Maybe I want to fuck him."

"Thanks for that, Anna Bell." Tracker grimaces.

I fight a smile. "I'm sorry, you were the first person I thought of."

"Not happening," Arrow seethes, finally speaking again. "Not fucking happening."

Ha! So he doesn't want me, but he doesn't want anyone else to have me either.

I look around at all their varying expressions and roll my eyes. "I was trying to make a point."

Sin looks at my brother. "Like I said, give her some space, Rake, she isn't a kid."

Rake's eyes harden, but he doesn't say anything.

"She might actually want to come to the clubhouse if you give her a little freedom," Tracker adds, earning himself a glare from both Arrow and Rake.

"You're no one's club whore, Anna," Rake says between clenched teeth. "I won't have it."

I put my hand on his shoulder. "I know that! You're missing the point here."

He shakes his head. "No brothers. But I'll lay off you dating anyone else. As long as he's good to you."

There was no one I was interested in besides Arrow, but at least it was something. My eyes find his to see him already watching me, a scowl etched on his face.

I nod, keeping my gaze trained on Arrow but answering Rake. "Deal."

Arrow didn't want me, so what the hell? I just saved the next man I dated from my brother and his goons.

It's the small things in life.

"But, Anna . . ." my brother adds. "If they hurt you, they die. Painfully."

I bend over, leaning on my knees, laughing so hard that I have to gasp for air.

"What did I miss?" Ryan asks as he walks in carrying a huge box in his hands.

My laughs turn to giggles as I look over at Summer, who is shaking her head at me, covering her mouth with her hand. "Nothing much, just the usual."

He raises an eyebrow and places the box down on the floor. "This is the usual?"

Summer shrugs and leans back against the bar. "Dude, it's dead. We have to amuse ourselves somehow, so we were doing a quiz."

Summer had brought in one of those girly magazines and we were having a good laugh over this month's quiz: Is He All Man, or Part Pansy? Ryan picks up the magazine and reads one of the questions. "Is it okay for a man to go to the movies alone?"

Summer looks at me and starts laughing again.

I look at Ryan and shrug. "What? I was just saying, who cares if a man goes to the movies alone. As long as he doesn't have his hand down his pants, it's okay with me."

Ryan blinks, then starts laughing too. "You're something else, Anna."

My shift goes by quickly, and then Tracker is here to take me to the clubhouse. My stuff is already there. I walk up to Tracker with a smile on my face until I see his own. He has a red scratch mark down his jaw, fingernails by the look of it.

"What did you do?" I ask, cupping his jaw for a closer inspection. "You let that bitch hit you?"

He walks with me to his bike before he speaks. "Don't worry about it."

"Since you can't hit a woman, can I do it for you?"

He smirks. "Thank you for wanting to defend my honor, Anna Bell, but don't worry about Allie. I'm done with her."

"I'm guessing she didn't take it well," I say in a dry tone.

I squeal as he suddenly lifts me onto the bike. "You'd be guessing right."

What's the bet they'll be back together tomorrow? That's how their relationship seems to be. Two people who were never meant to be together yet stuck with each other because they'd gotten too comfortable. But hey, who am I to judge? I didn't even have anyone special in my life. Maybe Tracker just didn't want to be alone and Allie was a sure bet who knew his lifestyle and didn't have a problem with it.

When we arrive at the clubhouse, Arrow walks out to greet us. "Hey, Anna."

I look around. He's talking to me now?

"Hey, Arrow," I say, a little unsure. I walk in with him and Tracker on either side of me. No one is around, for which I'm grateful. "Where is everyone?"

"Getting ready to go on a run," Arrow replies, opening my room door for me. I walk in and toss my handbag on the bed before flopping onto the mattress.

"So who's going to be here? How is this safe when no one is even here, and what exactly is the danger anyway?" I ask.

He closes the door and comes and sits next to me on my bed. "I'm staying, and a few of the prospects are staying. Everyone else is needed."

"Why do you get to stay?" I ask, looking into his eyes.

"Just because," he answers a little gruffly. "It's my turn to stay behind."

"And the danger? If you say club business I swear I'll scream."

A lip twitch. "Something's going down, that's all you need to know. If another MC sees a weakness, they will take that opportunity to use it against us and we can't take the chance. Because of where you work, people know you belong to the club, and they might use that to their advantage."

I remember Reid saying something similar.

"Why do they call you Arrow?" I blurt out, something I've been wondering for a while now. Is he good with a bow and arrow? Maybe he has an arrow tattoo. For some reason he finds the question really amusing, his eyes sparkling with humor. I can tell he's trying not to laugh.

It's a good look on him.

Really good.

Damn him, he isn't making this easy on me.

"If you ask Faye, I'm sure she will tell you why," he starts. "But she would be wrong."

"What does Faye think?" I ask, assuming it's going to be something dirty. Has he been with Faye? In my mind I picture myself strangling her.

He smirks. "Doesn't matter what she thinks, the truth is much less interesting."

"Well, come on," I say, nudging him with my shoulder. "Keep going."

"My surname," he says.

"Arrow is your surname?"

He shakes his head. "My surname is Arrowsmith. Killian Arrowsmith."

I bite my bottom lip. "You're right, that is boring."

He laughs this time. "I know. I think Faye's story is a lot more creative."

I make a note to find out just what that is.

"Why are you in such a good mood?" I ask him, feeling suspicious. I don't think I've ever seen him this lighthearted, especially around me. "You're usually grumpy."

He stands up and holds out his hand. "A man's not allowed to be in a good mood now and again?"

I place my hand in his large callused one. I wonder if this Jill is the reason for his sudden happiness. That thought instantly kills *my* good mood. "What are you doing, Arrow? You've stayed away from me all this time and suddenly we're best friends?"

"I'll be keeping an eye on you for the next few days. Don't make this difficult," he says, letting go of my hand as he opens the door.

"Is Lana going to be safe?"

"Lana isn't on anyone's radar, of course she's safe," he says patiently. "Come on. Faye wanted to see you as soon as you got here."

"I don't know Faye."

"I know; that's why she wants to get to know you."

"Why?"

He looks at me then. "'Cause you're family, darlin'."

Well, when he says it like that, it doesn't sound so bad after all.

"It's a little weird being around her," I admit to him.

"Why?" he asks, studying me.

"I don't know," I say, shuffling my feet.

"Tell me the real reason, Anna. You know you can trust me," he cajoles, his expression not giving away anything.

I wring my hands together. "Fine, but don't repeat this."

"You know I won't."

I expel a deep sigh. "She knows my own brother better than I do, and he's closer to her, so it's . . . I don't know."

I can't believe I just admitted that out loud. Nothing like letting a man with the power to break you see your weakness.

Arrow's eyes flare in realization. "Your brother fuckin' adores you, Anna, don't worry about anything else. You let Faye in, she'll be a good friend to you. Trust me."

My phone rings. Damien's name flashes on-screen.

Arrow sees it.

"Who the fuck is Damien?" he asks, in an even tone filled with restrained anger.

I roll my eyes. "A *friend* from school."

"Why is he calling you?" he demands.

I lift my shoulder in a shrug. "How am I supposed to know? I didn't answer the call."

"You fucking him?" he asks.

I gasp. "What right do you have to ask me that?"

He looks away from me.

My phone rings again. Damien. It must be important.

Before I know what he intends, Arrow snatches the phone from me and presses the green button. "Hello," he sneers into the line. "This is Anna's man, call her again and I'll be paying you a little visit."

"Arrow, what the fuck?" I yell, trying to grab my phone back from him. "He's a friend, you asshole! And I'm going to have to face him in class, so thanks a lot!"

Arrow steps back and I'm jumping in the air trying to get my phone back. He hangs up on poor Damien, who is probably traumatized, and looks down at me like I'm the one who did something wrong.

"At least now he knows where he stands," he says in a smug tone.

"I've never wanted to punch someone more in my life," I muse, poking him in the arm. "You're turning me to violence!"

He has the audacity to laugh. "You're fuckin' cute when you're angry, you know that?"

I huff. "Well, expect to see a lot of cute from me, then."

He grins and hands me my phone. "Looking forward to it. Now let's go and see Faye."

I follow him out to the living area, quickly texting Damien that I was sorry and I would talk to him in class. He doesn't reply, but then again I didn't really expect him to. He's seen the men who drive me home, so he's probably scared shitless.

There goes my only friend in college. Guess I'll have to make a new one next week. Arrow stops in his tracks, so I do the same. The place is still empty, but Arrow yells out Faye's name, and she soon walks in.

"Hello, Anna," she says to me, then hugs Arrow. "I hear you're stuck with us for the next few days."

"Looks like it," I tell her, sitting down on the couch. "Where is everyone?"

"The women are out getting supplies. We like to stay stocked before we go on a lockdown," she explains.

She really is beautiful. Wait, did she just say lockdown?

"Lockdown?" I repeat, looking at Arrow for an answer.

"What?" he asks.

"What about work?" I ask him. "I have to go to work!"

"I told Reid you aren't coming in," he says, leaning back against the couch.

"I'm sorry, what?" I whisper, my hands clenching into fists.

Faye cringes, obviously picking up on my anger before Arrow does.

I stand up. "You controlling bastard! I didn't know I was literally stuck under this roof with nowhere to go!"

"Anna, calm down," Arrow says, looking up at me. "It's for your own safety, so I'm not fuckin' sorry, and I know Rake isn't sorry either."

I see Faye look at Arrow curiously, a thoughtful look on her face. "You could have warned the girl."

Arrow shoots her a look. "You think she would have come? She's a fuckin' spitfire."

"Just how exactly do you plan to keep me here?" I ask him. "You can't watch me twenty-four-seven, and with you being a man-whore and all, I assume there will be times when you're busy getting your dick wet."

Faye surprises me by bursting out laughing.

"Oh, fuck!" she says, tapping her hand on her thigh. She looks at me and grins. "I've never seen a woman, other than me of course, put Arrow in his place. This is gold."

Arrow, on the other hand, doesn't look so impressed.

"Don't test me, Anna," is all he says.

Don't test him?

I look to Faye, the woman I didn't think I liked but somehow in the last few minutes has become my ally. "I heard you're a good fighter."

She tilts her head, probably wondering what I'm getting at, but then nods.

"Want to spar?" I ask. "I could work out some frustration."

She grins, widely, showing off perfect white teeth. "Hell yeah. Let's go."

"Anna . . ." Arrow says, warning in his voice.

I ignore him and walk off.

"Don't say I didn't warn you," I hear him call out behind me.

Has no faith in me, does he?

I'm going to love proving him wrong.

NINE

"DON'T worry," Faye says, sounding genuine. "I'll take it easy on you."

I smirk. "No need to do that on my account."

I tie my hair up so it's off my face and stretch my arms above my head.

"You know, this is the first time we've actually been alone with each other," she says, watching me.

I turn to the door to see Arrow standing there in the frame, his eyes on me. "Except for Arrow watching us."

Turning my back on him, I face Faye and say, "You're right. Even though these aren't normal circumstances."

Faye laughs. "Hey, you're the one who wanted to spar."

"I know."

"A lot of frustration to get out?" she asks with a knowing smirk.

I purse my lips. "Something like that."

When was the last time I'd even had an orgasm? I should really get that taken care of, and stat.

"Shall we?" I ask, as Faye stretches a little.

"We shall. Show me what you've got, Anna," she says, stepping to me, raising her clenched fists in front of her body. "If you want to stop, just say when, all right?"

I nod and step closer to her. She strikes first, her punch aiming for my jaw. I block her arm before it reaches my face and strike back with my own hit. Neither of us is hitting with all our strength—it's more about who can get in the hits than how hard they are. She somehow gets me in a hold, turning me around and wrapping her arm around my neck, applying only a little pressure. I elbow her in the stomach, which has her stepping back, her eyes full of excitement, and the corners of her lips turned upward. "I think I'm going to like you, Anna."

I grin. "I hope I can say the same."

She laughs then, and shakes her head at me. "Let me teach you something I learned last week."

I perk up at the prospect of learning something new. "I'd like that."

We share a smile.

Looks like I found some common ground with the queen bee after all.

Sweaty, my sports bra and yoga pants plastered to my skin, I walk out of the club's gym and head straight to my room, wanting a shower more than anything.

"Now I see what Rake was talking about when he said you were badass," Arrow says, leaning against the wall with one leg bent. "You held your own."

I smirk. "I know. Now let me pass, I have to take a shower."

His gaze rakes over me from head to toe, making me feel as

though he missed nothing. When his eyes hit mine again, I can see the heat in them.

"Fuck," he whispers. "You're perfect."

He takes a step closer to me, but then we hear voices. Sounds like the women are back.

"I'm so glad Arrow is the one staying behind," we hear one woman say. Arrow's eyes don't leave mine as we listen to them chatter.

"Looks like I'll be the only one getting laid while the men are away."

I don't look away, but I try with everything in me to not let the hurt shine through. Arrow reaches out and cups my jaw.

"Beautiful," he murmurs, longing in his gruff voice. "But not for me."

"Only because you don't care enough to fight for what you want," I reply, lifting my chin. "Now let me go."

He knows what I mean, because he breaks contact between us and rubs the back of his neck.

He needs to let me go. No more of this *I want you but I can't have you* shit. If he really wanted me, he would damn well take me.

"Arrow, there you are!" a woman says as she walks up to us; seeing me, she frowns. "Who are you?"

Arrow turns to her and winces. "Get the fuck out of here, Jill."

She nods and retreats, following his orders like an obedient dog. I'd seen enough. I know there's more to Arrow, so much more, but it's like he doesn't care. He doesn't *want* to be that person. I read somewhere that the worst mistake a woman can make is to fall in love with a man's potential.

I will not be making that mistake.

It also seems I am locked in a house for a few days with Arrow and his girlfriend.

Just fucking great.

I avoid his gaze and push past him, our bodies touching, my arm rubbing against his chest. That small bit of contact makes me want to moan, the feel of his hard, muscled body.

It's official—I need to get laid.

Faye introduces me to all the women. Names and faces blur, but there's Allie, a redhead named Jess, a cute girl named Katie, and, of course, Jill. Jill was, according to Faye, a club whore who had clung on to Arrow, and she now only serviced him. Her words, not mine. Then there was Clover, Faye and Sin's beautiful little girl. The biker princess, I liked to call her—she was absolutely adorable.

I watched Sin and Clover together, and I couldn't look away. He is so sweet with her, and it made me wish I had that growing up. I'm blessed to have Rake, but he didn't compensate for lack of a father figure. Watching Sin lift Clover up on his shoulders and her giggling and calling out "Daddy!" made me miss something I'd stopped yearning for years ago. The wishes and dreams of a young little girl, waiting for her father to come and save her. A father who never did.

"I'm trying to find a nanny," Faye says, looking down at her sleeping daughter. We were alone, sitting in the living room. "The club is keeping me busy working for them, and Sin can't watch her all the time."

An idea pops into my head.

"I could ask my best friend, Lana. She's great with kids, completely trustworthy, and she needs a job while she's still in school," I reply.

Faye nods. "I met her once. You think she'd be interested?"

"I could ask," I say. "There isn't anyone I would trust more with my own kid. And she would keep quiet about club shit."

Faye grins, opening an apple juice box and taking a sip. "Club shit—don't let Dex hear you say that."

I pick up my glass from the coffee table in front of me and take a sip. "Duly noted."

"So what the hell is going on with you and Arrow?" she asks.

I look down into my drink, which has suddenly become very interesting. "I have no idea what you're talking about."

"Really," she purrs. "The sexual tension is so high even I'm getting turned on."

I choke on my drink, orange and vodka dripping down my chin.

"Sexy." She smirks as I wipe it away with the back of my hand.

"Arrow is Arrow," I say, sighing.

"That he is," she says, giving me an inquisitive look. "I love him like he is my own brother, you know, but even I know his flaws. However, he has a heart of gold and a reason for being like he is. He used to be a lot more easygoing. When I first met him, sure, he had his grumpy side, but he was also quick to joke and put up with all my shit."

Interested, I lean forward and gesture for her to continue.

"Mary," she whispers. "She was a good friend of mine, and Arrow's woman. The men went on a run and she was shot when another MC broke into the compound."

My eyes widen. "So when they say dangerous, they aren't fucking around."

"I know," she says. "Anyway, Arrow took that on himself, and he's been miserable ever since. Except . . . when he's around you."

I put my hand up. "Don't read into that. He's been clear as crystal about where the two of us stand. And let's not forget Jill."

"I can't pretend to know what goes through his head, but I know that since Mary I haven't seen him have any interest in another woman—"

"Except for sex."

She cringes. "Well, yeah. When I saw him with you it was like you breathed the life back into him. It was a good thing to see."

"So he loved Mary?" I ask, already knowing the answer.

She nods, a sad look taking over her expression. "There's no one who didn't love Mary. She was kind, sweet, and gentle. How she ended up with a biker like Arrow I never knew, but she was all things good in the world."

I bite the inside of my cheek. I could never compare to that, and I shouldn't be expected to. It's obvious that Arrow isn't the man for me. If only I could curb this stupid attraction I have for him. It's bad enough he's hooking up with random skanks every night—competing with the ghost of his ex-lover is not something I want to do. I'm sorry for his loss; in fact, I wish he still had Mary. Arrow deserves to be happy; I'd want that for him.

"Why are you telling me this?" I ask her.

She wrings her hands. "I think you'll be good for him. I think that he wants you but is fighting it. He's letting the past control his future. He's not letting himself be happy because of the guilt and pain he's still carrying over Mary's death."

Why does he feel guilt, I have to wonder. It wasn't his fault. His lifestyle is a dangerous one, and I'm sure Mary knew that. Maybe because he couldn't protect her . . . Yeah, I could see a man like Arrow being guilty over that. He's probably carrying a whole lot of shit on his shoulders.

"Why do they call him Arrow?" I ask, changing the subject. I don't need to wonder how Arrow's mind works. What I need to do is forget about anything to do with him. If only it were that easy.

She laughs. Hard. "I remember one morning I walked out into the kitchen and he was standing there, cooking breakfast butt naked. I was horrified. He turned around, smiling and cheerful, like there was nothing wrong with his nudity. Then I looked down and saw his . . ."

She trails off, blushing.

"Penis," I offer.

"Yes," she says. "His penis, and it was huge. Long, straight, thick, and aimed right at me, like it was pointing at its next victim or something."

"Like an arrow," I surmise.

"Yes." She giggles. "Like an arrow."

We both break out in a fit of laughter.

"What's so funny?" Arrow asks as he enters the room, taking a seat and looking from Faye to me.

"Nothing," we say at the same time.

He raises an eyebrow at us and says, "I knew the two of you together would be trouble."

"Trouble? No idea what you're talking about," Faye replies, innocently staring down at her manicure.

"We were just talking about—"

Faye raises her eyes to me and we start laughing again.

Arrow shakes his head. "Spill it now. Look at the two of you, giggling like fuckin' teenagers."

I sober. "Faye was just telling me why she thinks everyone calls you Arrow."

I look down at his crotch for emphasis.

Arrow's eyes crinkle. "You both talkin' 'bout my cock?"

Faye gasps. "Don't let Dex hear you say that."

"It's the truth," Arrow scoffs.

"I was just telling her the story," Faye says, smirking. "Good times."

"Anna?" Arrow growls.

Oh, shit, I was still staring at his crotch.

"Yes?" I reply sweetly, my expression a picture of innocence.

He does something then that makes me want to rip his clothes off and lick him inch by delicious inch.

He smiles.

His lips curve up on both sides, and his eyes dance with amusement.

"What you looking at, Anna?" he asks, looking on the verge of laughter.

My gaze darts to Faye, who is staring wide-eyed at Arrow.

"Nothing," I mumble. But it wasn't nothing; it was something.

Something huge.

His phone rings, ruining the moment, and he instantly stands up, barking into the receiver, "Talk to me."

He leaves the room and walks into the clubroom for privacy.

"Do you have any idea what's going on?" I ask in a soft voice.

She sighs and rubs her forehead. "Arrow killed the president of another MC a couple years ago. Sin and their new president negotiated a truce, but I honestly think they're going to be at each other's throats for the rest of their lives. Every time something goes wrong, our men blame the Wild Men MC; I don't know if it's really them or not."

"So what went wrong this time?" I ask.

"A deal went wrong, and Dex and the others went there to sort it out and smooth things over with the other party."

"Do they sell drugs?" I whisper, looking around to make sure no one was listening.

She shakes her head. "Not anymore."

Okkaaaayyyyy.

"I do know things, Anna, but there isn't much I can say. As their lawyer I keep my ears open and my lips sealed."

She was their lawyer?

So she must know more than she is letting on. Everything about every member, Rake included.

I want to kill my brother for getting me into this shit. I twirl a lock of hair around my finger and sigh heavily.

Faye smirks. "Don't worry, it's nothing too bad."

I stare at her face and wonder how she wound up where she is. "How did you end up as Sin's old lady?"

She smiles. "Long story short, Dex and I used to be neighbors when we were growing up. We ran into each other one night at a bar and ended up hooking up. That's how I became pregnant with Clover. I was leaving the city, planning on being a single mother, when Dex found me and brought me back. He actually brought me to the clubhouse, so I was thrown into this world just as you've been."

"That's quite a story," I say, blinking slowly, trying to absorb that information.

She nods. "To be honest I didn't know if Dex could give me what I needed. But we fell in love and there's no one else for me; he's it. I accepted the club with him, and I love these guys. They're my family now."

I could see that her words were the truth. They were one huge, unconventional family.

"They're all good guys, I could tell that from the start. Rough, but good nonetheless."

Faye smiles, her eyes shining. "They are that. Don't get me wrong, I wouldn't want to be on their bad side."

I laugh. "Yeah, definitely not, but they're loyal to those they care about. To be honest, I was surprised at how easily I was accepted here by the men. They welcomed me with open arms just because I was Rake's sister. I think Sin was the one who was most cautious around me, to be honest."

Faye tilts her head to the side, a thoughtful expression on her face. "I think Dex didn't want Rake to get hurt in case you decided you didn't want to have anything to do with us. This isn't the life for everyone, you know. So I think he was a little wary. As president he takes things a little more seriously than he used to. He cares about each of his brothers and takes a lot on his shoulders, wanting everyone to be happy. He also knew Rake was forthcoming with you, and didn't know if he could trust you with information about the club. But trust me, he knows now that you're a good, honest woman and that you love your brother and would never betray him."

I swallow. "I never thought of it that way. But you're right, I'd never do anything to hurt Rake or this club."

Arrow walks back into the room, looking pissed. Jill walks into the living room trailing behind him, sliding next to him. He moves away from her, punches the wall, and then storms out of the room. Faye and I exchange glances.

"I'll go talk to him," Jill says, fixing her hair before going in the direction Arrow went.

"Clueless," Faye mutters under her breath. "Where the fuck did he find that one?"

"Toxic?" I guess, referring to one of the popular strip clubs in the city.

She laughs. "He doesn't give a shit about her."

That didn't make it hurt any less.

"She didn't sleep in his room though; she's been sleeping with the girls."

I knew that. In fact I have a feeling Arrow was making sure I knew that, because last night he told Jill in front of me that he was going to bed alone.

"You were a little standoffish with me," Faye blurts out. "Or was that my imagination? I kind of thought maybe you didn't like me."

I bite my lips. "It wasn't that I didn't like you. I guess I was kind of jealous."

Her eyes widen. "Jealous about what?"

I rub my cheek, wondering how best to explain it. "It was stupid, and it really had nothing to do with *you* exactly; it was just that you and Rake had spent a lot of time together and were so close. As close as he and I should have been, but we were still getting to know each other again, and Rake was trying to protect me from everything, including his true self."

Her eyes flash in understanding. "Trust me, your brother

loves you more than anyone. I think he just took a little time testing the waters, hoping that you would stick around in this crazy place with these crazy-ass people."

We both laugh.

"He told me he didn't want you to leave again, so he was stuck between wanting to show you the man he is now and not wanting you to cut him out of your life if you saw something you didn't like," she explains further.

"He should know me better than that," I mumble.

Faye shrugs her shoulders. "You were gone awhile. Time changes people."

She could say that again.

"I love my brother, and I guess I was acting a little possessive," I say, when the realization hits me. "Great, I'm more like him than I want to admit."

Faye laughs at that. "As the president's old lady, I take care of all my guys. I think half of them already love you, and I hope you stick around. It's good to have a woman to spar with, one who can take my hits and return them full force."

I smirk. "Women bonding over violence, what a great pair we are."

"Biker women, baby, we have to be tough," she says. "If we're not, we end up being treated like her." She cocks a thumb at Jill, still knocking on Arrow's door.

"Fuck off!" I hear him bellow.

Faye and I cringe.

Jill starts crying.

Just my first official day in the biker clubhouse.

 **TEN**

ARROW paces the game room of the clubhouse, running his hands through his hair in frustration. "I should be there with them."

"Why aren't you?" I ask, lifting the pool cue off the table after playing my shot.

He scoffs. "I'm not letting history repeat itself."

He downs some Scotch. I almost want to tell him that if anything did happen right now, he'd be too drunk to do anything about it.

Instead, I bite my tongue.

Blade, one of the prospects, walks in and whispers something to Arrow, who nods. I haven't really spoken to any of the three prospects, and they don't seem too eager to get to know me either.

"Hello, Blade," I say, trying to be friendly.

Blade looks to Arrow quickly, before nodding his head at me. "Anna."

Arrow narrows his eyes on him. "Don't you have work to do?"

I scowl at Arrow and speak as soon as Blade leaves the room. "You don't have to be so rude."

His answer is to drink some more.

Jill and Allie walk in, their own drinks in their hands, and stand on either side of Arrow. I don't take my eyes off Allie, who I can tell is a little tipsy. But when she puts her hand on Arrow's chest, I've had enough. I look at Arrow, and it's him I speak to. "Get that whore's hand off your chest right now, Arrow, before I break it."

He glances down as if only just realizing Allie is touching him, then quickly shrugs off her hand. "The fuck," he rumbles. "If you think I would ever touch a brother's woman, you don't fuckin' know me at all. Now get out of here!" He looks at Jill and sneers, his upper lip curling. "Both of you."

I swallow hard as they leave, then step forward to make my exit.

"Stay," he demands, not even bothering to look at me.

He wants me to stay, by asking me like that and in that tone? Riiiggghhht.

I storm past him and into my room. I'm about to close the door when he pushes himself inside. "You don't know how to listen, do you?"

"I listen just fine, thank you. I just don't see why the hell I have to listen to *you*. Now, I'm going to take a shower and go to bed, so I'm asking you kindly to fuck off."

He blinks at me, and then I see his lip twitch.

It pisses me off even more.

"I really don't see what's so amusing," I say, sitting on my bed and glaring up at him. Instead of storming out of my room as I'd hoped, he sits on the floor by my feet. "And do you talk to all women like that?"

I didn't even like Allie or Jill, but still.

"Most women don't talk back to me. I guess it amuses me that you do it at every turn," he replies, pausing. "And I'd never talk to you like that, Anna, so no, I don't talk to all women like that."

He leans his head back on the mattress, and I can't help but let my hand reach out and feel his hair. When he moans, I massage his scalp and continue to run my fingers through his thick, silky hair.

"Feels so good," he says quietly, followed by a contented sigh. "What is it about you?"

"I could ask you the same question," I mutter, continuing my administrations. "How much longer am I stuck here with you?"

"I'm not that bad," he says, reaching his hand out and casually resting it on my thigh. My body tingles with just that simple touch, and I both want and don't want him to reach his hand up higher.

"You're not that good either," I say, remembering our previous conversation.

"No, I guess I'm not. Tonight I will be though."

I have no idea what he's talking about, but when he gets up and lifts my blanket, sliding under my sheets, my eyes widen. "You can't sleep here."

He ignores me, trying to get comfortable. When he sits up and pulls off his T-shirt, my mouth waters and I decide that maybe he *can* sleep here. His body is perfectly cut and defined, and I get a flash of ripped abs before he pulls the sheet up to cover himself. I feel my nipples pebble, unable to get that image out of my head.

Holy shit, he's a fine specimen.

"You going to sleep or just stand there with your mouth open all night? If you stay like that I might get ideas that will get both of us into shit," he says in a husky voice. Is that his sex voice? Because I could get on board with that. I head to the bathroom, shower and brush my teeth, then change into my pajamas. When I walk back into the room Arrow is still awake and watching me. Am I really going to sleep next to him? My feet take me to the other side of the bed. I lift up the blanket and slide in next to him.

I guess that's a yes.

"Your feet are fuckin' cold," he complains, but pulls me closer, into the safety of his arms. How am I supposed to sleep, being pressed up against him like this? His whole body is rock-hard, steel against my softness. I feel protected. Swallowed by his big body, wrapped in his strength.

I also feel more turned on than I ever remember feeling.

"Arrow?" I whisper.

"Sleep," he replies, kissing the back of my head.

For once, I do as he says.

I wake up feeling warm and safe. When I open my eyes, the first things I see are two sleepy, smiling brown eyes staring at me.

I almost scream, quickly lifting my head up. "Arrow, what the hell?"

He smirks. "You look so cute when you sleep. And the little snoring sounds you make are—"

"I do not snore!" I reply indignantly, scooting away from him on the bed. I can see that he's already had a shower: his hair is damp and I can smell his clean scent from here.

He pulls me back, right up against his body. "You do."

"I don't."

"Darlin'," he says, smiling. "You do."

"Prove it," I demand, sounding smug.

My eyes widen in horror as he says, "Okay," and grabs his phone from the side table.

"Tell me you didn't," I groan, rolling over and burying my face in my pillow.

But he did.

I hear a soft snoring noise playing through the phone.

I turn my head to the side to look at him, giving him the dirtiest look I can fathom. "You just crossed a line."

He laughs, eyes crinkling. "I wasn't going to show anyone."

"Not the point," I grit out, trying to hide my embarrassment. Who wants to actually hear themselves snoring?

There is no way to make that shit cute.

Someone please kill me now.

"That is the point. You can trust me; I just wanted to annoy you a little. See, I'll delete it," he says, unable to hide a grin.

I go to grab the phone off him to delete it myself but instead end up pinned under him. Before I know what he's about to do, before I can think of the consequences, his mouth is on mine, firm and demanding.

And perfect.

Better than I had imagined, and trust me, I had imagined a lot.

His lips are full and soft and his tongue knows exactly what it's doing as it licks my own, tasting me. He tastes delicious, like strawberry candy.

It's not just *a* kiss, it's *the* kiss.

And I lose myself in it.

My arms wrap around his neck as I put my all into the kiss, showing him without words how much I've wanted him.

He grinds his pelvis into me and I feel his hardness, feel the size of his cock Faye was telling me about.

He's huge.

And so hard.

I raise my hips up, wanting more friction. Arrow suddenly lifts his head, moving his mouth away, ignoring my noise of protest. He peers down at me, watching me through gentle, heavy-lidded eyes. He swallows, his throat working as his gaze lowers to my lips. He licks his own, as if wanting another taste.

I make a soft mewling noise and gently grab on to his beard, wanting him to come back to me.

Wanting more of what he'd given me. I knew he had so much more to give, and I wanted it. I wanted everything he had to offer. In this moment, nothing else mattered.

"Sweet Anna," he murmurs, eyes still on my lips.

"Arrow—"

"I know," he says, the two words sounding like they were pulled from his throat. "Fuck, I shouldn't have kissed you. I was selfish, I just wanted another taste."

Just a taste? Does that mean that it isn't going to happen again? I don't like that. Not one bit. He thinks he is selfish, but I want him to be. I want to yell at him.

Be selfish.

Be selfish!

I don't care. To me, it is selfish to keep himself away from me, especially after that kiss.

"Arrow—"

"Fuck."

Yes, please.

He gently pulls away from me then, and I don't like it. His index finger grazes my cheek, a touch so soft that goose bumps appear on my skin. He exhales, his finger now running down my jawline. Then, he drops his hand and pushes off the bed, standing next to it and staring at me, indecision written all over his expression.

As for me, I feel confused. How could he feel what I just did and not want any more? Why is he pulling away from me? I'm not an expert on love, but I don't think that a connection like this comes along every day. I'd never experienced it before, but then Arrow was older than me, and had loved before me. I knew he didn't love me, but surely he felt at least lust?

His hands turn to fists at his sides.

Then I watch him, almost as if in slow motion, as he walks out of my room, closing the door behind him.

I stare at that door for what feels like an hour. I'm feeling hurt, lonely, and sexually frustrated as hell, not a good mix. Why do I keep going in deeper with him when I know it will always turn out like this? We both know nothing can happen, so why do we keep playing this game? It is almost like we come together whenever one of us gives in to their weakness, but then pull apart when that moment is over. It isn't meant to be like that in a relationship, but that isn't what we have, is it?

I take a long shower, ignoring my needy body. Bringing myself to orgasm wouldn't satisfy me as much as Arrow could, so even though I'm tempted to let my fingers wander, I don't. Instead, I brush my teeth and get ready for the day, all the while thinking about Arrow's lips on mine. How could he just walk away? I know that I couldn't have done it, especially as easily as he did. Does he not want me as much as I want him?

Anger fuels my next decision.

I leave my room in search of Arrow. I need an explanation, I need . . . something. Either we're all in or all out. I can't keep going on like this. I stop at his door and lift my hand to knock, but the door opens before my knuckles touch the wood.

Jill walks out, a satisfied smirk on her face.

My breath hitches and I try to keep my face from falling.

"He might be a little tired," she whispers so only I can hear. I look behind her and see Arrow walk out of the bathroom as naked as the day he was born. For once, his beautiful body does nothing for me.

I feel nothing but pure pain and anger.

How. Dare. He.

I give him a look that shows him exactly what I think right now. I let the pain seep through my eyes, letting my guard down for a moment so he can feel what I'm feeling.

He flinches.

"Anna . . ." he says, reaching his hand out to me.

But I'm done.

I walk away in search of a distraction. When I find nothing, I get angrier.

When Arrow doesn't come after me, I decide that I don't need this shit. I don't need to be stuck here in a club that isn't mine, with people who care about me only because of who my brother is.

I don't need *him*.

And I sure as hell don't belong here.

I walk outside, and when I don't see anyone, I smirk to myself. Everyone must still be sleeping—except Jill of course. Who knew whores were such early risers?

Darting my gaze around the exit, I walk briskly until I come to the fence. Making sure to lock it before I leave so no one else can get in, I slide outside and straight into freedom. I wouldn't jeopardize anyone else in any way, and I wouldn't take a chance with their safety. But as for me, I'm done.

D.O.N.E.

I walk up the street until I come to the main road. Sliding my phone out of my jeans, I call Lana.

"I'm escaping and I need someone to pick me up," I say into the phone. I had messaged Lana and updated her on everything, the lockdown, Arrow, and why I was going to be missing in action. So she knows where I am, and why I'm here.

There's a slight pause on the other end before she speaks. "Text me the name of the street you're on."

"Okay, 'bye."

I hang up and text the name of the street, then press SEND. Phone in my hand, I look up at the sun in the sky. It's a beautiful day and freedom never felt sweeter.

Who needs Arrow?

That was my last thought before everything went black.

ELEVEN

WAKE up disoriented, my body resting on a soft mattress, my wrists tied together above my head.

Where am I?

My eyes flutter open as I stare at the ceiling, momentarily confused. What happened?

A man clears his throat and my body stiffens, my heart racing with fear. I slowly look toward the far corner of the room, at the man standing there, casually leaning against the wall. I've never seen him before in my life, and I have no idea what he wants with me now, but I know I am in a lot of shit.

Why did I do something so stupid? The Arrow situation was messing with my head *and* my common sense, and now I am fucked.

Great going, Anna.

"Good morning, sunshine," the man says with a smirk.

I open my mouth to scream, but faster than lightning, he's on me, covering my mouth with his hand. "I'm not going to hurt you, okay?"

I nod.

Isn't that what they always say? How do I play this one out? I don't know. I need to be smart about the situation, because I know that the wrong move can have deadly consequences.

Like my ending up dead.

Yeah—the stakes are kind of high.

He removes his hand.

"I won't hurt you, I promise," he cajoles.

Right, like I'm supposed to believe him.

"The bump on the back of my head says otherwise," I grit out, licking my bottom lip. My mouth is dry and feels like I haven't had any water in a long time. "Who are you? And what do you want with me?"

He stands there studying me. "Wind Dragons sent a shipment up north that we tried to intercept. Two of my men were captured. You, my dear, are all I need to make sure my men make it out of there alive."

I bite the inside of my cheek. What did he mean I was all that he needed? Was he going to trade me—or do something to me?

"What are you going to do with me?" I ask in a small voice, my lower lip trembling slightly.

He tilts his head to the side, watching me with an intense expression on his face. "You won't be hurt, Anna, as long as you listen to what I have to say."

I consider what he's told me. Rake has taken two men? To do what to them? Teach them a lesson for messing with his stuff? He never did play nice with others.

"What's in the shipment?" I ask quietly, wanting to learn all I can about the MC I know nothing about. I regret the words, however, as soon as they leave my mouth. I really don't need to anger this man right now, asking questions I know I have no right to know the answers to.

But lucky for me, the man just smirks, eyes brimmed with amusement. "Nothing for you to worry your little head about."

It's his amusement that makes me let out the next words from my mouth.

"Condescending bastard," I mutter, showing him my displeasure by the look on my face. "You know, you don't look like a kidnapping, abusive jerk."

He was actually good-looking. Tall, lean, and covered in tattoos, he had shaggy white-blond hair and crystal-green eyes.

He grunts. "I didn't do the kidnapping, and I told them not to hurt you, so I'm sorry for that."

He sounds sincere; still something doesn't add up. Why didn't he want to hurt me? Just because I am a woman? I didn't think it would matter, considering they'd had no problem shooting Mary.

"Wild Men MC, right?" I ask, taking a gamble. He isn't wearing a cut, just dark jeans and a white shirt rolled up at the sleeves.

He nods, his eyes darkening. "I see our reputation precedes us."

The way he says it makes it sound like that's not exactly a good thing, and he'd be right.

"If I untie you, are you gonna be a problem?" he asks, staring at my tied hands. "There are other men around the compound, and I can assure you, none of them are as nice as I am."

"I'll be good," I reply. "Can you just untie me? The ropes are cutting into my wrists."

He quickly stands and cuts the binds. I consider kicking him in the balls and making a run for it, but I need to examine the situation first. If there are men out there, there is no way I can get out of here. I also have no idea which way the exit is. I decide to bide my time and suss out the situation before I get myself killed. "Can I have some water, please?"

He nods and leaves the room, returning about a minute later with a bottle of water and some painkillers.

"Thanks," I say, taking both from him. "So who do I thank for the possible concussion?"

His lip twitches. "That would be Ranger."

These men give each other the stupidest names.

"And what is your name?" I ask.

A strange look appears on his face before he answers me. "Call me Talon."

"Talon it is."

He tilts his head to the side. "I'd expected hysterical screaming, crying at the least."

"Then you should have kidnapped a weaker woman."

I am trying not to let him see that I am shit scared, because I am.

He laughs at that and points to the door on the left. "Bathroom is there. Don't think of trying anything, Anna, or you will regret it."

With that warning lingering in the air, he leaves the room and locks the door behind him. I check out the bathroom, finding nothing I can use as a weapon. There isn't even a mirror in there, which makes me think that this is the room where they keep all their captives. Now that Talon has left the room, I allow myself to feel terrified. Rake will come for me, I know it. I just hope it will be soon. My stomach rumbles. It seems inappropriate to be hungry at a time like this, but unfortunately I have no control over it. Sitting back on the bed, my back against the headboard, I feel helpless.

I don't like to feel helpless.

My gaze darts around the room, looking for anything that can help me.

When Talon says he won't hurt me, I believe him. But if I push my luck I don't know if that will stay true. What feels like an hour passes before Talon walks in with a bag of food.

"Thought you might be hungry," he says, giving me a small smile.

He'd thought right, not that I was about to admit it.

"Are you the president?" I blurt out, wanting to know why it was him in here with me and no one else.

"I'm the vice president," he says, biting his bottom lip. "My dad was the president before he was killed."

"Oh. Family business, huh?" I say, not knowing how to respond to that. I take the bag from his hand and open it, peering inside to see a burger and fries. "Any idea when I'll be able to leave here?"

His eyes shutter, expression darkening. "Told them we had you; they went crazy, as we expected. Thought I'd make them sweat a little, so I said I'd meet up with them tomorrow and we could trade."

I think about that. "That means you leave your men with them for longer than necessary."

He resumes his spot against the wall, standing how he was when I first saw him. "They'll survive."

"Do the clubs always use their women against them?" I can't stop myself from asking. This wasn't a world I wanted to live in, yet was thrust upon me. It somehow didn't seem fair that I was to be used as a bargaining chip in a world that I didn't belong in.

A muscle tics in Talon's jaw. "You haven't known the club for long, have you?"

I shake my head. "Not at all. But I heard about Mary, the woman who was killed."

Talon looks away then, his Adam's apple bobbing as he swallows. "The men did that against their president's orders. They went rogue, and our club suffered for it. My father would never have wanted an innocent woman harmed—he wasn't like that—though that's now our burden to bear."

"What happened to the men?" I ask.

Talon clenches his fist. "All dead. My father died too, because of them. If they weren't killed I would have done it myself."

"Your own club brothers?" I ask, raising an eyebrow.

"They betrayed us," is all he says. "Now eat, you must be hungry."

I wake up, horrified with myself for falling asleep in the first place. I'm alone in the room, luckily, and seem to have been left alone. I walk to the door and try to pull it open, but it's still locked and doesn't budge. Of course I'm not *that* lucky, but at least no one has hurt me. I use the bathroom as quickly as I can, just in case they decide to come in, then sit back on the bed. With nothing else to do, my mind races, thinking up different scenarios. Where is Rake? I hope he is okay, and not too worried about me. He must think they're doing God knows what to me, and I can only imagine how frantic he must be.

Where is Arrow? How is he reacting right now?

Probably back in bed with Jill.

Well, wasn't that a mood killer.

The door opens with a creak and Talon walks in, followed by another man—a scary-looking one at that.

"We're going to the meet," Talon says, holding his hand out to me. I hesitantly take it and look up at the other man.

"Let me guess, you're Ranger?" I ask, gulping. Dressed in all leather, he is a massive man with shrewd dark eyes and a Mohawk.

He laughs at me, his shoulders shaking. "No, sweetheart, I'm not Ranger. I'm Slice."

"Slice," I repeat, tasting the ridiculous name on my tongue. "I don't even want to know why they call you that."

"And I don't want to tell you," he replies smoothly.

With a man on each side of me, we exit the room and I get my first look at where I'm being held. The Wild Men clubhouse is different from the Wind Dragons'. Less homey for one, less clean for another. Men sit around a table, drinking and carrying on. I know it's morning, although I don't know what time, but I'm assuming they've been up all night.

"Well, what do we have here?" one man croons, making all the other men turn to look at me.

Just great.

Talon ignores them and ushers me into a garage and to an expensive-looking black four-wheel drive. He opens the door for me, waits for me to slide into the car, but hesitates as he's about to close the door.

"Anna," he says quietly, eyes boring into mine. "Are they good to you there? They treat you right?"

My brows furrow, wondering why he is concerned at all. "They're good to me."

He nods once, seemingly satisfied. "Good."

Then he closes the door, leaving me even more confused. Slice gets into the passenger seat after me and Talon drives. The car ride is tense, the air thick between the two men, obviously anticipating facing the Wind Dragons face-to-face. Did they think this was going to run smoothly? Or were they worried that something might happen?

"Where are we going?" I ask nosily, breaking the strained silence and looking between the two men.

"A secure location," Talon replies, his fingers squeezing the steering wheel. "Don't worry, you'll be safe with your brother before you know it."

"How does everyone know so much about me?" I ask him, frowning. It is a little weird. There are many people connected to the club, but it seems like they had homed in on me. Was I an easy target? I didn't like the sound of that.

"You work at one of the most popular bars in town, and the club keeps an eye on you everywhere you go. Everyone knows who you are," Slice says in a dry tone. "Don't know why you were stupid enough to be walking around alone. I'd kick your ass if you were my sister."

"Well, luckily I'm not," I snap. "I'm not a club member, I live my own life. I work at the bar; I go to school. I'm a fucking scientist. I didn't think anyone would do anything to me because my only crime is being related to Rake!"

The men go quiet at my outburst, and Talon uncomfortably clears his throat. "You should listen to your brother. Other men might not be as nice as I am."

My eyes narrow. "What I should do is move back to the

other side of the country and live a peaceful life away from over-bearing assholes."

Slice chuckles, a really annoying sound. "Sweetheart, we both have chapters over there. You can't get away no matter what. If you think your brother didn't keep tabs on you while you were living away, you're one stupid scientist."

I blink. It never even occurred to me that Rake would have an eye on me while I was living on the other side of the country, but it does sound like something he would do.

I rub my forehead. "I'll move somewhere far away. Scotland maybe? How about Ireland? I heard Galway is a beautiful place to visit this time of the year."

"Shut it," Slice demands as we drive into a warehouse.

"Is this the place?" I ask, sticking my face against the window. It is a large, dark, empty space in the middle of nowhere. Perfect for such dealings as this.

"Quiet, Anna," Talon says, looking around the warehouse. I follow his lead and do the same. Where are the men? Goose bumps appear on my arms as I wait for something to happen.

Then, one by one from the darkness, they appear.

First I see Arrow, then Rake. Tracker and Sin step out from the shadows.

They look pissed.

And I mean *pissed*.

Deadly.

My gaze lingers on Arrow, whose posture is rigid, his fists clenched at his sides.

Suddenly I can't help but feel sorry for Talon. Why did they come with only two people? If it was me I'd make sure

I had a man for each man I was up against, but what did I know?

The Wind Dragon men step toward the car, like a unit, united by their fury. What was I supposed to do? Did they want me to get out of the car? Talon and Slice both get out at the same time, and Slice opens my door and drags me out, nowhere near as gentle as Talon had been. I give him a dirty look that he doesn't see because he's staring over my head. Then I'm spun around and my eyes instantly connect with Arrow's. His gaze scans me from head to toe, maybe looking for any injuries? His mouth is tight, and his eyes are narrowed but alert. He looks imposing, and ready to do murder. Something I probably shouldn't joke about, seeing as it's something he's extremely capable of.

"Where are my men?" Talon asks, gritting his teeth. "You said they would be here."

I look around and feel like something is going on.

Because the two men they were supposed to deliver aren't here.

TWELVE

ARE you okay?" my brother asks, taking a step toward me. "Anna, answer me!"

He sounds panicked, so I quickly reply. "I'm fine, I wasn't hurt."

"You will pay for touching her," Arrow grits out, and I raise my eyebrow. *How nice of him to care.* I cringe. Okay, that was catty of me. There are bigger things to worry about right now than my unrequited love and the fact that Arrow fucked Jill instead of me.

Talon's grip on my upper arm tightens, pulling me from my thoughts.

"Talon, you're hurting me," I say softly, and he instantly lets go of my arm.

"Where are they?" Slice demands, looking like he wants to hit something. "Or don't the Wind Dragons keep their word?"

"In the van," Sin replies, nodding toward the black van parked in the corner. "Let Anna walk to us, then you can go and get them. We kept our word, and we always do. This way everyone walks out of here unharmed."

They wanted to control the situation. They did keep their word, but they also wanted assurances that I was going to be leaving with them today. It was a smart plan.

"Are they hurt?" Talon asks, staring toward the van.

Sin grins, all teeth. I never realized just how scary the man could be until this very moment. "They might be a little banged up, but they'll live."

Talon pushes gently on my back, silently telling me that I'm free to go. I step one small step forward, then another.

"Anna," Rake says softly, making me look up at him.

I run to him, closing the space between us, and wrap my arms around him, finally feeling completely safe.

"Jesus, you scared me half to death. I'm so fuckin' sorry, Anna," Rake whispers in my ear. I squeeze my eyes shut and just hold on to him. Talon and Slice get their men and put them in their car.

"Be careful who you trust, Anna," Talon calls out, sending me an apologetic look before he gets in and drives away. Be careful who I trust? What the hell is he talking about? I am going to let future me worry about it because right now I am where I want to be, in my brother's arms, safe and untouchable once more.

"Come on. Let's get you home, little warrior princess," my brother says, leading me to the van. Arrow walks up to me, blocking my way. He has a cut lip, looks like he took a punch to the face. He reaches his arm out but then retracts it at the last moment. He curses and then takes another step to me, so close we're almost touching. I can feel the heat from his body, smell his delicious scent. I stand still, not saying anything or moving.

Just watching.

"What the fuck were you thinking?" he whispers angrily. His hands have come up to cup my cheeks, almost as if he hasn't noticed.

My body shivers at his touch.

"Fucking hell, Anna!"

The emotion in his eyes kills me. The raw pain etched in them looks so wrong on his usually stoic expression.

"I'm sorry," I whisper. This was all my fault, I never should have left.

"Let her be," Rake demands, pulling me away from Arrow and lifting me into the back of the van. Tracker comes and sits next to me, and lets me put my head on his shoulder.

The ride home is silent, strained and tense. I can tell everyone is spitting mad at me, but they're also relieved that I'm safe. I wonder which emotion will win out in the end. Considering their alpha-male tendencies, I am going to place my vote on anger.

I soon find out I am right.

Once we were safely inside the clubhouse, and the relief of my being safe wore off, the yelling began. It was no more than I deserved, but that didn't mean I enjoyed it. I did, however, have to listen to them tell me exactly what I put them through, and how worried they were about me. I was so sorry, so damn sorry, and I told them as much. I know it didn't make up for anything, but I wanted them to know that I had learned my lesson. This wasn't a game. I always said I wasn't a kid when Rake treated me like one, but today I'd acted like one.

I felt like utter shit.

"Why the hell would you just walk out when we told you that it wasn't safe?" Rake asks, pacing up and down. "I think I lost ten years of my life! Christ, Anna! If something had happened to you . . ."

"I was fine," I say for what feels like the tenth time. "I wasn't hurt. I know I screwed up and I'm sorry, okay?"

I'd been so busy feeling hurt over Arrow that I acted without thought. I knew it was all on me. But right now I just want to go to bed. I need a good cry, but I don't want anyone to witness it.

I look up to find Arrow staring at me, a lost look on his face.

"Who hit you?" I ask quietly, my voice subdued.

He looks at Rake, and my eyes widen.

"You hit him?" I ask Rake.

Fuck, I caused this. I didn't think it was possible to feel worse, but I just proved myself wrong.

"He should have kept a better eye on you," Rake says, rubbing his hands through his hair. "I need a fuckin' drink, some weed, and a warm, willing woman."

With that, he storms out. Looks like he's not holding back from me anymore, that's for damn sure.

"You were lucky this time, Anna," Tracker says to me, softly, yet his gaze is full of disapproval. "You should have listened to us. I hope you learned your lesson this time and don't try to do something so foolish again."

Sin gives me a look that would frighten a lesser woman. "I'm so fuckin' glad you're not my sister."

Well, ouch. That hurt. After seeing Rake's face I think that Sin's speaking the truth. My brother didn't deserve to have to worry about me after I put myself in danger. Sin leaves after that, and I for one am grateful for his absence. My shoulders droop. Only one man left in the room.

I turn to him, giving him my full attention.

"I'm sorry Rake hit you because of me," I tell Arrow, our eyes connected. "I don't want to cause trouble between you guys, and trust me, I've learned my lesson."

"Anna—"

I flash back to seeing him with Jill, and the hurt returns in full force. I might feel connected to Arrow, but nothing can come of it. After how I acted today I doubt he even wants me like that anymore. Jill is definitely an easier option for him.

"I guess we're even now," I say, forcing my lips to move.

I needed to sever the tie between the two of us.

Standing up, I move to leave the room when he finally speaks.

"How so?"

I shrug. "You hurt me and I got you hurt in return. We're even in my book."

"Anna—"

I ignore him and leave.

Then I'm finally alone, and I let the tears pour.

After crying until I had no tears left, and explaining and apologizing to Lana, I take a bath, taking my time soaking in the water. It turns out Lana came to pick me up and when I wasn't there, she rang Tracker. How she had his number is something I plan on asking her the next time I see her. Tracker had called Arrow, and everyone panicked, knowing what they think they know about the Wild Men's history and violence toward women. The men had worked quickly, wanting me back and worrying when Talon said he was keeping me overnight. All in all, I was exhausted. Being kidnapped and held hostage was damn exhausting, and I'd rather not do it ever again. I understand I was lucky, in the sense I wasn't hurt or raped or tortured, but still, I'd been scared.

I'd wanted to go back to my apartment tonight but I was told no, to stay at least another two nights, and for once, I listened without complaint. I didn't need to start any more trouble— that was for sure. When the bubbles disappear and my wine finished, I drag myself out of the bath and walk into my room wrapped in nothing but a towel. I come to a standstill at the sight of Arrow sitting on my bed, his head in his hands. This whole thing must have brought back memories of Mary, of her being hurt and his not being there to do anything about it. I feel for him, I do, but right now I'm kind of stuck on my own issues. I need to be selfish.

"Arrow—"

"Why did you leave, Anna?" he asks, lifting his head and watching me.

"I was angry," I say. "I didn't think I was in any actual danger; I mean, what were the chances? I was stupid, arrogant, and naïve."

And I wish I could take it back.

"Why?" he demands, brown eyes flashing. "Why were you angry?"

Why was I angry? Was he seriously asking me that?

"Surely you aren't that stupid, Arrow? You went from my bed to fucking Jill, from kissing me to being inside her. You may not have any feelings for me, but that doesn't mean that I don't. I'm sick of you playing with me, so please, just leave and let me get some rest."

I'm not at my best, my shields are down, my resilience tested, my will temporarily shattered.

I want to wake up to a new day and start fresh. I need time to regain my strength.

"So that's why you left? Endangering yourself to, what, get back at me?" he asks, steel in his tone.

"No—"

"Well, it worked. I was fucking worried about you; if anything happened to you . . . For fuck's sake, Anna, if you're pissed you come to me and let me know. If we're in private, say whatever you have to say, but you bring it to me. What you don't do is walk off when we're on a fuckin' lockdown, scaring half the men to death. We protect what's ours, Anna, and whether you like it or not, you are ours."

I was happy to be theirs, but that didn't mean I was perfect either.

I sit down on the bed and stare at the wall. "I messed up. I wasn't thinking."

"No, you weren't," he says with a grunt. "You should have known better."

"I'm sorry, okay? I'm not used to this, but I know this is my brother's world, and I love him enough to try better. I won't fuck up again, okay?" I say, scared he is going to tell me to leave the clubhouse and never come back.

Arrow turns his head to me and scoots closer, gently wrapping me in his arms.

"I'm sorry," I tell him. "But Talon isn't a bad guy. At least I don't think he is."

His body stiffens. "Don't even mention that fucker's name to me. You were lucky, Anna, I need you to realize just how much. You could have been raped or fuckin' tortured, do you hear me?"

I close my eyes. "I know."

"I'm not telling you this to upset you," he says, his tone turning gentle. "You just need to know that you lucked out this time. Talon didn't hurt you, and that's why he's breathing right now, but someone else might not act the same way. There's a lot of evil out there in this world, Anna, and they're just dying to suck the life out of something as beautiful and innocent as you."

"I have to get dressed, Arrow," I tell him. "We can talk in the morning."

About anything except the two of us, of course.

He stands and I think he's going to leave, but instead he picks up the nightie I'd laid out on my bed and kneels before me, sliding the cotton over my head and pulling it down. He removes the towel, letting it drop to the floor, but his eyes stay locked on mine as the material covers my naked body. I open my mouth to ask him what he's doing when he pulls me into his arms and stands, pulls down the blanket and lays me down. Just like the other night, he lifts off his shirt and slides into the bed on the opposite side. He then reaches over and turns off my lamp, leaving the room in darkness.

"Sleep," he says, wrapping me in his arms, my head leaning on his warm chest. "Let me hold you."

Was the situation with me reminding him of what happened with Mary? It was the same MC after all; maybe this brought back bad memories, resurrected old demons.

"Okay, but, Arrow," I whisper. "If I could bring Mary back to you, I would. I want you to know that."

His body stiffens. "Why would you say that, Anna?"

He loved her. I would do anything for him to be happy, even if it wasn't with me.

I shrug. "I thought maybe she would be on your mind after what happened. I really am sorry, you know. I don't want you to hurt. You deserve to be happy, Arrow. I want you to be."

Mary was perfect to him. How did one compete with that?

Simple—they didn't.

I fall asleep before I can hear his reply.

THIRTEEN

'M alone in the bed when I wake up, and although I feel a pang of disappointment I tell myself it's for the best. I take my time getting dressed, brushing my hair slowly, even taking my time with my makeup—anything to avoid walking out there and facing everyone. I'm watching a video on how to do my hair in an intricate braid that would have taken me all day when Faye walks into my room without knocking.

I hold up my free hand. "I know, I know. I'm a selfish jerk."

"Well, as long as you know it," she replies with a smirk. "How are you feeling?" She sits next to me. "Turn around, I'll braid your hair for you."

I turn my back to her and tilt my head back, closing my eyes as she runs her fingers through my hair.

"You going to tell me what made you run yesterday? I thought we were having an okay time here."

Guilt floods me. "I was pissed off about something."

Or someone.

My excuse sounds more and more stupid each time I have to say it.

"Arrow," she guesses, her hands stilling for a second.

"Yeah, but it doesn't matter. Nothing can come of us anyway, unless I want to start shit between him and Rake."

And that was only one of the many issues standing in our way.

She pauses. "Is that the real reason?"

"One of them," I say. "The other is that he clearly has issues he needs to work out. I think that he thinks I won't be safe if I'm with him. But I'm already in deep with the MC; it wouldn't make a difference. Maybe he feels like he can't love anyone other than Mary? I honestly don't know."

She sighs heavily. "He's worth the fight, you know. And fight is what you would have to do to get him to see things clearly."

I let those words sink in.

"I don't know if I'd make a good biker's old lady."

Faye scoffs behind me. "You should have seen me when I first came in here. I was a law student with my nose in the air, judging Dex's every move until I finally got it. You're a strong woman, Anna, and that's all you need to be to be a biker's woman. Keep your head up and just do you."

"He slept with Jill!" I grit out, hating saying the words because that makes it real. "How could he do that to me knowing how much it would hurt me?"

"Says who?" Faye asks.

"I saw it."

"You saw them boning?" she asks, her voice taking on a higher pitch.

I rub my forehead. "No, I saw her leaving his room and him naked inside the room. And of course she had to say something to rub it in."

"Hmmmm," she says. "You know, Arrow told her to get the fuck out of the clubhouse. After you left he lost it. Don't even look inside the game room, because he smashed the shit out of it. I think he feels so much for you but doesn't know what to do with it or how to handle it."

He probably kicked her out because he felt guilty after sleeping in my bed, then going and fucking her.

And he should.

"Maybe I should just find a guy and have some hot, filthy sex and work out my frustrations, instead of chasing after a man who doesn't want me," I say.

"Faye, leave the room," Arrow grits out, the fury in his tone notable.

We both jump and look to the door where he's standing, half in, half out.

Faye had left the door open just an inch, so Arrow must have opened it without us hearing.

Well, this is awkward.

What's the bet he came just in time to hear the last words out of my mouth?

Such is my luck.

"I haven't finished doing her hair," Faye complains.

"Faye—"

He isn't amused.

"Okay, okay," she murmurs, giving me a wide-eyed look before she leaves. Arrow slams the door behind her and turns the lock.

I gulp.

"Yes?" I ask, trying to keep my voice even. "What do you want, Arrow? How about another kiss from me so you get turned on enough to go and fuck another, easier woman?"

He looks around the room before meeting my eyes. "I didn't fuck her, Anna."

I pretend to not know what he's talking about. I have to try and retain some of my pride. "Who?"

"Anna," he says softly. "I came out of the shower and she was there, waiting. I sent her on her way. It wasn't her I wanted, although it would be a hell of a lot easier if I did. And that was my second, extremely cold shower for the day, because I was so fuckin' turned on but was trying to do the right thing by staying away from you. It wasn't fuckin' easy."

"Oh," I say, my mouth hanging open a little. "She said—"

"Doesn't matter what she said; that's the truth, all right? So don't go around fuckin' threatening to go fuck some other guy, because you don't want to push me, Anna."

"Arrow—"

"I'm not used to having to explain myself, Anna, and I don't fuckin' like having to do it now. You either have faith in me and trust me, or you don't."

It wasn't that simple, was it?

My eyes narrow slightly. "We can't do this, Arrow. You either want me or you don't. You either take me or you don't. I can't do this back-and-forth shit."

He rubs the back of his neck. "Why?"

"Why what?" I ask.

"Why the fuck do you have to be so beautiful that I can't get you out of my head?"

"Oh," I say again, blinking furiously. Did he really think that about me? Of course he did, Arrow didn't say things he didn't mean. Fuck, that compliment feels good. It is nice to know he wants me as much as I want him.

"Here's something no one knows. Before I gave in and fucked Jill, I hadn't been with anyone since Mary. Five years, Anna. I only fucked her to try to get you out of my head, and I fucking regret it. It should have been you. I don't give a fuck about Jill. I just didn't want to hurt you."

He didn't have sex for five years? Because of Mary?

"Why?" I ask.

He looks me straight in the eye. "I don't deserve you. I don't deserve anything. How is it fair that I caused her death and now I get to be happy?" He stops and takes a breath. "I can't go through something like that again. And with you . . . it's worse, Anna. It's fuckin' worse."

I speak in a soft, gentle tone. "I'm not going to end up like Mary, Arrow. And what happened to her wasn't your fault. It could have been anyone that day."

"Anna—"

"I know you loved Mary, but she would want you to be happy, Arrow," I say, my eyes pleading with his to believe me.

"She would," he replies, smiling sadly. "She was always so good, so perfect, you know? It was hard to live up to that. She was soft. She never disagreed with me; she never raised her voice. She wasn't made for me."

He pauses and takes a deep breath.

"But you, Anna? You're *my* perfect match. You were made for me, because you not only take me as I am but make me want to be a better man at the same time. Because you challenge me and aren't afraid to give me your opinion. You're a fighter, Anna, and exactly what I want. I thought fucking Jill would take some of the want away, but it didn't. I won't be satisfied until I have you."

"It should have been with me, not Jill, and I'm fucking pissed off that she took what's mine."

I seriously hated that bitch.

His eyes darken. "Fuck, hearing you talk like this . . ."

"What? What does it do to you, Arrow?" I demand.

He reaches down and adjusts himself. "I've never wanted to be inside someone more in my entire life."

We stare at each other for a few tense moments. "Rake wants someone better for you—"

"Rake is going to have to deal," I say, lifting my chin stubbornly. "You think I'd choose some overbearing criminal if I had the choice? You're it for me, whether I like it or not."

His lip twitches at that.

"I tried not to want you, Arrow, but these things don't work like that," I murmur softly. "It's making me crazy. I'm overthinking everything, trying to understand it all, but really what it all comes down to is that I want you. More than I've ever wanted anything in my life."

He smiles, walks over to the bed, sits down and pulls me on top of his lap. "I don't know what this is with us. It's making me crazy too. You're a gift I didn't expect and sure as hell don't deserve."

I don't believe that is true.

I lean my forehead against his. "Arrow. Kiss me."

"Anna—"

I take matters into my own hands. Grabbing his beard and pulling his face to me, I capture his lips in a kiss he isn't going to soon forget. I move so I'm straddling his lap, my hands on his shoulders, gripping him in place. He moans, his hands moving to cup each globe of my ass. He squeezes. I slowly grind myself onto him, feeling his hard cock standing to attention. He holds me in place, so I can't move anymore. I wonder why, until I hear the sound of someone knocking on my door.

"Anna! Come on, breakfast is ready," my brother calls out, interrupting us.

Arrow's cock goes a little soft at that.

I sigh, burying my face in his neck. "Surely being this frustrated with no release isn't good for my health."

"You aren't the one with blue balls," he says, puffing out a breath.

I lift my head. "I didn't have women at my beck and call these last few weeks."

He slaps my ass. "You going to hold that against me forever? And don't say it was cheating, because it wasn't. We weren't together, and I was trying to get you off my mind. Not that it fuckin' worked, but I tried."

"So what are you saying? We're together now?" I ask, wanting to clarify this once and for all.

"What I'm saying is," he says as his hands move up my thighs, stroking lazily, "I see no other option for us. You're mine, Anna, that's all there is to it. It's not a choice, it's a fact."

"You don't need to sound so happy about it." I sniff. It sounds like he's talking about a prison sentence or something.

He lifts one hand to grip my chin between his thumb and index finger. "I'm not happy about it. I never thought I'd feel anything for a woman again, and I'm not sure I'm capable of being what you need. I don't want to hurt you, Anna—"

"Anna! Hurry up!" Rake bellows again.

I kiss Arrow once, gently, just a simple touch of our lips, then slide off his lap. Without another word, I unlock the door and walk out of the room. I find my brother in the kitchen, sitting there with a plate full of food in front of him. He points to the seat next to him with his fork, silently inviting me.

"Who cooked?" I ask, grabbing a plate and serving some of the scrambled eggs and bacon.

Rake shrugs. "One of the women. Jess, I think."

I take my place next to him. "You still angry at me?"

His eyes soften when he looks at me. "You know I can't stay mad at you long."

I'm glad he feels that way.

I eat my food in silence, wondering how best to approach the Arrow subject. I don't want the two of them to fight over me. They've been friends a long time, and I don't want to come between that. Arrow is right; it would be so much easier if we could just stay away from each other. In a way, I guess we're being selfish, but at the same time, feelings like this don't come around very often. They haven't ever for me before. I've never felt such an instant attraction to someone before. Is it an attraction? Or fascination? There is something tethering us together, a connection. I can't explain it, and I'm done questioning it.

"I'm sorry I worried you," I say. "And I'm sorry that I got involved in something that I wasn't meant to."

Rake puts his fork down and pins me with his green eyes. "You're my baby sister, Anna. I heard what Sin said to you, but I couldn't ask for a better sister. Yes, you're strong-willed, opinionated, and a general pain in my ass, but what sister isn't?"

I smile at that. "I learned from the best, after all."

He smiles, now staring down at his plate. "You've got that right."

"Everything else went well on your . . . run?" I ask.

He nods once but doesn't say anything else on the topic.

"What are your plans for today?" I ask, easily changing the subject.

"Tonight I'm going to Rift to see how it's running. Are you going to class today?"

"Yeah, I need to work on my thesis. Now that my kidnapping is over, I guess it's back to reality."

He grins. "Only you would play it off like that."

"Yeah, well, I wasn't hurt, so it could have been a whole lot worse," I say quietly.

Rake puts his piece of bread down. "And that's why they are still breathing."

"I don't want anyone hurt because of me," I tell him, taking a bite of the eggs and chewing slowly. "So who do I need to thank for your good mood this morning?"

He smirks. "They're still in my bed sleeping if you want to go and take a peek."

"They? You're a pig sometimes, Adam," I say in disgust, enunciating his real name.

"Hey, you asked."

"And you overshared."

"Not my fault only one woman can't satisfy me."

Bailey had, but I didn't bring her up.

Instead, I roll my eyes. "When you find the right one, trust me, she'll be more than you can handle."

"And until that day," he replies, "I'm free to explore the many beautiful women who come my way."

Arrow comes into the kitchen just as I'm cleaning up. His hair is damp and he smells delicious, like lime and soap. If he were mine to run my hands over right now, I'd be a happy woman.

"What happened to Jill?" Rake asks him, brows furrowing and completely oblivious to the tension now filling the room.

Arrow's gaze darts to me quickly, before he clears his throat and answers. "Was done with her."

"So? You could have passed her on, she was great at giving h—"

I slam the plate I was washing down in the sink, then turn to see the two of them staring at me. "Could you please have this conversation when I'm not here?"

I walk past them and go to find Faye.

Time in the gym is exactly what I need right now.

I plop down on the mat, breathing hard, my knees bent in front of me. "That was an awesome kick."

Faye, lying on her back, turns her head to me. "I know, right? And a man wouldn't expect it."

"How long have we been at it?"

"An hour."

"I better take another shower and get ready for class."

"What happened with Arrow?" Faye asks, sitting up and looking at me.

"Nosy."

"Yep," she replies, grinning. "I love the man and I want him happy. So please tell me there was some progress."

I nibble on my lip before I reply. "We kissed, and admitted our feelings. I think we're going to try and make this work, but Arrow needs to talk to Rake first. I'd do it, but I think with how the club works Arrow needs to do what he has to do first."

"You're right, let Arrow handle it. You know," she says, hesitating slightly, "I was good friends with Mary. She was an amazing woman, beautiful and sweet. Never once did Arrow tell her how much he wanted her, or admit his feelings to her."

"I know I could never replace Mary—"

Faye cuts me off. "Arrow shouldn't make you feel like you have to."

I swallow. "He hasn't. I think it's more me overthinking things and . . ." I puff out a breath. "I don't know. But it feels right between us, you know? And I want to explore what we could have. I don't want Rake to be angry though; I couldn't handle that."

Faye nods, understanding flashing in her eyes. "If there's anything I can do to help, let me know. Although Dex would kick my ass for getting involved. But Arrow deserves to be happy. He's stopped drinking as much; we've all noticed it. He hasn't gone to Toxic as much either, and he's happier, more focused. I think you've given him a purpose, Anna, and he needed that."

"I don't know about all that," I say a little shyly, staring down at my hands. "I mean, I think I can make him happy, you know? I hope I can."

Faye giggles. "You have it *bad,* Anna Bell."

I groan at the nickname. "Not you too."

But really, I was happy. Faye was now my friend, and Arrow was right—she was a good friend to have.

"Hey, it's catchy," she replies, standing up and dusting off her pants. "I have to go pick up Clover. I'll see you tonight, if you're coming back here."

"Okay. Thanks for the workout."

She smirks. "That totally sounded dirty."

I roll my eyes, my lip twitching. "Seriously?"

She grins and pulls her hair down from its ponytail. "See you around, Arrow's woman."

I shake my head to myself as she exits the gym, then I force myself to stand up.

Arrow's woman.

Damn if I didn't like how that sounded.

ave you seen Tracker?" Allie asks me, sticking her head inside my door. Why the hell is she asking me? I'm not Tracker's keeper. I don't understand Allie. Is she just a shit person? Or a woman who hides behind her defenses, which in her case would be her bitchiness and general unpleasantness.

"Nope," I reply. "Haven't seen him all day."

He is probably hiding from her. That's what I would be doing.

She makes a noise of irritation and stomps her foot. "I'm so sick of this shit!"

"Why don't you just call him?" I murmur, staring down at my textbook and wishing that she would spontaneously combust. "And why the fuck are you in my room?"

"He's not answering," she reluctantly replies. "If he's with another bitch I'm gonna kill him! And her!"

I slam the textbook shut. "Can you please fuck off and leave me out of your shit? I'm trying to study."

"Fuck, you're a bitch," she replies, sounding a little surprised. "How about some fucking help finding him?"

My phone beeps with a message from Lana.

Come over, I'm bored.

"Is that Tracker messaging you?" Allie asks, crossing her arms over her chest and trying to peer at my phone. Was she serious right now?

"You're still here?" I ask, raising an eyebrow. I put down my phone and sigh. "I don't know where he is, Allie, but if I do I'll tell him you're looking for him, okay?"

"Anna, I have to go out for a bit," Rake says as he enters the room. He looks at Allie. "Everything okay in here?"

"She won't leave me alone," I say dramatically. "You should make her leave."

Rake ignores my outburst. "Do you wanna come with me, Anna?"

"Will you drop me off at Lana's after? She's in need of some Anna time. I've done my time here anyway; I get to go home now."

His face falls slightly at that. "Is that how you feel about staying here? Comparing it to prison time? Fuck, Anna. I love having you here."

Shit, now I feel like a bitch.

"I'll come back on the weekend, how about that? You know I just like having my own space," I tell him, trying to get him to understand. Allie silently leaves the room, clearly bored with our conversation.

"Yeah, yeah," he mutters. "Come on, I need to stop at Rift, then we can have some lunch before I take you to Lana's."

I smile widely. "Thanks, bro."

His eyes soften. "Get your shit together then."

"Okay," I say, standing up and grabbing my bag. Arrow walks in a few seconds later, just in time to find me in a compromising position, bent over, searching under the bed for my pen.

"Trying to kill me, aren't you, darlin'?" he says, clearing his throat.

I sit abruptly on the bed. "Yes, I purposely waited in that position in hopes you would drop by."

He chuckles at that. "Lucky it was me then." He looks behind him, then murmurs, "Fuck it."

Closing and locking the door, he steps to me and lifts me up to a standing position. Then, without a word, his lips are fused to mine. Hands on my ass, he lifts me in the air, and I wrap my legs around his narrow waist. "Need to be inside you," he says against my mouth. "But I can't."

"Why not?" I whisper, digging my fingers into his back, trying to get myself as close to his body as I can.

"I can't do that to him," he grits out. "I fucking can't. I need to talk to him first. I need to tell him."

I groan in frustration and lay my forehead against his chest. Suddenly he lays me back on the bed and starts lifting up my maxi skirt.

"Arrow?"

"Shhh," he soothes, running his hands up my thighs and pulling down my white lace panties. I gulp in air as he spreads my legs wide, making a sound of masculine appreciation deep in his throat.

"Beautiful," he says in a soft, husky tone, then his mouth is on me, licking gently. I arch off the bed as he pays attention to my clit, gripping the sheets and slamming my head back into the pillow.

"Arrow, holy shit," I whisper, looking down to see his head between my thighs, the sight so erotic that a whimper escapes my lips. His large hands are on my thighs, spreading me to him, his head slightly bobbing as he worships me with his talented mouth. The orgasm creeps up on me, hitting me with full force. I take the pillow next to me and cover my face so no one can hear me scream. Arrow keeps at it, sucking my clit until he wrings every possible cry from me, each wave of pleasure making my thighs tremble and my eyes roll back into my head. I move the pillow away from my face and squirm silently, letting him know I've had enough. It's too much; it's too sensitive. He raises his head and looks at me with a smug, satisfied look.

"That tongue should come with a warning," I pant out.

He wipes his mouth with the back of his hand, then kisses the inside of my thigh, once. I hear Rake call out my name, and I quickly jump out of bed on shaky legs. Arrow stands and grimaces, adjusting himself, his arousal straining through his jeans. I lick my lips, wishing nothing more than I could take care of that *big* problem for him.

"Later," he says, staring at me, promise in his eyes.

I pick up my bag from the floor, then realize that I'm not wearing any panties. "Where are my panties?"

He looks to the ground, picks them up and lifts them in front of him. Grinning, he hands them over to me, but not before smelling them first.

"Weirdo," I say as I take them from his hands, then slide them on. "When will I see you next?"

He rubs the back of his neck, considering. "I'll talk with Rake tomorrow, then come and see you afterward."

I swallow hard. "Okay."

I close the space between us and press a sweet kiss to his lips, unable to stop myself from running my hand over the bulge in his jeans. "You better not use anyone else to relieve this."

His eyes darken. "I'm going for a cold shower as soon as you leave."

"Is that your promise to not screw around with anyone else until we sort out whatever this is between us?" I ask boldly, my eyes not leaving his.

He tilts his head slightly, which I take as agreement. Another quick kiss and I walk out of the room, where Rake is waiting for me in front of his bike.

"You know," I tell my brother, "maybe it's time I got my own bike."

His smile is so wide that I can't help but smile with him.

"I'll teach you how to ride, then I'll happily buy you a bike," he says, handing me a helmet.

"A hot-pink bike?"

He laughs at that. "If that's what you want."

I get on the back of his bike, still smiling.

Life is looking up.

I was having the worst day ever.

After a long and tiring day of observations at the zoo, I wait at the bus stop. I finished classes early and didn't bother to message Rake because it was just easier to take the bus than hassle someone for a ride.

"Hey, Anna," Damien calls out, coming up to stand next to me.

"Hey, Damien," I say, smiling. "How was your day? I saw you talking with some of the students and didn't want to interrupt."

He grins. "That would have been a welcome interruption considering I was on babysitting duty all day."

"Got stuck showing around the freshmen, huh?" I tease.

He puts his hands in his pockets. "Something like that. Do you need a ride home? I'm parked just over there," he says, nodding his head to the student parking lot to the right.

I look to his car and consider it. "Thanks, but it's all right. I live close by."

"Are you sure?" he asks, frowning. "I honestly don't mind."

He is sweet, Damien. We talk in class sometimes, usually about the work we were doing, nothing personal. But like I said, he is sweet, and I didn't need Rake or Arrow scaring the shit out of him.

"I'm good," I say as the bus arrives. "I'll see you around."

I get on the bus before he can protest.

Ten minutes later, as soon as I step off, it starts pouring.

Just my luck.

Dripping wet and moody, I walk from the stop to my apartment, which takes a couple of minutes. As I walk to my front door, dying for a hot shower, I notice something that makes me stop in my tracks.

The door is open.

What the hell?

Taking two steps backward, I pull out my phone and walk to the parking lot, where there would be people around. I dial Rake.

"Anna?"

"Hey, Rake, can you come to my apartment, please?"

He's silent for a second. "Talk to me, Anna."

"I just got home and the door is open. Something doesn't feel right. I mean, it could be nothing; maybe I left the door open?"

But I know I didn't.

"Are you safe?" he barks into the phone, and I can hear movement around him.

"Yeah, I'm in the lot, so I'm in clear view of the main road," I say, shuffling my feet.

"Good girl," he croons. "I'm on my way."

"Thanks, Rake."

"Oh, and, Anna?"

"Yeah?"

"You should have fuckin' called me when you finished class."

He hangs up, leaving me cringing at the phone.

I sit on the curb, lifting my head when I hear the sound of rumbling motorcycles about ten minutes later. I can just imagine the lecture I'm going to get from Rake, about how all of this could be avoided if I just lived at the clubhouse like he wanted. Resigned to my fate, I stand as Rake and Arrow approach, both wearing identical scowls on their faces. Arrow lifts his hands to me as he walks up but drops them at the last second. Rake pulls me into his arms as Arrow watches, staring at my face. He looks like he wants to touch me badly but can't because of my brother's presence. I know the feeling, because I want to be in his arms too.

"You okay?" he asks me, our eyes connected. I nod.

"I'll go in and check it out," he says, giving me a gentle look before he walks in the direction of my apartment. Rake and I follow behind and watch as he disappears inside my apartment.

"Fuckin' hell, Anna, you'd be safe if you weren't so stubborn and just stayed where you belong."

"Don't start, Rake," I mumble, staring at the door, waiting for Arrow to reappear. When he does, he's empty-handed.

"Place is a wreck," he says. "Doesn't look like anything is missing though. Lock's broken."

Probably because I had nothing of value to steal. Luckily Lana wasn't over, since she has a key and drops by whenever she feels like it. A key I actually gave her, unlike my brother.

Arrow removes his leather jacket and places it over my shoulders. "You look freezing, Anna."

I sigh. "It's been a long day."

"I can see that. Come on, I'll help you clean up the place," Arrow says, leading me inside with an arm around my shoulder.

Sweet, so fucking sweet.

"Thanks," I sniff, walking into my home. Arrow removes his arm as we step into my kitchen and I take in the disaster that is my apartment.

"Fuck! Shouldn't I call the cops?" I ask.

"No cops," Rake says. "Unless you want one of us to get arrested."

I roll my eyes. "You guys can leave then, you haven't done shit. I'll call the cops."

"They aren't going to do anything, Anna," Arrow says. "Let us handle it. Don't worry, all right?"

Sighing, I turn around to see Arrow and Rake having a silent conversation I'm obviously not meant to hear. Or in this case, see.

"What?" I demand. "What aren't you telling me?"

"Nothing," they both say at the same time, trying to look innocent.

And failing.

I point my finger. "Don't fuck around, tell me what's going on."

I'm ignored.

"Call in the women to help," Arrow tells Rake. "It will be quicker, and Anna looks exhausted. She doesn't need to be doing this shit."

Rake grins. "Shall I call Jill?"

I grit my teeth together. Why is that woman's name still being said?

"Fuck Jill," Arrow replies. "I was thinking more along the lines of Faye and Jess."

"Oh," Rake replies, deflated. "The old ladies."

We really don't have the time for this. I step into my living room, to see the place trashed. Everything is turned upside down, though I can't come up with one reason why someone would do this. I clearly have nothing of value; they can see that. Tying my hair up in a messy bun, I quickly step into my room and change into some dry clothes, then start to arrange the place. Faye and Jess drop by, along with Tracker and even Allie. I appreciate the help. It takes two hours before everything is back in place. Arrow opted to help me put my room back together, and I literally cringe when he starts snooping through my drawers.

"Arrow, can you stop?" I ask, scowling at him as he opens my panty drawer.

"Just making sure everything is in working order."

I don't even know what to reply to that.

"You know you're coming back to the clubhouse tonight, don't you?" he says casually, pulling out a pink thong and stretching it between his fingers.

"No, I'm not. Everything is fine now. I can stay here. And I can see you still haven't spoken to Rake."

Rake walks in just after I say those words. "We'll get this sorted out, then Arrow and I are going out later tonight."

"Going out where?" I ask. "And I'm not moving back to the clubhouse full-time, but I'll stay there until whatever this is is sorted out."

"Fine. For now, that works."

"Where are you going out?" I ask again.

Rake grins. "Strip club, having a couple of drinks."

The look I send Arrow is judge, jury, and executioner.

He flashes me an apologetic look and mouths the word *later*.

"Fine," I mumble.

I have other things to worry about right now.

Faye sticks her head through my door as I'm finishing off my room. "Anna, let's go out tonight. I heard the men were too."

"Sounds good," I tell her. No way I want to sit at home while Arrow is out at a strip club.

I see Faye grin mischievously, her gaze darting to Arrow before landing back on me. "You need to get laid, and I think tonight should be the night."

My eyes widen.

The shit stirrer.

I smile innocently at both Arrow and Rake, playing along. "I know just what to wear."

Rake scowls at Faye while Arrow stares me down, his eye starting to twitch a little.

Yeah, he doesn't like that idea much.

"Faye, don't say my sister's name and 'get laid' in the same sentence ever again," my brother groans.

Faye raises an eyebrow. "The things I could tell Anna. The things I've seen!"

Rake grabs her and covers her mouth with his hand. He looks up. "Arrow, meet you out front. Faye will take you to the clubhouse, Anna."

He walks backward with her, probably going to give her a talking-to.

Arrow kisses my brow. "I'll be in your bed tonight, Anna."

"That spot might already be taken tonight, Mr. Arrow-smith," I reply, a smug smile playing on my lips.

Arrow surprises me by grinning. "We both know that won't be the case, darlin'."

Cocky bastard.

A quick kiss on my mouth, and he's gone.

FIFTEEN

FAYE walks back from the bar with two shots in her hand. Sin stands at the corner, watching his woman, a hungry look on his face. The two of them are an amazing couple, strong and so very in love. I'd spent a little time with their daughter this evening too, and Clover was a treat. She's a bright, witty five-year-old and I could tell she was going to be an absolute stunner when she was older. She even told me how her uncle Arrow sneaked her strawberry candy.

I glance around Knox's Tavern once, then look at Faye as she hands me a shot glass. This wasn't exactly how I pictured the night going, but I just pretend our every move isn't being scrutinized and try to enjoy the drinks.

"I love this song!" Faye calls out, doing an exaggerated grinding move that has me laughing. She drags me to the dance floor, and it's not long before her man is there, grabbing her by the hips and looking like he wants to fuck her right here on the dance floor. I head back to the bar, feeling like a third wheel, and sit in front of Reid.

"When you getting your ass back to work?" he asks.

"Why?" I reply. "Do you miss me?"

He grins and pours me another shot. "I just don't want to have to train anyone else."

I roll my eyes. "You love me. Admit it, Reid Knox, badass MMA fighter. You luuurvvve me."

He pulls the shot back. "On second thought, maybe you've had enough."

I lean closer. "I have a question. What do you know about that Talon dude?"

Reid seems to know everything about everyone.

His eyebrows raise. "Talon?"

"Wild Men Talon," I explain further.

Reid studies me for a few tense seconds. "I know that no one will be happy you're asking about him."

I shrug. "I'm curious. He wasn't a bad guy—you know, kidnapping aside."

Reid scrubs a hand down his face. "So happy you're not my sister."

I gape. "Why does everyone keep saying that?"

"Maybe because you're a troublemaker," he suggests.

I pout. "Where's Ryan? He's nicer."

He chuckles at that. "It's his wedding anniversary, so he's out spoiling his wife. How's Arrow?"

I narrow my eyes. "What about Arrow?"

He doesn't reply, just gives me a *How stupid do you think I am?* look.

"Does everyone know?" I grumble.

"Everyone except Rake."

Okay, that makes me feel like total shit. I don't want everyone except Rake to know. Rake should be the first to know.

Even though Arrow and I haven't really made anything official and won't until Rake knows, it still feels wrong, and I don't like it. Arrow better talk to Rake tonight. Surely the strippers will have him in a more amicable mood. Arrow should buy him a lap dance or something.

"Nothing is going on . . . yet," I evade.

"You better be back here tomorrow night," Reid says, changing the subject, which I appreciated.

"I'll be here," I tell him. "I actually like working at this place."

"Well, lucky me then," he says with a smirk, then walks off to serve a customer. When someone wraps their arms around me from behind, I elbow them in the stomach out of instinct.

"Ouch," Tracker says, lifting up his shirt and rubbing his hand over an impressive set of abs.

"Like that hurt," I say. "You just want to show off your sexy abs."

He smiles and puts his hand out. "It's nice to be appreciated. Want to dance?"

I give him my hand. "Lead the way."

We enter the dance floor and Tracker immediately pulls me into him. I raise my eyebrow at his apparent lack of boundaries, but he just flashes me a boyish grin and starts to dance.

"Where's the old ball and chain?" I say into his ear so he can hear me.

He waves his hand in the air dismissively. "Fuck her."

I shake my head and start to move in sync with him to the music. Tracker turns out to be a good dancer. He moves his hips in a bump and grind that has me seeing exactly what Lana sees in him.

Holy hell, he's sex on a stick.

One minute I'm pressed against Tracker, the next minute I'm pulled away from his body and pushed behind Arrow. I hear Arrow angrily say something to Tracker, a lot of swearing involved, and then he's dragging me out of the bar by my wrist.

"What the fuck happened?" I ask when we're standing by his bike, lifting my hand to touch his swollen cheek.

He moves his face away. "While I'm with your brother, trying my fuckin' best for us to be together without losing him, you're here, pressed up against another one of my brothers?"

Okay, he's angry.

And even though it was an innocent dance, he does have a point.

His chest is heaving up and down and the look he's giving me makes me want to cringe.

I need to apologize.

"Arrow—"

"You better be worth all this shit, Anna," he says through clenched teeth. "Mary would have never—"

My gasp stops him in his tracks. I can't fucking believe he went there. I just can't.

"Well, unfortunately, Arrow, Mary isn't here," I snap, my chest tightening. "But I am. I was sitting alone and Tracker asked me to dance. As a friend, so I wasn't bored out of my mind. You're the only one I have eyes for, even though you're usually a dick! You know I would never even think about being with someone other than you. I'm fuckin' crazy about you!"

His mood instantly changes, lightening the air around us. "Anna, I—"

I hold up my hand. "I'm going to *try* and enjoy the rest of my night."

"I told Rake," he says. "He wasn't happy. In fact, he was fucking pissed. He's probably on his way here now to grab you."

My head falls back against my neck. "Can you just take me home, please? Or shall I call a cab?"

He nods, rubbing the back of his neck. "You're not taking a fuckin' cab, Anna. Can you hold on, or have you had too much to drink?"

"I'm fine," I tell him, staying silent as he puts the helmet on me and helps me onto the bike.

Mary would have never . . .

That's what it all comes down to, doesn't it?

I'm not Mary; I'll never be Mary. She's gone, and I'm here.

I just hope he sees that before it's too late.

Arrow doesn't take me home.

He takes me back to the clubhouse, where I ignore him, have a shower, and slide into bed. He stands in front of the bed, watching me while I try to pretend like he isn't there.

"I didn't mean it," he says into the silence. "I shouldn't have said it. I mean, it's messed up of me to compare you two, I know that. It just slipped out."

I pretend to sleep, and after a few moments he leaves the room.

When I wake up the next morning, I realize Arrow never returned to my room, and for some reason that annoys me. After I'm dressed I walk into the kitchen to see Arrow and Rake standing there, face-to-face.

"Rake?"

He spins to me. "Anna, what the fuck?"

I shrink into myself. "Can we talk alone, please?"

"We will talk after," he says, staring at Arrow, who is a little taller than him, and bigger built, but Rake is scrappy. Like me, he had no choice but to be. "Arrow and I are going to sort some shit out in the ring, aren't we?"

Arrow nods but doesn't look happy about it like Rake does.

Sin storms into the kitchen with Faye on his heels, sends me a scowl, then demands, "Church, now!"

Great.

Everyone with a penis disappears into the club-only room while the women stand there with curious expressions on their faces. Then, one by one, they all turn to stare at me.

I shrug, feeling helpless.

Faye and I sit down on the couch, waiting to see what happens next.

"What happened?" she whispers.

"Arrow told Rake last night. Rake didn't take it very well. And I think your husband is just angry that I'm getting in between his club members."

Faye doesn't bother to deny it.

I see her biting her lip. "What?"

"Nothing, it's just . . . This is so out of character for Arrow. And kind of . . . hot."

I purse my lips. "Seriously?"

She smirks. "What? I'm still a woman, after all."

I roll my eyes at her, my focus back on Arrow. I am still mad at him over the Mary thing, but this is a time where I need to have his back. I should be in there with him; we got into this together.

What feels like an hour later but is actually fifteen minutes, the men all walk out. Arrow and Rake beeline to me straight-away, and I gulp at the expression on their faces.

Both of them are not fucking happy.

"Anna," they say at the same time. I stand and look from one to the other.

"Yes?"

Sin walks up behind them and stares me down. "You caused this, so you're going to watch."

I gape. "I *caused* this? What the fuck, we aren't in the Middle Ages! What I do and who I do it with is my business and mine only."

Arrow leans down and whispers in my ear. "Calm down, Anna. Rake and I are going to fight it out. I need you to hold your shit together right now. Can you do that?"

I nod, then turn to Rake, who looks even more pissed off now.

Great.

I put my arm on my brother's shoulder and give him my best puppy-dog look, which usually works on him.

Nothing.

Wow, he's really angry.

"I'm sorry, Rake. I don't want to hurt you, but I can't seem to forget the bastard."

He looks at me then and sighs. "I wanted better for you, Anna."

I swallow hard at the disappointment in his eyes. "You wanted me here with you in this lifestyle. Please don't be mad now that I've decided to be a part of it."

"Fuck," he curses, then kisses me on my forehead. "He hurts you and I'll kill him. Slowly."

"So you aren't going to fight?" I ask, hearing the hope in my voice.

Rake smiles slowly. An evil glint in his eye that sends a shiver down my spine.

"Fuck no, I need this." He looks down at me. "And stay out of it, Anna. You wanted to be a biker's woman—now sit here, bite your tongue, and let me take what I'm owed."

My eyes widen. Rake has never spoken to me like that in my entire life. I step away from him, not seeing my brother, but Rake—the club member. Arrow wraps his arms around my waist from behind and spins me around. Then, with everyone watching, his mouth settles possessively on mine.

Point made.

I'm his, and he's mine.

And now everyone knows it.

SIXTEEN

DREAD fills my stomach as Rake and Arrow face each other. Why do these men have to act so barbaric? And screw Sin for making me watch it. Arrow pulls off his T-shirt, exposing his smooth, toned chest, and I perk up a little. Faye sends me a knowing smirk before her gaze returns to the two impressive men, staring at each other, waiting for the fight to begin. Rake pulls his shirt off as well, and they both face away from me, talking to Sin. I stare at the dragon tattoos on their backs, both staring at me.

These men live by their own rules, and there is nothing I can do about it. If I want Arrow I know I can't change him. I have to accept him as he is, and I do.

That, however, doesn't mean that I will stop being me. It just means that I have to think before I speak.

I'm trying.

Arrow looks over at me just before they get the go-ahead from Sin to start. He lets Rake hit him once, square in the face, then says something to him in a low tone. After that, he gets into the fight. I close my eyes as I hear the sounds of flesh hitting flesh, knowing that, to me, it doesn't matter who wins this fight. The two men I care about the most are beating the shit out of each other, and all I can do is sit here and let them act like idiots. I hope after they work off all this aggression, Rake can forgive Arrow and let it go. This isn't the olden days, where he needs to defend my honor because some man took my innocence. Arrow and I haven't even had sex yet. I look up to see blood dripping down my brother's face and Arrow's lip cut open once more. I shoot Sin a dirty look, but he just grins at me.

Why do I want anything to do with these men again?

I stand up and yell at the top of my lungs, "ENOUGH!"

Surprisingly they both turn to me.

"Enough," I say again, my voice shaky. I grab a first-aid kit from the bathroom, then tend to Arrow's face. Rake already has two women fussing over him. I gently cup Arrow's face, lifting it up for me to inspect closely. I don't like seeing him hurt, even though I now know to expect this kind of shit.

"Fucking stupid," I mutter to myself, wiping the blood away and checking out the cut. It looks painful, but he is acting like he can't feel a thing.

He smiles, blood on his teeth. "Nothing like a good fight."

I wrinkle my nose and look over his ribs. "Anything else hurt?"

He shakes his head and gets on his feet. "I'm fine; now let's go to bed."

My head snaps to him. "I'm sorry?"

He smirks. "I'm full of adrenaline, darlin', and I won the prize. Now let's go fuck."

He's so romantic.

Not.

I look around to see everyone watching us.

"Don't you all have things to do?" I ask the peanut gallery.

Faye shakes her head and grins.

Arrow, apparently done waiting, lifts me in his arms and carries me bride-style to my bedroom. Throwing me on the bed, he braces himself over me and kisses me, wincing a little because of his cut lip.

"If you're not up for this, Arrow . . ." I tease, lifting my hips up and feeling just how much he wants it. "I can take care of it myself."

"No chance in hell, darlin'," he replies with a smirk, then undoes my jeans and slides them off. Next to go is my black tank top, my bra, and then last of all my panties. I lie there, completely bare before him, but instead of feeling shy, I feel empowered by the look in his eyes.

He likes what he sees, and I like that he likes what he sees.

I lick at my bottom lip. He doesn't miss the motion.

"So worth the wait," he says in a low rumble. "So worth it."

"Glad to please," I whisper. "Now, your turn."

He takes off his jeans. He isn't wearing any underwear.

My mouth waters at the size of his cock, my eyes widening.

Now *that* is a cock.

Before I'm finished with my perusal, he lies down and rolls me on top of him.

"I want to enjoy this view," he says as his thumbs swipe over my nipples. "Kiss me."

He doesn't have to tell me twice.

I lean down and kiss his mouth gently, as his hands wander, not leaving any part of me untouched.

"Love this ass," he sighs, feeling each cheek and slapping twice for good measure. "I want to be inside you, Anna."

I want the exact same thing.

"Condom?"

He curses.

"I'm on the pill, if you're—"

He exhales, eyes on my mouth. "I'm clean, Anna."

"Jill?"

"Got tested after her, I wouldn't put you in any danger, Anna."

Staring into his brown eyes, I nod and take his hard cock in my hand and slide him into me. I'm dripping wet, but I go slowly, the wide girth of him stretching me. I push down, lowering myself on him until he's completely inside me. His jaw clenches, but his eyes never leave mine, the connection between us stronger than ever before.

"Fuck me, Anna," he demands, sitting up slightly and capturing a beaded nipple into his mouth. I move forward, my body doing as it's naturally inclined, lifting myself up and down on his length.

I've never felt anything better.

My jaw drops open and my eyes squeeze shut as I just feel, surrendering to the pleasure. Suddenly Arrow rolls us over so he's on top and starts to fuck me with an intensity that should scare me but doesn't. It turns me on even more.

"Eyes open, Anna," he commands as mine fall shut. "I want to see those beautiful green eyes as I'm fucking you."

I moan in response, spreading my legs wider, silently begging for more, my eyes fluttering open. "Arrow—"

He kisses me, cutting off my begging. My nipples rub against his chest and he reaches down to play with my clit. When he starts to kiss and lick my neck, my orgasm builds to a point of no return. I come—saying his name over and over again, as he continues to pleasure my body with exquisite torture.

Too much.

Not enough.

I wanted more.

I never want him to stop.

When I come back to myself, I study his expression.

He cups my face, staring down at me as he comes, his body jerking above me.

I've never seen something so spectacular as his body.

Muscles rippling, covered with a light sheen of sweat, braced above me. His hair falling into his face, his eyes—filled with pleasure—drilling into mine. I pull his beard down, lowering his face so I can kiss his mouth.

He smiles then, and it lights up my world.

Grinding his hips into me, he says, "I want to stay here forever."

I smile, then lower his head to my breast, which is waiting for attention.

There is no way in hell we are done with each other just yet.

It is official.

I need to increase my stamina.

"I can't feel my legs," I complain, sitting up and letting my eyes roam over his naked body. I don't think I'll ever get sick of the view.

Arrow chuckles deeply. "You'll get used to me soon enough."

Gripping my waist with his fingers, he pulls me back to rest against his body.

"Do you think anyone heard me?" I ask quietly, the thought of Rake hearing me making me cringe. "If my brother heard me screaming your name I'm leaving this clubhouse and never coming back."

"There's nothing the people around here haven't seen or heard, so don't stress over it," is all he says.

Was I that loud?

I kind of want to die.

I bury my face in his chest and groan. Arrow runs his hand through my hair, gently pulling apart the tangles.

"Does your face hurt?" I ask.

He sighs. "No, it doesn't."

"You lie."

"No, I don't."

"Stubborn."

"Babe, we get into fights all the time. It isn't a big deal," he says softly.

"It should be," I mutter, then press my lips against his chest.

He kisses the top of my head. "You working tonight?"

I nod and pick up my phone. It is three o'clock already.

"Holy shit, we've been in bed for hours! Yeah, and Reid will kick my ass if I'm not there."

"No one's going near your ass except me."

I roll my eyes at that, then slide out of bed. "I'm going to take a shower, eat something, then get ready for work."

Arrow rolls onto his stomach, showing off his tight ass.

"Nice buns."

He makes a sound of amusement, glancing up at me while I check him out. Moving from that delectable ass, I take in his dragon tattoo and the muscles in his back. "Not bad for an old man."

He flashes me a boyish grin. "Who you calling old?"

"Not me, that's for sure."

He pushes up on all fours, grabs me and pins me underneath him. "Yet you're the one who couldn't keep up with me, hmmmm."

I narrow my eyes. "I haven't had sex in a while, so excuse me if I was tired after three rounds."

He presses his lips to mine, his tongue licking—begging entrance. When I open for him, he kisses me hungrily, hands on either side of my face. When he pulls back he looks at me and says, "Can't wait to be back inside you tonight."

"Tonight? I'm going back to my apartment after work tonight," I tell him.

"The fuck you are. You think you can give me one taste, then walk away?"

I purse my lips at his dramatics. "I'm not walking away, I'm going home. I have class tomorrow."

He tilts his head to the side. "I'll stay at yours then. After I pick you up from the bar."

"Fine. What are your plans tonight?"

He lifts an eyebrow at my question.

"What?" I ask.

"You gonna try to demand that I explain my every move now? Because I think you need to know right now that that isn't me."

My mouth drops open.

What the hell?

"What are you talking about?" I ask, forehead creasing in confusion. "I just asked what you were doing tonight."

He nods. "Yeah, a word of advice, darlin', don't ask. I'll be where I tell you I'll be, and that's to pick you up after your shift."

How did he go from sweet to asshole in 2.5 seconds?

I try to push him off me but he doesn't budge. "I need to go or I'm going to be late."

"You're pissed?"

One point for him.

I ignore his question and just shove him again. "Arrow, get off me!" I demand through clenched teeth.

He lets me go, and I quickly get off the bed and head into the bathroom, locking the door behind me.

I guess I was wrong to think that Arrow considered me his equal.

I don't know if I can be with someone like that.

Turning the shower on, I close my eyes and let the hot water wash over my body as I try to clear my head.

It doesn't help.

And for the rest of the day, I avoid Arrow.

SEVENTEEN

LANA surprises me by showing up at the bar.

I hug her and get her a drink, waiting for everyone to be served before I return and stop in front of her. "I feel like I haven't spoken to you in ages."

"I know," she says. "That's why I decided to come and see you. What's been going on?"

I give her a quick rundown, which has her brown eyes wide and a smile playing on her lips.

"So you're dating Arrow?" she repeats for the third time.

I shrug. "I don't think *dating* is the word. *Fucking* is probably more apt."

Since apparently I couldn't even ask the man a freaking question without it stepping over a line.

She downs her drink. "That's quite a story."

"I know," I reply. "Do you want to go out for lunch tomorrow after my morning class?"

She nods. "Sounds good. I'm going shopping with my mother in the morning, but apart from that I have nothing else to do."

"Why don't you keep in touch with any of your friends from school?" I ask her.

She shrugs. "After you left I was kind of a loner; I don't really keep in touch with anyone."

I frown. "Why?"

She shifts in her seat and looks away. "I guess I just kind of kept to myself, I don't know."

Okay, there is definitely a story there, one she doesn't want to share. I make a mental note to try and get her to open up about it another time. If anyone has hurt my Lana, they better run.

"Their loss," I reply, meaning it 100 percent.

She smirks into her drink. "Your life is much more interesting than mine."

"Yeah, I'm not sure that's a good thing," I reply, but a small smile plays on my lips. A seriously hot guy with violet eyes and dark hair comes into the bar and chats with Reid and Ryan. He has twin dimples that I find seriously hot, and the perfect amount of stubble on his jaw. I glance at Lana to see her checking him out as well.

"He could make my life more interesting," she says with a grin.

I exhale. "I have no doubt of that."

The man glances over at us, and Lana and I quickly look away, Lana's cheeks burning at being caught. From the corner of my eye, I see him approach. Lana feigns noninterest, staring down at her drink, while I lift my head and offer him a friendly smile.

"Hello," I say.

"Hi, I'm Dash," he says, flashing a smile that I'm sure has dropped many panties.

"Anna. And this is Lana," I say, nodding toward my bestie.

Lana looks up and smiles tentatively. "Hi."

Dash nods at the seat next to Lana. "Can I sit here?"

Lana glances at me, then nods.

I hide my grin.

"Can I get you another drink, Dash?" I ask.

"I'm good, thanks," he says, and I take that as my cue to leave, ignoring Lana's pleading looks.

I go over to Reid and Ryan and stand between them. "Your friend is a hottie."

Reid ignores my comment, but Ryan flashes me an amused look. The rest of the evening passes quickly. Thirty minutes before my shift is over, Arrow walks in. I'm looking down at the cash register when he enters, but I know he's there.

It's like I can feel him.

The atmosphere in the room changes, thickens. I raise my eyes and he's standing there, arms crossed over his chest and his gaze locked on me. He takes a seat at the corner of the bar. I'm still angry with him, but at the same time I kind of want to rip his clothes off and have my way with him. Maybe the only way to survive Arrow is to be his fuck buddy? It's clear that a deeper relationship with him doesn't look like it will ever happen. He's so closed off, and if he expects me to not even ask him any questions? Yeah, I can't live like that. I want an open, trusting relationship. A safe place where I can say what I want and be who I am.

I want a partner, not someone who thinks he can control me. I understand with the club there are times I have to back away. I get that. I know that the club business doesn't really have anything to do with me, but at the same time I'm the one who got kidnapped because of them. Knowledge is power, and without it, I feel like I'm stumbling around a room blind. And then there's the fact that Arrow's obviously carrying around some heavy emotions concerning Mary.

I don't even want to touch that subject.

After ignoring him a few minutes, I walk over. "Beer?"

He nods, eyes narrowed slightly. "That's how you greet your man when you see him?"

"I'm working," I reply.

He rakes his teeth over his bottom lip.

I look away and grab him a beer from the fridge. "I'll be done soon."

He nods once, then turns to scan the bar. It's not very busy tonight, with only a few tables filled with people. Lana left about an hour ago, Dash offering to walk her to her car. I wonder what happened there.

I'm wiping down the counters when Reid tells me I can go home. I throw the dishrag down and grab my bag, not looking forward to facing the tension with Arrow. He stands without a word and walks me to the door. He even opens it for me. We walk to his bike and ride back to my apartment in complete silence. I fumble with my keys while Arrow waits patiently for me to unlock the door. I finally get it open and walk in before him. He locks the door while I put the light on and lay my handbag on the table.

"You want something to drink or eat?" I ask, glancing at him before heading to the kitchen.

"No, I'm good," he replies. "Faye fed me before I went to Knox's."

I know that shouldn't annoy me, but it does. I should be

the one feeding him. I push the ridiculous feeling away and head straight for the bathroom, where I take a quick shower and prepare for bed. Arrow is lying on my bed when I walk out, checking something on his phone. He puts it down as soon as he realizes I'm standing here.

"Come here," he says. A soft, yet firm demand.

Dressed in a long T-shirt and nothing else, I climb up on the bed and crawl to him, then lay my head on his warm chest.

"If you're pissed at me, you tell me why, Anna. I'm not a mind reader," he says quietly. "I don't like the silent treatment or your ignoring me. I know we're still getting to know each other, so I'm letting it slide this time, but next time, I expect you to open that luscious mouth of yours and tell me what has your knickers in a twist."

I swallow. "Arrow, I asked you a simple question, like one would ask anyone else, and you shut me down. If you want it that way, why bother to talk at all? Let's just fuck and then go on our merry way."

The tension in the room spikes. He's quiet, but I can actually feel him silently fuming. He's trying to control it.

"I don't like being questioned," he says after a few moments. "At least not by pussy."

He did *not* just say that.

I lift my head and try to push myself off his body. "You fucking arrogant jerk—"

He puts his hand over my mouth. "I wasn't finished. You aren't just pussy, so you're right, I shouldn't have cut out like that. This is new for me too, darlin'."

"How is this new for you? What about—"

I don't even want to say her name.

"Mary was different. She didn't ask questions," he says softly, cringing slightly. "I'm not trying to upset you by saying that, you know? You're a different woman—you're a strong woman, and I like that about you, a lot. I can be myself with you and know you won't go running scared. Instead, you will give shit back to me in full force. Fuckin' love that, Anna. Obviously there's shit I can't and won't tell you, and you can't push me on that."

I nod. "I get that."

"Good, then there's no problem here. Now give me the kiss that you should have given me when you first saw me tonight," he demands.

I reluctantly give in, leaning over him and pressing my lips to his. He takes over the kiss instantly, taking control. His hand slides up my thigh, and he makes a growling sound when he realizes I'm wearing nothing underneath.

"Came to bed wanting to get fucked, didn't you?" he rumbles into my ear, biting down on it gently before kissing my neck, licking and sucking just hard enough to not leave a mark behind. I make a needy sound, letting him know I need more. He lifts the T-shirt off me, throwing it somewhere on the floor, and gets up, standing next to the bed, removing his own clothes. I watch his every move, enjoying the view, licking my lips in anticipation. He knows it, giving me a little show, rubbing a hand down his abs and over his erect cock. I think of what Faye said about it "pointing like an arrow" and can't help the giggle that escapes me. It is literally pointing in my face. Arrow lifts an eyebrow at me, then grabs me and kisses me greedily, wrapping my hair around his hand and pulling gently.

"What's so amusing?" he asks in a deep voice.

"Nothing," I pant.

He flips me over and pulls my back to his front. I groan at the skin-on-skin contact, how nice he feels pressed against me. Lips on my favorite spot, the crook between my neck and my shoulder, one hand plays with my breasts while the other one trails lower, stroking me intimately.

"So wet for me," he murmurs, pulling back, holding my hips and pushing me forward so I'm on all fours. Without further preamble, he slides into me from behind with one smooth thrust that has me gripping the sheets and begging for more.

"Beautiful," he grits out, and I look behind to see him staring down at where we're joined. "Touch your clit, Anna."

I reach down and touch myself, my thighs starting to tremble. Just as I'm about to come, Arrow pulls out, flips me over, and then his mouth is on me, devouring me as I come in his mouth.

"Oh my God," I pant as I come back to myself.

He leans over me and smiles, his eyes dark and full of passion. "Not done with you yet, Anna."

I smile as he slides back into me.

EIGHTEEN

I F you're here to kidnap me again, I'm going to be really fucking mad," I tell Talon when I see him on my front doorstep. "Do you have a death wish? Why are you here?"

I reach into my handbag and fumble for my hot-pink pocketknife.

Talon just smirks at me. "I was in the neighborhood."

I blink slowly. "Do you visit everyone you kidnap? Or am I special?"

He wets his lips before he speaks. "Just wanted to make sure you were okay and say sorry about what happened. It was fucked-up to bring you into it, but it was my only choice at the time. Know that if there was another way, I would have taken it, okay?"

He looks like he's serious, like it's important that I believe him.

I move my hand from my pocketknife to my house keys. "Are you alone?"

He puts his hand in his pocket and nods.

"Why are you really here, Talon?" I ask, my eyes searching his.

He looks down. "I just wanted to talk to you about something."

"About what?" I ask.

"There's something I need to explain about—"

It's then that I hear the rumble of a motorcycle and cringe. "You better get out of here, Talon."

He rubs the back of his neck. "Just let me fuckin' say this to you, Anna."

I narrow my eyes. "Do you want Arrow to beat the shit out of you?"

He scoffs. "I can handle myself, don't you worry about me."

I exhale slowly, gathering patience. "It's not about that. I don't want any more drama. So please, for me, just go."

A muscle tics in his jaw, betraying his anger, but he nods and walks off.

Why the hell did I just save the man who kidnapped me?

There is something seriously wrong with me, but my gut instinct is that Talon would never hurt me.

I sigh in relief when I see him disappear on foot through the side of the apartment complex, and unlock my door, waiting for Arrow. He swaggers up the pathway, dressed in all black, tight T-shirt with his cut over it and black jeans. His hair looks damp and combed back, and he's holding something in his hands.

"Hey, beautiful," he says as he reaches me, lifting me in his arms and kissing me sweetly.

"Hi," I say when his mouth finally leaves mine. "What have you got in your hand?"

"Oh, right," he says, looking down as if only just realizing. "I bought you something. A present." He looks unsure, which I can't help but find adorable. "I hope you like it."

He takes my hand and places the box in my palm, closing my fingers around it. I open my hand and lift it up closer.

"Don't open it right now," he says, cheeks heating. "Wait until I leave." He looks around. "Please."

I nod and try to hide my smile. "Can you just turn around so I can open it now?"

"Anna—"

"Please," I say, sticking my lower lip out and giving him my best puppy dog–eyed look.

"Okay," he says, exhaling deeply. "Open it."

I open the box and sitting in a bed of velvet is a bracelet. It's gold and embedded with diamonds. I flip it over, where I see an inscription.

K.A. & A.W.

Killian Arrowsmith & Anna Ward.

Was Arrow a closet romantic?

I glance up at him, amused at his red cheeks and touched by his present. I didn't need gifts, but the inscription really made it special to me.

"I love it," I tell him. "Thank you, Arrow. It's beautiful. Will you help me put it on?" He nods and relaxes, helping me put the stunning piece of jewelry on my wrist. He then guides me into the house with his hand on the small of my back.

"Got some business to take care of tonight, so I can't stay," he says. "I just wanted to see you before I had to leave."

"Okay," I reply.

"I'd prefer it if you stayed at the clubhouse."

"Duly noted," I reply, having no intention of going anywhere.

His eyes cut to me, and his mouth tightens. "Anna—"

"Lana's coming over later, okay? So I won't be alone."

"Ask her to stay the night," Arrow says, relenting. "Deal?"

"Are you making a deal with me, Arrow? With *me*? A measly woman? I'm shocked," I reply in a high falsetto.

"Cute," he replies, looking amused. "It takes more than a measly woman to get my attention, Anna."

I take his hand and lead him to the living room, then put the gift he gave me on the coffee table. "I'll take that as a compliment."

"It was meant as one," he replies, taking a seat.

"How's Rake been?" I ask, sitting down next to him. I haven't seen him since the fight, and even though I've called him a few times he hasn't returned my calls. It hurts like a hole in my chest. Never in my wildest dreams did I think he would shut me out after we'd only just reconnected.

Arrow's eyes soften as he glances at me. "Don't worry about Rake; he'll come around. Let him sulk for the time being."

"My brother doesn't sulk," I say, indignant.

"Of course he doesn't." Arrow smirks. "You want to go out for dinner?"

"Are you asking me out on a date?"

Arrow's eyes widen.

He clears his throat.

"Fuck," he blurts out.

"What?"

"I don't remember the last time I went on a date," he admits, looking a little sheepish. "I generally don't have the time or the need to do anything but fuck."

"Charming," I mutter, pursing my lips. "I can see that I've picked a real winner here."

He chuckles. "You didn't pick me, darlin'. I picked you, and don't you forget that."

I roll my eyes. "Oh, please, I wanted you from the first time I saw you."

"And I wanted you before that."

"What?" I ask, searching his face. "What do you mean?"

He licks his bottom lip before he speaks. "Rake showed me a picture of you once. It was years ago. My dick got so hard and I knew that I wanted you even then."

My eyes flare. "From a picture?"

"From a picture," he deadpans. "You were the most beautiful woman I'd ever seen. And it fuckin' sucked you were his sister."

I make a scoffing sound. "Didn't stop you though, did it?"

He pushes me back, laying me across the couch. "I always get what I want, Anna. Best you realize that now."

"It's cute that you think so," I tell him, feeling amused. "That was obviously before you met me."

His lip twitches. "Full of sass, Anna. Maybe I should fuck some of it out of you?"

My heart races. "You could try."

He lowers his face and kisses my jawline. "I think you'd like that, wouldn't you?"

My breath hitches as he kisses below my ear, then down my neck. When his warm breath blows over my nipple, through the thin cotton of my T-shirt, I moan out loud.

"Do you know what I want right now?" he asks softly.

Hopefully the answer to that involves his mouth and my pussy.

"What?"

He lifts his head and grins at me. "To go out to dinner. I'm fuckin' hungry."

I slap at his shoulder. "If you don't make me come right now, Arrow, I'm not going to be very good company!"

He smirks. "I'm just playing, I'd never leave my woman wanting. Never."

Thank goodness for that.

When he chuckles I realize I'd said that out loud. Sitting up I pull off my T-shirt and unclip my bra, throwing them both on the floor.

"Eager, are we?" he asks with a teasing glint in his eyes.

"Less talking, more fucking!" I tell him, throwing myself at him and kissing him passionately. He groans and cups my ass, pulling me closer against his body.

It hit me then.

It hit me hard.

I've fallen in love with Arrow.

I love him, but I know I shouldn't.

Shutting my thoughts off, I concentrate on the man himself, on his tongue in my mouth, on his hand sliding down my leggings.

I lose myself in him, so I don't question myself.

So I don't ask myself if I think he can ever love me back.

Because I'm not sure I want to know the answer.

"Take off your clothes," I practically growl as I take my mouth away from his. "I want you, now."

"I give the orders here, Anna," he rumbles deeply, then lowers his head to my nipple.

Okay, I could work with this.

Eventually, after he gives me the best foreplay of my life, he removes his clothes.

And then he makes love to me.

After dinner Arrow waits with me until Lana arrives. With a long kiss he leaves, and I turn to face Lana, who is watching me with a knowing look on her face.

"Now that was a kiss," she says, pushing her glasses up on her nose.

"Indeed," I say, watching Arrow's retreating back for a moment before closing and locking the door. "What happened with Dash the other night?"

We wander into the living room, my face flushing slightly as I remember what happened in here just hours before. I sit down on the spot where we had sex, just so poor Lana doesn't have to sit there.

"He walked me to my car and asked for my number. I gave it to him, and we've been texting and calling, but . . ."

She trails off. Who are we talking about again? Oh, Dash.

"But what?" I ask.

She cringes. "Tracker's been calling me as well."

My head snaps to hers. "That's right. I wanted to ask you how you had each other's numbers."

She raises an eyebrow at me and plays with the end of her ponytail. "He got it from your phone. You must have left it lying around somewhere."

"That jerk," I grumble. "What does he message you? I love Tracker like my own brother, but he's not done with Allie—she's still living in the clubhouse. Don't get involved in that mess; I don't want you to get hurt."

"He just needs a friend, Anna," Lana says softly.

"Hey, I'm his friend," I mutter.

She giggles at that. "We're just friends, don't have an Anna attack. I wouldn't be with someone who has a girlfriend; I'm not a home wrecker."

I start to laugh. "An Anna attack? I haven't heard that since grade school."

She leans back and grins. "Every time you lost your temper . . . There was no other word for it."

"Ha!" I say loudly, making her jump a little. "Look who's talking, little innocent Lana. I've seen you lose your temper, and it's not pretty. Hell, even I'm scared."

Her face goes red. "The difference between us is, you lose your temper every day. Mine is more like once a year."

That was the truth.

"Well," I say, crossing my legs under me, "your annual tantrum is worse than all of mine put together. Everyone runs for cover. Have you used up your tantrum quota for the year? I should sic you on Allie."

We both laugh at that.

"What do you want to do tonight?" she asks.

I give her a *Duh* look. "Watch *Outlander* and perve on Jamie Fraser, of course."

She grins. "Good thing I brought my pajamas for the occasion!"

"What pajamas?" I ask, perking up.

She gets her bag and pulls out a sleep top that reads "I'd rather be sleeping with Jamie."

My eyes go wide. "I need that, like now."

She rolls her eyes. "I got you a set. Obviously."

"I love you," I tell her on a sigh.

"I love you too," she replies. "But I don't think you should wear these around Arrow."

I smirk, picturing his face. "I think you might be right on that one."

We settle in for the night, some good old quality Lana time.

I love every second.

Even though I'm kind of missing Arrow.

NINETEEN

"HOW long are you going to be mad at me?" I ask Rake, hand on my hip. I came to the clubhouse this morning to resolve two things. One, Arrow still isn't back from wherever he is, and two, Rake is avoiding me.

"I'm not mad," he says, eyeing but not eating the breakfast I brought him.

I throw my hands up. "Are you not going to eat the food I brought you because you're holding a grudge against me?"

He pouts, actually pouts.

I point at the bag filled with his favorite breakfast foods—a croissant, a bagel, and a couple of hash browns. "Please eat it, or I will."

He slowly moves the bag closer to his chest so I can't take it.

I hide my smirk.

He sighs.

"Adam," I say, wanting to get through to him. "This is my family too, now. Think about it—I'm safer with Arrow than on my own." I lower my voice. "I love him."

His eyes dart to mine. "I don't want to see what happened to Mary happen to you."

"Anyone could have died that night," I say. "It wasn't Arrow's fault."

He lowers his head. "I know that! Fuck. You're my baby sister, Anna. It's me who fucked up. I'm the selfish one. I wanted you around me, so I brought you here, and now you're shacked up with one of the baddest motherfuckers in the club."

He looks at me. "You couldn't have chosen Tracker or someone, could you?"

Tracker? Did Rake think he was the best out of them all? I think over the rest of the men and realize, sadly, that he may be right. Tracker was a good guy, even though he had his own issues with Allie.

I step closer to him and wrap my arm around him. "I love you, you know that, right? I never want to hurt you, or disappoint you, and it kills me that you're avoiding me right now. You were my only family, Rake; you were all that I had. Now you've given me your MC family, and at first I wasn't too thrilled," I admit. "But I wouldn't have it any other way. So thank you. And Arrow has been a perfect gentleman to me."

Except in the sheets—but he doesn't need to know that.

"A gentleman?" he repeats, sounding incredulous. "I've heard Arrow called many things, but definitely never that."

I smirk. "Now will you eat your breakfast?"

He smiles and looks down into the bag. "I suppose so."

I kiss him on the cheek. "Will you spend the day with me?"

He nods and takes a huge bite out of his croissant, half of it disappearing into his mouth.

"Good. Any idea when Arrow gets back?" I ask, hiding my annoyance that he didn't mention he would be gone for longer than a night.

Rake looks up at me and grins boyishly. "Not so great to be an old lady now, is it?"

Old lady? No one said anything about that.

"Hmmph."

He chuckles. "At least now I won't have to threaten you to get you to the clubhouse."

Tracker walks in at that moment with Trace, Jess's husband.

"You," he says, pointing at me.

"Me what?" I ask, looking around.

"I have a favor to ask you."

I instantly become suspicious.

"I'm listening," I reply warily.

He walks over to me and casually puts his hand on my waist. "Let's talk about this in my bedroom."

My eyebrows rise at that. "I don't think so, buddy, unless you want me to finally get the chance to punch Allie in the face."

He rubs the back of his neck. "She isn't here—just come."

He grabs my arm and walks me to his room. I glance back at Rake, who just shrugs his broad shoulders.

"So, what?" I call out to him. "Before, no club members could touch me, now any of them can lure me into their rooms?"

He laughs at my poor excuse of a joke. "You're Arrow's now. No one would dare touch you." In his room, Tracker turns and looks down at me. "I want to ask Lana out," he says.

I should have seen this one coming.

"And?"

"And I want you to tell me where her favorite place to eat is," he says, blue eyes pleading with mine.

I cross my arms over my chest. "You know I love you, Tracker, but for fuck's sake, Allie still lives here with you! I don't think you should ask anyone out, *especially* Lana, until you sort out your shit."

His expression darkens, but I don't regret my words. They're the truth—whether he wants to hear them or not.

"You don't think I'm good enough for her?" he grits out, jaw tense.

"Tracker—"

He laughs mirthlessly. "Look, I know no one is probably good enough for Lana; I see what she's worth. But it's nice to know that someone I consider a good friend doesn't see *my* worth."

"Tracker—"

He opens the door to his room and walks out, leaving me sitting here alone, feeling like complete shit. I sit there for a few minutes, thinking. I see a pad of paper and a pen by the bed. It's pink, so I'm assuming it's Allie's. I rip off a sheet and write Tracker a note.

> You're wrong; I know what you're worth.
> But do you?
> I'm sorry I'm a jerk.
> Love, Anna Bell.

Why does he keep Allie around? As a safety net? Is it a comfort thing? I have no idea, but I realize I'm being judgmental and poking my nose into shit that's not really my business. I'm very protective of Lana, but I should be asking *her* if she wants this. It's not my decision to make. I leave the note on his bed, then go to find Rake.

We have some catching up to do.

*   *   *

Wetness on my face.

I force my eyes open and stare up at Rake, who is dripping water on my face from a water bottle.

"What the hell are you doing?" I ask, sitting up and looking for something to throw at him.

"You fell asleep," he says, shaking his head. "Some party animal you are."

"What time is it?" I ask, rubbing my eyes with the bottom of my palm.

"One a.m., Anna, let's go out!" he says cheerfully, bouncing on the balls of his feet.

I blink. "Are you on drugs?"

It's a legitimate question with the way he's acting.

"You want to go where?" I ask. We'd hung out all day, went to see a movie, spent some time playing pool, and had dinner. Then, everyone started drinking and I may have joined in for one or two drinks.

Or five.

"Let's go to the club," he says. "Rift, remember?"

"The one you guys dragged me out of last time?" I ask in a dry tone.

Good times.

"Yep," he says, starting to tip more water on me.

"Do it and die!" I yell, standing up and pushing my hair out of my face. "Let me get dressed."

"You have ten minutes," he says. "I'm going to round everyone up."

I look at him and only just notice he's dressed and ready to go, in jeans and the black T-shirt I bought him when I first came back.

"Fine," I say, following him to the door and locking it as he leaves. I'm wearing jeans and a plain white top, which won't do. Knowing I don't have time for a shower, I wash my face, brush my teeth, and put on some light makeup. My hair looks like I just got fucked, but there's no fixing it. I get changed into tight jeans and a black top that shows off my stomach. I slide my feet into some stiletto heels, spritz a little perfume, and grab my handbag on the way out.

Rake, Tracker, Trace, Sin, and Vinnie are standing in the game room, laughing and drinking. They all look at me as I walk in.

"What?" I ask, feeling a little self-conscious.

"You actually got dressed in like fifteen minutes," Tracker says, any earlier anger vanished. "Impressive. Arrow is a lucky fucker."

That earns him a slap on the back of the head from Rake.

I roll my eyes and look at Sin. "Is Faye coming out?"

He shakes his head but gives no explanation for her absence. Okaaaay then.

"Where's Arrow?" I ask Tracker. He still hasn't contacted me since last night, and I'm really put out over it.

"He'll be at Rift," Tracker replies, then snaps his head back to me. "And you need to be on your best behavior because men from other Wind Dragon chapters are going to be there tonight."

"Define *best behavior*."

"Have fun but keep your mouth shut," he replies. "And stick to us at all times."

I can do that.

Maybe.

He hands me my drink, and I take a sip.

Then I cough. "Holy shit, Tracker!"

He chuckles. "What? Can't handle a little vodka?"

"Not straight! I'm not an alcoholic, you bastard!" I snap, putting my drink back down.

"Why are you grumpy?" he asks. "You had a nap and everything."

Rake laughs.

I pick up a pool cue and threaten them with it.

They laugh harder.

"Why am I the only woman going out tonight?" I ask the group of them.

They all look at one another.

"The other women know their place," Tracker inserts, laughing at his own joke.

I slap his shoulder. "How you get women at all, I have no idea."

"Probably my huge pierced cock," he replies. "Or my charm."

My eyes widen as I look down at his crotch area. "Your dick is pierced?"

He undoes his button. "Yep. Want to see?"

Another slap from Rake.

The truth was, I did want to see. But I didn't want to get Tracker killed.

Vinnie walks over and takes a gulp of my vodka, then pours in some juice and hands me back the glass. "Thanks, Vinnie," I tell him.

I pound the whole glass.

"That's the spirit," Rake says, wrapping an arm around me. "Let's do a shot, then get out of here."

I slam the glass down and nod.

Why not?

One of the prospects, Blade, drops us off at Rift. A few of them tried to argue with me and wanted to take their bikes, but I made a big scene over it. No drunk riding. When we walk in, the vibe in the club is different from last time. There are a lot of bikers around, and a lot more practically naked women. Tracker stands to my left, Rake to my right. I feel like I'm walking in with a group of bodyguards. I see Arrow standing at the bar, his back to me. He's talking with a man I've never seen before, also wearing a cut. The conversation doesn't look too friendly, and I don't want to interrupt.

"I'm going to the bathroom," I tell Rake, raising my voice over the music. After having broken the seal before we left, I know I am going to have to pee a hundred times tonight. I do my business in the bathroom, then wash my hands in the sink. A woman walks in, and I realize she looks familiar. Where have I seen her before? I try to rack my brain but come up with nothing.

"I know you," she says suddenly, smirking as she looks at her own reflection in the mirror. "You were waiting outside my house when Arrow came by."

So that's who she is. I remember now, Arrow said he had to make a stop while I waited by his bike outside.

I shrug. "That doesn't mean you know me."

Her lip twitches. "You're nothing like Mary. I guess he went for her opposite this time."

I pretend that doesn't hurt, unwilling to let this woman see any weakness in me.

I stare her right in the eye. "If you have something to say, then say it."

She smiles then. "Arrow won't ever love anyone the way he loved my sister."

She's Mary's sister? I didn't see that one coming.

I force a smirk. "Why are you here, then? Trying to pick up your sister's seconds?"

She raises her hand to hit me, but I catch her arm and twist it back.

"I'm not someone to fuck with," I grit out. "I've never said one bad word about your sister, and I never will. But if you want to be on my bad side, you're going to need a whole fuckin' army to take me down, because I'm not like any other woman you know."

"Let me go!" she gasps.

"Do you understand me?" I ask, steel in my tone.

She nods.

I let her go.

I check myself in the mirror, then glance at her one last time.

"Have a good night," I tell her in a saccharine sweet tone.

Then I walk out, leaving her wide-eyed and cradling her arm.

Bitch.

The worst part is that I think she may be right.

TWENTY

W HEN I walk back to Tracker and Rake, Arrow finally notices me. He instantly storms over and pulls me into his big arms. I'm about to scold the shit out of him when his mouth lands on mine, kissing me quickly before pulling back and whispering into my ear, "I've missed you so fuckin' much. I'm sorry I didn't call, I've been dealing with these fucks and didn't know when they would leave."

He cups my face and kisses me again, cutting off anything I was about to say. "Do you want a drink?"

I shake my head. "No, I had enough of those."

"Water?"

"Okay."

He holds my hand and walks me back to the bar.

"Water," he tells the bartender, then focuses his attention back to me. "You look fuckin' edible tonight, Anna."

"I try," I reply, grinning.

"You don't need to try, you have a natural beauty most women could only dream of."

"Well, aren't you the charmer," I reply, taking the bottle of water from his hand and opening the lid. I take a sip and let the cool, delicious water slide down my throat.

"So this is why you turned down our hospitality," the man Arrow was talking to before says as he stares me up and down. "Beautiful woman."

I don't miss the way Arrow creeps closer to me. "Yes, she is, isn't she?"

"*She* is right here," I mutter.

The man smirks. He looks to be in his fifties but carries himself well for his age. "A firecracker."

He can tell that from one sentence? The man must be a genius.

I see Mary's sister out of the corner of my eye, but she turns away the second I look back at her.

Good.

Arrow runs his hand down my body, resting it on my lower back, almost on my ass. "We done here?" he asks the man, his eyes on me.

"I'll meet up with Sin tomorrow to go over the details," the man replies.

Arrow nods once sharply, then leads me to the dance floor. One hand cupping my jaw, the other on my hip, he kisses me, then moves to the music.

"I was mad at you."

"I knew you would be." He smirks. "And I thought I handled you pretty well."

My mouth falls open. "You did not handle me."

"I did," he replies, a smug look on his face. "If that didn't work I was going to take you out for sushi."

Dammit! He knows my weakness.

"Now let's go home, I want to be buried inside you. Unless you want me to take you right here?"

I look around. "My brother is here, so no, thank you."

Not that that was the only reason. I'd never had public sex, but I don't think it was something I was going to be into.

He grunts. "Let's go, then. I'm tired of being around all these people."

We say our good-byes to everyone.

Rake kisses me on top of my head, letting me know that we're good, and I leave the club with a smile plastered on my face.

I'm about to slide onto Arrow's bike when Mary's sister runs out, looking panicked.

She starts to cry, her shoulders shaking uncontrollably.

An uneasy feeling spreads through my body.

"What's wrong, Janet?" Arrow asks, walking over to her. "Why are you crying?"

She lifts her finger and points at me. "How can you be with her?"

Arrow frowns and glances at me briefly. "That's none of your business."

"It is when she says shit about my sister! About how you never loved her and how she was a whore!"

My eyes flare, my fists clenching.

She can't be serious right now.

"You conniving bitch!" I sneer, losing my composure. "I never said anything like that!"

Janet cries more, laying it on really thick. She looks pathetic ,really.

The bitch should get an Oscar.

After I punch her in the face.

I step forward, but Arrow grips my upper arm, holding me back.

"She threatened me too, in the bathroom. She hurt me, Arrow. What would Mary say?" Janet adds.

Arrow peers down at me; I can see that he's thinking about Mary right now.

This woman is Mary's sister. Mary obviously cared about her, and that means Arrow must either care or feel responsible for her in some way.

Arrow looks down at Janet. "Come on, Janet, I'm calling you a cab."

"No!" she cries. "Not until you say you believe me."

I stare up at Arrow with an arched brow, daring him to say that he believes her.

He rubs the back of his neck.

"Did you say that shit?" he asks me quietly.

"No," I reply, staring him straight in the eye.

"Did you threaten her?" he asks then.

I bite my bottom lip. "I did. After she spoke shit to me and raised her hand to me."

He stares down at Janet, and even I can see the pity on his face.

"I'll take her home, Anna," he says. "You wait with Rake. I'll be back for you. I just don't want to have to be worrying about her ass all night."

Wow.

Even after how he looked at her, like he knew what her game was, he's still choosing her over me.

I pretend that I don't see her smug look, and walk back into the club without another glance.

"Anna!" he calls once, but I don't turn around.

I'm too pissed.

I hear him rev his engine as I walk back into the club, looking around for my brother.

I just want to go home.

I don't end up going straight home.

Instead, I have a few more drinks, then head to another biker bar.

"What's this bar called again?" I ask Tracker, who's texting someone.

"Your words are slurring, Anna Bell, that means no more tequila," he replies.

I stick out my lower lip. "What about vodka?"

He laughs. "Only water."

I lean my head on his shoulder. "You're a great man, Tracker; why don't you dump that whore once and for all so you can ask out Lana?"

"I thought you didn't want me with Lana?"

"I want you to do right by her, and that means no Allie baggage. And I'm sorry for being a bitch; Lana is just really important to me, you know?"

He messes my hair. "I know."

"Good."

"Allie is the daughter of a club member who passed away, that's why she lives in the clubhouse," he explains to me. "It's a little complicated."

"It always is," I say sagely.

"Arrow?"

"Last person I want to talk about right now."

"That's a shame, since he just messaged me asking where the fuck you are."

"Yeah, well," I sigh. "He chose that Janet bitch over me."

Tracker studies me. "Let him explain himself, Anna Bell. I know that man is crazy about you."

"You're, like, ten times better-looking when I'm drunk," I blurt out.

"Thanks, I think," Tracker replies, his eyes narrowing on me.

Rake hears my comment and starts to laugh, the woman that was perched on his lap falling on the floor.

"Ooops," he says, retrieving her with a lopsided grin.

"Why do I hang around with you guys?" I muse out loud as the woman runs her hand over his crotch.

"Because your man ditched you," Tracker unhelpfully supplies.

"Oh. Right."

He grins. "Come here, I'm just playing with you."

"Ew, save that for Lana please."

"*Ew?* What are you, fourteen?"

I sigh heavily. "Sex with you isn't appealing. You're like family and you belong to Lana."

"And I've already told you, you look too much like Rake for my dick to even pay attention to you."

I smile. "Good to know. That's why we're friends. Like, best friends. And ha! You didn't deny belonging to Lana."

He laughs and shakes his head, looking amused.

"Thanks for the pierced cock picture by the way, it looks like it would have hurt," I tell him. "Oh, and you also have a pretty huge cock."

And that's when Arrow walks up to us.

"The fuck?" he growls, his eyes darting between Tracker and me. If only he were here one minute earlier, he wouldn't be looking at us like he is.

"What are you doing here?" I ask, sitting up straighter.

"Claiming what's mine," he snaps. "Come on, now."

I lift my chin stubbornly. "I'm not going anywhere with you. I'll get a ride home with the guys."

"Anna, don't fucking test me," he says through clenched teeth.

I scoff. "You were already tested tonight, Arrow, and you failed. So leave me the hell alone, because you're the last person I want to see right now."

He lifts me in the air, carrying me out over his shoulder.

I have déjà vu.

Is it always going to be like this with us?

"Arrow, trust me, you don't want—"

"Don't tell me what I want, Anna," he says, rudely cutting me off. We exit the bar, and I ignore the catcalls and whistles from the peanut gallery.

Arrow puts me down, then pulls out his phone and barks into it. "Blade, I need a lift."

He hangs up and looks down at me, an unhappy expression pasted on his too-damn-handsome face.

"Where's your bike?" I ask, looking around.

"You're too drunk to get on the bike," he says, looking away. "Blade's going to give us a lift and bring back my bike later."

"Can you just take me home?" I ask in a small voice, looking down at the ground. "I just want to sleep."

"You can sleep as soon as we get back to the clubhouse."

"Alone."

"Not happening, Anna. I don't care how mad you get at me, you're sleeping right next to me, where you fuckin' belong," he says. "Don't push me."

"*Don't push me*," I mock him, digging through my handbag looking for my phone.

He sighs.

I look up when I hear someone approach us. A woman stands next to Arrow, but not too close, and licks her lips. "Hi, I was wondering if you guys were having a party tonight at the clubhouse. My friends and I would like to come."

She sticks her chest out and I watch Arrow—but he doesn't move his gaze from her face.

"Why don't you go in the bar and see if any of my brothers are interested," Arrow tells her, sounding bored.

"Oh," she says, face falling. "I was kind of hoping—"

"Do you not see me standing right here?" I ask loudly.

She turns to me, as if only just noticing I was there. "Oh, I just assumed—"

I step closer to her. "Right, well, next time don't assume. I'm not in a good mood, and it would be a shame if I had to take that out on you, wouldn't it?"

"Anna," Arrow snaps, stepping closer to me and grabbing my arm. "Cut it out."

Blade pulls up at that moment, and Arrow all but throws me into the backseat. He gets in next to me and closes the door.

"Hi, Blade!" I greet him too loudly.

"Hey," he says to me, twisting his body around, then looks to Arrow. "Clubhouse?"

"Yep," Arrow replies. "Thanks, man."

"No problem. Good night?" he asks Arrow.

Arrow glances at me, then replies, "Could have been better."

"Mine could have been better too," I add sulkily. "Much better."

Blade chuckles until Arrow tells him to shut up.

The two of them talk as I close my eyes, the motion of the car making me feel slightly nauseous.

"You okay, Anna?" Arrow asks. The car comes to a stop and he carries me into the clubhouse. The place is still loud, with music and laughter being heard as soon as we exit the car.

Gently he lays me down on my bed. "Stay here. I'll get you some water," he says, then disappears. I use that time to clean up and use the bathroom, then strip down to nothing.

I walk out of the bathroom and scream.

Tracker stands there, grinning and staring at my naked breasts. Realizing he isn't going to leave or close his eyes, I grab the sheet and cover my body.

"Okay," he says slowly. "You don't look anything like Rake."

I purse my lips. "You pervert! You could have turned around."

He holds his hands up. "I was just coming in to check on you. Now I'm leaving before Arrow—"

"What the fuck?" comes the growl from behind us.

Great.

"Just leaving," Tracker says, leaving in haste.

"How come every time I turn around that bastard is with you?" Arrow asks, his jaw tense.

"He's my friend. Who puts my feelings first," I can't help but add.

"Fuck, you're stubborn," he adds, handing me a cold bottle of water.

"And you're an asshole."

"Never claimed I wasn't."

"I'm going to bed," I say after I take a sip of water. I get comfortable, then turn to the side and close my eyes.

Arrow slides in and curses. "You're fuckin' naked under here and Tracker was in here? I'm going to kill that fucker."

I inwardly roll my eyes.

I'm about to fall asleep—in that dreamy state just before you lose consciousness—when I hear him say in a soft voice, "I know you didn't say or do what she said. You're not a liar, Anna. But she's all I have left of Mary. I feel responsible for her."

His voice wavers a little when he says her name.

TWENTY-ONE

WHO was that man you were talking to at the bar?" I ask Arrow the next morning. I am still angry with him, but I am also curious. My curiosity wins out.

"You didn't recognize him?" Arrow asks me. "He's famous."

"Nope. Who is he?"

"He's a local legend. Rock star. Before your time, I suppose."

"So you were with him the entire night and couldn't even send me a message?"

He cuts his eyes to me at my tone. "We had some issues; I was busy. Now cut it out."

"Cut what out?" I ask in a sugary-sweet tone.

"Being a bitch."

Well, then.

I narrow my gaze on him. "Trust me, you haven't seen me be a bitch yet."

He rolls his eyes heavenward.

"God isn't going to help you," I mumble under my breath.

"Yes," he replies, suddenly sounding amused. "I'm starting to see that."

I pick up my piece of toast and devour it.

"Will you take me home, please?" I ask him once I'm done. Rake walks in, looking like he'd had a wild night.

"Is that a hickey on your neck?" I ask him. "Who were you with? A sixteen-year-old who wanted to show off that she's sexually active?"

He isn't amused. "Anna, not so fuckin' loud."

I smirk. "You want me to make you some breakfast?"

He sets his puppy-dog eyes on me. "Would you?"

I stand. "Yes I would. Go take a shower. You stink."

He leaves the room.

"Yeah, for him you're sweet," Arrow grumbles.

"Yes, well, Rake didn't ditch me last night," I snap. I remember the words he said to me last night about Janet being all that he has left of Mary, but I still feel like he shouldn't have treated me the way he did. I also feel like Janet knows how guilty Arrow feels and is using it to her advantage.

"Anna, I told you—"

"What did you drop off with Janet that day we stopped at her house?" I ask him, wanting to see if my theory is correct. Janet is using Arrow, and I'm sure he's been supporting her too.

"Why?" he asks, like it's of no consequence.

"Answer the question, Arrow."

He shrugs, playing it off. "She was behind on her rent."

Aha! I knew it.

I turn my back on him to hide my expression and start to fry some eggs for Rake. Arrow comes up behind me and presses his front to my back. "You need to curb your jealousy, Anna."

I scoff. "Like you can talk."

"I'm a man."

He *is* a man.

A man with a currently hard cock pressing into my ass.

But that is no excuse.

"Are you saying that just to piss me off?" I ask, purposely rubbing my ass against him.

"Darlin', don't fight with me for the sake of fighting, because you're going to lose," he whispers in my ear.

Two women walk by and Arrow calls them over. "Can you finish this breakfast off for Rake? Anna is about to become very busy."

They nod.

Arrow leads me to his room, leaving the women to the task of feeding my brother. He slams the door behind him and sits on the bed, lifting me on his lap so I'm straddling him.

"Stop being angry about last night. I wasn't choosing her over you, okay? She was Mary's sister so I keep an eye on her, because I know Mary would want that. You're strong, baby, she's not."

"I don't deserve to be anything but first place, Arrow," I tell him. "Janet lied. I would never say anything bad about Mary. I've only ever heard good things about her, especially from Faye. Janet is a manipulative bitch, and I'm not going to put up with her shit just because you have a soft spot for her."

He licks his bottom lip. "You are my priority, Anna, and I'm sorry I've made you think otherwise. I'm telling you now, you're who I want; I'm not fuckin' touching anyone else, and I don't want to. Janet doesn't mean shit compared to you. If I'm honest, it was my guilt taking care of her, since it was my fault Mary died."

"It wasn't your fault," I tell him. "She knew what she was doing, getting involved in an MC."

He makes a deep sound in his throat but doesn't reply. I know he doesn't believe what I'm trying to say; I guess it's something he's going to have to figure out for himself.

"I'm serious," I tell him.

"Don't know what I did to deserve you, Anna," he says softly, our eyes connected.

"Then don't fuck it up, Arrow," I whisper back. "Treat me how I deserve to be treated."

"Quinn was right," he muses. "You are a firecracker."

Quinn? The older man at the bar last night?

"Well," I say. "Are you going to kiss me or not?"

He slides his hand up my thigh. "Where do you want to be kissed, Anna? Your mouth, or your pussy?"

My cheeks flush.

I clear my throat. "Maybe we can do both."

He grins, then slams his mouth down on mine.

A few days later, I'm having the day from hell.

After missing the bus from campus I call a cab. The one day I need an escort, and no one shows up.

Typical.

After paying the cabdriver, who smiles at me with no teeth, I can't get into my apartment because I can't find my keys. I knock on the maintenance man's door, but he isn't home. I sit on the front step, and then it starts raining. I try to call Arrow again, and luckily this time he answers.

"Anna?" he says as he picks up.

"I'm locked out of my apartment," I tell him.

"I'll be right there," he says, then hangs up.

Five minutes later he shows up, dangling my spare set of keys in his hand.

"Hi," I say, wrapping my arm around his torso. "Looks like Rake having a set came in handy."

He kisses the top of my head. "I know. Come on, let's get you inside."

When we're in, Arrow starts packing some of my things.

"What are you doing?" I ask, as he grabs my suitcase from the spare room.

"You're moving in. Rake and I decided," he says. "You're at our place most of the time anyway, Anna. And if you don't want to stay at the clubhouse, then I'll move in here with you. Your choice."

I look around my crummy apartment. "I don't know, Arrow."

"You want me to buy us a place?" he asks casually. "And you need a car too. Rake said he offered to buy you a car and you said no. What's up with that?"

"I'm saving for my own car, I don't want anyone else to buy it for me," I say.

He scrubs a hand down his face. "Of course you are. You need to choose your battles, Anna."

I arch a brow. "Looks like you need to take your own advice right now."

He stops packing and closes the space between us, a smile playing on his lips. "You're something else, you know that?"

He lowers his head and kisses me gently, taking it slowly like he has all the time in the world. "I want you to live with me, this is what I'm asking you."

"That's what you should have started with," I tell him, smiling. I wrap my arms around his neck, using his body to lift me up, and wrap my legs around him. "Why don't we stay in the clubhouse for now, and see where we go from there?"

He looks relieved. "Okay. Fuck, I'm glad you agreed. Rake told me to call him if we had to kidnap you."

I place a kiss on his neck. "I can be agreeable sometimes."

"Good to know," he says, his breath hitching as I trail open-mouthed kisses down his neck.

"You know, we've never fucked on a kitchen table before," I say, glancing behind me at the table.

Arrow palms my ass, gripping each globe. "No, no, we haven't. You're insatiable, Anna."

"Are you complaining?" I ask, running my fingers through his hair and gripping it.

"Fuck no," he replies, walking back with me and leaning me on the table. "You're more than I imagined, Anna."

I smile as he kisses me, a warm feeling in my chest at his words. Could Arrow love again? Could he love me?

Later that night at the clubhouse, I find Arrow's side of the bed empty. I wander into the kitchen to get a drink and hear the men in the game room. As I'm about to enter the room, I hear something I'm obviously not meant to hear.

"It's safer for her here. Thanks for getting her here, bro," Rake says.

Did Arrow want me to move in? Or was he just doing my brother's bidding?

"I think you should tell her who ransacked her house," I hear

Arrow say. "Knowledge is power, Rake—it's wrong to keep her in the dark."

They know who did it?

"I'm her brother."

"And I'm her man," Arrow inserts. "I'm all for keeping her safe, but she needs to know, so you have a couple of days to tell her or I will."

"Fuck you, Arrow, she's my fuckin' baby sister and you know her history. Now I'm able to protect her from a lot of things. She's smart, educated, and beautiful. She has a good life going for her, even though you're in it—which wasn't part of the plan by the way."

Arrow grunts. "She's safer with me, and you know it. No one with half a brain fucks with me, Rake. You need to tell Anna the truth."

Rake's cold voice stops me. "Trust me, Arrow; you of all people don't want me telling Anna the truth."

"Why?" Arrow asks, voice booming.

I open the door and step in. "Tell me what, Rake?"

Two pairs of guilty eyes look my way.

TWENTY-TWO

AKE shoots Arrow an accusing look, then looks at me again, his green eyes softening.

He sighs. "Come and sit down, Anna."

I take a seat next to him, feeling nervous. "We know who messed up your apartment. It was one of the Wild Men MC members."

"Why?" I ask, feeling confused. "How do you know?"

Would Talon let them do that to me?

Rake sighs. "Someone saw him leave your apartment. We tracked him down. It was one of the men we caught messing with our shipment, one that we traded to Talon for you."

"I don't understand," I say, my voice shaking.

Rake sighs. "He obviously wanted revenge, and he was going to take it out on you. You need to be careful, Anna. We only found out everything yesterday, and that's why you needed to be here with us where we can keep you safe."

I look at Arrow. "So you didn't actually want to live with me, you were just doing what you had to. I get it."

"No, Anna, you don't. I did want you here," Arrow quickly says.

"Right."

"Anna," both of them say at the same time.

"Talon never hurt me; how come this man wants to?" I ask them.

"Talon isn't innocent, Anna; why do you keep acting as if he is?" Rake snaps, scowling.

"Hey, you weren't held captive by him, okay? I was. Trust me, he didn't hurt me, and I don't think he would."

"So he has a soft spot for you," Rake replies flippantly. "That doesn't mean it's going to be enough to save you if his men want you. He's not the president, Anna; he's the VP. He doesn't call all the shots."

"So, what? This man came to hurt me? But I wasn't there, so he got angry and destroyed the place?"

Arrow answers this time. "That's what it looks like. We don't know for sure."

"I thought you caught up with him?" I ask, frowning. "What did he say?"

Arrow flinches and Rake cringes.

"What did you do?" I yell, standing up.

"Nothing for you to worry about," Arrow replies curtly. "Come on, let's go back to bed."

I open my mouth, then close it with a snap. "You two are unbelievable, you know that?"

Did they kill that man? I don't want one of them going to prison. I don't think I could handle that.

Arrow takes my hand, but I pull it away and storm back to his room.

When we get into bed, he pulls me into his arms. My body is stiff for a moment before I relax.

"Sleep," he whispers.

Even angry, I dream of him.

"Two vodka and cranberries please," the young woman says. I smile at her and make the drinks while Summer takes her money and gives her change.

"When does Reid get here?" I ask Summer. It's been unexpectedly busy, and we're holding down the fort, waiting for Reid and Tag to arrive.

"He's on his way," she replies, then goes to serve the next customer.

I woke up this morning angry with both Arrow and Rake, for different reasons. Arrow because I don't know if he truly wanted me living with him, and Rake because he was hiding shit from me. I'd crept out of bed early this morning and gone to Lana's, then came straight to work. An hour early, might I add—that's how desperate I was to keep busy and not have to deal with my own thoughts. I know Arrow will come to pick me up tonight, demanding that I be reasonable. I know they're both trying to protect me, but if something involves me I have the right to know. They can keep their club secrets, but when some man is out to hurt me . . . Well, forewarned is forearmed.

Reid arrives and tells me to take a break. I check my phone and see a text from Arrow.

> Want to go out for sushi after your shift?

I try and fight my smile but it wins.

I'm not that easy, I type back.

My phone beeps a few seconds later.

How about sushi followed by a bath, a massage, and multiple orgasms?

I shake my head, amused.
Putting my phone away, I head back to work.

"You can't still be angry, I took you out for sushi!" he calls behind me as I walk into the bathroom. He holds me by my hips and stares at me in the mirror, our eyes connected. He looks down, then starts to slowly slide my pants and panties off, leaving me naked from the waist down.

"Anna," he rumbles.

"Hmmmm?"

"I want you, darlin'. I want you badly," he says with a throaty groan. He undoes his jeans, letting them pool at his ankles.

"Then take me," I softly demand, tilting my neck to the side as he starts to kiss me there. He sucks on my neck until I'm squirming, then reaches his hands around to cup my breasts. He plumps them, sliding his thumbs over my beaded nipples, grinding his cock against me. Multitasking—I like it.

"Arrow," I whimper.

He slides his hand down, gently stroking me with his thick finger, sliding it inside me, then playing with my clit.

"I wanted you to move in with me, Anna," he rasps into my ear. "I wanted you with me, so don't try and hold that against me."

He grips my hips, bends me over the sink, and slides into me with one smooth thrust. I curse as he slaps my ass, then moan as he moves in and out, hitting all the right spots.

"You're mine, Anna," he says, sliding out of me. "I don't care how fuckin' angry you get at me, how mouthy you get. I love your sass, your attitude. It gets me hard every fuckin' time."

He thrusts again, harder this time. "This pussy is mine, and no one else will ever get a taste of it now."

He grabs my hair and pulls my head back, then bends over and captures my mouth in a fierce, possessive kiss. I love it when he gets rough with me, when he lets his passion for me take over. I kiss him greedily, taking everything he offers and demanding more. He bites on my bottom lip before letting my hair go.

We come together, both of us loudly.

Arrow eases out of me gently, and places sweet kisses on my lower back, on both of my dimples.

"Let me fill a bath for you. You can read in there and drink wine," he says, giving me a gentle look. My heart warms. I was telling him the other day that that was one of my favorite things to do. My legs wobble a little, so he carries me in his arms, letting me sit on his lap and hold on to him while he fills up the tub, then he places me down in the warm water.

"Thanks, Arrow," I tell him. "Are you going to join me?"

He smirks. "We both know there's no way I can fit in that tub."

I look over at him. He is a big man, tall, broad, and packed with muscle.

"I could sit on your lap," I tell him.

He grins then. "Okay, darlin', if that's what you want."

"I do," I reply.

"Let me get us some drinks," he says, kissing me on top of my head, then leaving the room.

I relax into the tub, closing my eyes and enjoying myself. Arrow returns with a glass of red wine for me and an ice-cold beer for himself. He undresses and I scoot forward so he can slide in behind me. I sit between his legs, his knees sticking out of the water, my head leaning back on his warm chest.

"Did you hurt that man?" I ask, my eyes still closed.

He stiffens, but replies. "Yes."

His hands cup my breasts, not asking for anything, just enjoying touching me.

"Does that upset you?" he asks when I stay silent.

"I just don't want you to go back to jail," I admit.

"I'm not going anywhere," he says. "Why would I when I have everything I want right in my arms?"

He squeezes my breasts to emphasize the *everything*.

I smile at that.

Arrow picks up the wineglass and brings it to my lips. The rich merlot slides down my parched throat, the taste flooding my tongue.

"Where did you get wine from?" I ask him.

"I sent Blade to the store to buy it today."

I smirk. "You couldn't go yourself?"

"I would have," he says. "But Sin needed me to do something for him."

I don't bother to ask him what that was.

"Arrow?"

"Yes, Anna."

"I believe you promised me multiple orgasms," I say with a grin.

His body shakes as he laughs. "I believe I did, and don't you worry, I always make good on my promises."

"I was counting on that," I say.

"I've been dying for a taste of your pussy all day, Anna. Trust me, as soon as we get out of here I'm going to lie you back on the bed with your legs in the air and feast."

My cheeks redden. "Fuck, you have a dirty mouth."

He kisses my shoulder. "You love it."

I love you, I think.

"Maybe we should get out now," I say, imagining what Arrow spoke of in my head.

He chuckles deeply and bites gently on my neck. "I think you're right. I'm suddenly famished."

I gulp.

He makes good on his word.

Three times.

TWENTY-THREE

THE next morning, I walked in on something I never wanted to see.

Like an idiot, I'd come into Tracker's room with a smile on my face and a plate full of food. What I'd come across was a very naked Tracker and Allie dressed in a nurse's costume, on her knees with his cock in her mouth.

In my shock, I placed the food down on the side table and ran.

Now I am hiding in my room, feeling both disappointed in Tracker and sorry for myself for having seen something I can't forget.

"Why are you hiding in here?" Arrow asks when he gets back from wherever the hell he goes for the club.

"I saw Allie choking on something."

"What?" he asks. "Is she okay?"

"It was Tracker's cock, so yes, I assume she's okay, but I'm not. I'm scarred for life and I'll never look at her or a nurse's outfit the same."

Arrow stares at me a moment, then bursts out laughing.

"How is this funny?" I ask, tapping my toes on the floor in impatience. "And Tracker said he didn't want Allie anymore, he really wants Lana."

Arrow sobers. "Stay out of it, Anna."

I say nothing.

Arrow takes that as me planning to start something—he already knows me too well. "I'm serious. It's not anyone's business except Tracker's. He doesn't need to feel judged here. He's free to do as he pleases."

"I'm not going to say anything," I say, knowing the disapproval on my face speaks for itself.

"That's right, you aren't," he says pointedly. "I thought we could go for a ride, get some lunch."

I stand up. "I'd like that. Can we go out the back way?"

He laughs harder. "Babe, stop acting like a prude. Going by the things we did last night, I know you aren't one."

My lips tighten. "It's not about that. I'm embarrassed that I walked in on them! Now I have to look them in the eye. Well, Tracker at least; fuck Allie."

He smirks. "You'll live. Not that I like you seeing any other man naked, but come on, you should see your face."

I square my shoulders. "Ha-ha, very funny. Now let's get out of here."

He reaches out and takes my hand, then brings it to his lips, kissing my knuckles.

My heart flutters.

"I'm not fuckin' eating sushi today though," he says, grinning at me. "I want a steak."

"Fine, I suppose I could go for a steak."

We walk out hand in hand to his bike. I'm putting my helmet on when Vinnie runs over to Arrow and tells him something in a low tone so I can't hear.

"Fuck!" Arrow yells, then looks to me. "Anna, I'm going to have to take a rain check, darlin'."

"Is everything okay?" I ask, stepping closer to him.

"Everything will be fine. I'll see you tonight. Only leave the clubhouse with an escort—I'm not asking, Anna, I'm telling."

He kisses me quickly, then gets on his bike and rides away.

I'm still standing there when Tracker walks up to me. "Get a nice show?"

I cringe, closing my eyes for a second. "I'm so sorry, Tracker. Impressive body though."

And it really is. The man looks like Adonis, all smooth skin and sculpted muscles.

Shame he is Tracker.

I see him smile. "Why you standing out here looking like someone kicked your puppy?"

"Arrow had to go somewhere, it seemed urgent. I hope everything is okay."

It's hard to just ignore the fact that things happen, but I'm not able to know what they are, or help out in any way. I just need to wait and hope that nothing goes wrong, that Arrow comes home every night.

Tracker quickly slides his phone out from his jean pocket and presses some buttons. "Fuck, yeah. I have to go too. Sin needs me. Go inside, Anna."

And just like that, I'm dismissed a second time within ten minutes.

I head back inside to look for a new lunch date, but no one's around except the prospects. Faye has her own house and is only around sometimes. The rest of the permanent couples all have their own places as well. The only people who live here full-time are Arrow, Vinnie, Rake, Tracker, Allie, and the three prospects who come and go, although it isn't uncommon for members of other chapters to drop by, or for Rake to bring home a harem of women who don't want to leave. I'm about to give in and just make myself a sandwich when Lana calls me.

"Hey," I say, leaning the phone between my shoulder and ear.

"Hey, you busy? I thought we could go out and have some lunch."

I smile. "I'll come pick you up in ten."

"Pick me up in what?" she asks, sounding confused.

"One of the guys will bring me in the four-wheel drive."

"Oh, okay. See you soon then."

We both hang up, and I go in search of a prospect.

"Do you think women prefer alpha males? Or cute, geeky men?" Lana asks me after a bite of pizza.

"Why have you been asking these weirder-than-usual questions?" I ask.

She shrugs, looking down at her plate. "Just curious."

"Alpha males, definitely."

She rolls her eyes. "We know that's you."

I cough. "Ahem. Tracker."

She flashes me a sheepish smile. "He's charming. Sue me."

"What happened to Dash?" I ask. I'd hoped they would hit it off.

"We've spoken a few times but haven't met up. He's great, but he's not Tracker."

That's probably a good thing.

"I don't know what to tell you, Lana. Tracker is my friend, but Allie is still there at the clubhouse with him. I guess you need to decide for yourself and know that I'll always have your back, no matter what you choose. Or who."

"Do you think he's still sleeping with Allie?" she asks, frowning.

Fuck my life.

She gasps. "You cringed, I saw it! That means he is."

"Lana—"

She holds her little hand up. "Say no more, Anna, say no more."

Thank goodness for that.

I open my mouth to speak when someone takes the seat next to me.

"Hey," Talon says, swiping my plate and taking a bite of my food.

I stare at him with my mouth hanging open.

"Ummm, Anna?"

I look at Lana and clear my throat. "Lana, this is Talon, my kidnapper. Talon, this is Lana, my best friend. Keep staring at her like that and I'll stick my fork in your eye."

Talon smiles. "Nice to meet you, Lana."

Lana doesn't look so thrilled. "You're the one who kidnapped her?"

"Well, Ranger actually did the kidnapping, if you want to get technical. I was just—"

"My babysitter," I interject.

He nods. "Right. We had some good times, didn't we, Anna?"

I don't bother to comment. "May I ask what you're doing here?"

He shrugs and leans back, his arm casually hanging on the back of the chair. "Was walking by and saw you, wanted to say hello."

Blade walks in then and sees Talon. His face turns to stone. Before I can even blink, he has his phone to his ear. Probably calling Arrow.

"Arrow is going to be pissed, Talon: you need to get out of here."

He gives me a weird look. "Do you love him, Anna?"

I swallow. "Why would you ask me that?"

"It's important."

"It's also none of your business," I snap, wondering what the hell his game is.

He's quiet for a few seconds before he speaks. "I need to talk to Arrow."

"So you're using me again to get the club's attention? This whole me-being-used-as-a-pawn thing is really getting old."

He sighs and crooks his head from side to side. "You're a lot more than that, Anna, trust me."

"More nonanswers. Just what I fuckin' need."

He arches an eyebrow. "Quite a mouth on you."

Blade sits down opposite Talon and glances around. "What do you want? Leave the women out of it."

"I'm not going to hurt the women," he says, glancing sideways at me. "I want a word with Arrow."

"Why?" Blade asks.

"That's between me and Arrow," Talon fires back.

"He'll be here," Blade says, his eyes on me. "And he won't be happy you involved Anna."

"I'm not a threat to Anna."

Lana gives me a wide-eyed look. "Yeah, I don't think I'm going to date a biker after all."

"Smart move," I mutter.

Talon flashes a charming smile at her. "Oh, come on now, we're not all that bad."

Lana purses her lips. "Right."

Talon sighs. "I miss the old days where women were afraid of me."

I grin at that. "I'm sure they still will be, just find ones who aren't badass like Lana and me."

He messes my hair. "You are kind of badass, aren't you?"

"Get your fuckin' hands off her," Blade grits out, his face going red.

Oh, dear.

I can see this escalating fast.

Blade's phone rings, and he looks to Talon. "He's out front."

Talon looks down at me, a sad expression flashing on his face. "Take care, Anna."

My brows furrow. What am I missing here? Something is going on, but I haven't the slightest idea what it could be.

"Both of you stay here," Blade says, following Talon outside.

"Holy shit," Lana mumbles.

I slide my plate back from Talon's side and take a bite of my salad.

"How can you eat at a time like this?" Lana whisper-yells.

I put my fork down. "What do you want to do?"

She stands up, grabbing her handbag. "Let's go and see what's going on."

I follow her to the front window, where she sticks her face against the glass.

People in the café start to stare.

"Seriously, Lana?"

She turns her head around. "What? All I can see is Talon and Arrow standing next to their bikes, talking."

I grab her hand and we walk outside.

I see Arrow shaking his head, and Talon reaching into his pocket and pulling out some papers. Arrow glances at them, then slams them against Talon's chest. Arrow looks down at the ground, while Talon's lips keep moving, obviously telling him something.

What the hell is going on?

I look at Lana, who looks even more confused than I, then back at Arrow in time to see him punch Talon square in the face. I try to run to him, but Blade appears and holds me back. Talon doesn't hit Arrow back, but for some reason he looks . . . almost pleased?

Arrow notices us standing there, and storms over, not even looking at me.

"Get them home," he demands to Blade. "*Now.*"

Then he walks back to his bike, gets on it, and rides away.

Talon watches him leave, then does the same.

"Come on," Blade says, herding us into the car.

We drop Lana off first, then drive back to the clubhouse.

I sit on our bed, and wait for Arrow to come home and explain.

TWENTY-FOUR

T'S midnight when the sound of the door opening wakes me. I turn on a light, watching as Arrow steps into the room, sitting down on the bed to take off his shoes.

"Hey, where were you?" I ask him.

Silence.

"Arrow?"

"Not tonight, Anna," he finally says, stripping down and sliding into the sheets. He reaches for me, and I go to him. He wraps me in his arms, but something doesn't feel right.

Something has changed.

He turns my head to him roughly and kisses me almost desperately.

"I need you, Anna," he says huskily, his hands wandering down my back. "Give yourself to me."

I kiss him back, wrapping my legs around his trim waist and running my hands through his hair.

"You have me," I tell him, moving back to pull off my T-shirt. He quickly takes advantage, leaning forward and licking my breasts one at a time. He bites down gently, while his hands try to remove my sleep shorts.

"Off," he growls. "Take them off."

I quickly remove my shorts and sit there before him.

"Beautiful," he whispers. "And all mine."

Our lips are once again joined as he lifts me to straddle his waist. When he pulls me up farther so I'm sitting on his face, I feel a little self-conscious. When he starts to lick me, making moaning noises of enjoyment, I relax, turned on to the point of no inhibitions. I look down at his face, unable to look away as he tastes me, his heavy-lidded eyes watching me back, making me even hotter. I can only imagine how I look, hands gripping the headboard, straddling his face—spread out for him so he can please me as he wishes. His hands roam, squeezing my behind and pulling me down onto him. My own fingers reach for my breasts, pinching my nipples as I feel myself about to explode.

"I'm going to come, Arrow," I moan, my head thrown back in pleasure. "Fuck!"

My thighs tremble as my orgasm hits me. I squeeze my eyes shut, lost in the pleasure.

Arrow sucks on my clit, prolonging my release. My fingers dig into my thighs until the final wave hits me.

I pant a little, look down at Arrow, and slide off him. "Shit."

He sits up and wipes his mouth. I take him in from head to toe, seeing his rock-hard cock and knowing that it needed attention. I slide down his body so I'm in between his legs and take him into my mouth with no preamble. His hands tangle in my hair, gently urging me on as he sits forward and watches me.

I stare up at him, taking him in as much I can, and then sliding back down.

He curses and slides out of my mouth.

"Stay like that," he demands, coming around me from behind. Holding my hips, he enters me quickly, fucking me like he owns me. His pace quickens, and I know he's almost ready to come. He pulls out and turns me over, sliding back in. "Want to see your face when I come."

He thrusts a few more times, his face contorting in pleasure as his orgasm hits him.

His eyes never leave mine.

I hold on to him, my fingers on his back, digging into his dragon tattoo.

"Anna," he whispers, bracing himself over me. I pull him down, so his weight is on me, but I don't mind. I like the feel of it.

"Hi," I say, smiling up at him.

His lip twitches. "Hi, darlin'."

"I missed you today," I say, but instantly regret it when his entire body stiffens, and his expression is suddenly devoid of any emotion.

"What's wrong?" I ask him softly.

He shakes his head and slides out of me, lying on his back. "Nothing, nothing's wrong."

I lay my head on his chest and wrap my arm around his waist.

"I love you, Arrow," I tell him.

"Anna—" he whispers, his voice sounding strangled.

"You don't have to say anything. I just wanted to let you know. From the first time I saw you, I knew I wanted you. I can't even explain it," I ramble, then kiss him on his chest.

He rubs his hand down my back in comforting circles but doesn't say anything back.

I didn't expect him to.

I close my eyes and let sleep take over.

Over the next two weeks, Arrow pulls away from me. It might not be noticeable to others—he was still caring and protective—but I could tell the difference.

Something had happened to make him put distance between us. And I'm thinking it had to do with me dropping the L-bomb on him. Why did I have to tell him that I loved him? Yes, it's the truth, but if I'd known he was going to act like this, I would have kept that bit of information to my damn self.

He comes to bed later and wakes up earlier. It's almost like he doesn't want to be around me as much. His playfulness is gone, and he's almost back to how he was when I first met him.

I don't like it one bit.

I don't like that I sit and wait for him to come home at night.

I don't like that he isn't being himself anymore.

Why does he think he has to guard himself from me?

One thing that hasn't changed is the sex. He still wants me, and that's a good thing, I think.

Okay, I don't know what to think anymore.

Yesterday, he came home with a present for me.

A car.

He bought me a fucking car.

A brand-new, expensive-looking car.

I don't want a car.

I want Arrow back.

I wake up in bed alone, which I'm still not used to. I don't want to get used to it. When I walk into the kitchen, I see him sitting there, nursing a beer. I look at the clock. It's 9:00 a.m.

"Mornin'," I say as I open the fridge and grab the milk.

"Mornin', Anna," he says quietly. "Do you want to take the car out for a drive today?"

With him? Sure.

"Sounds good," I tell him, smiling. "Maybe we could get some lunch or something."

He drinks his beer, eyeing me over the bottle. "Actually, I was going to ask Vinnie to take you. I got some stuff I need to do at Rift today."

"Oh, right," I say, looking down so he doesn't see my disappointment. "Don't bother Vinnie, I'll ask Tracker to take me."

His jaw tightens. "What's wrong with Vinnie?"

"Nothing. I'm just more comfortable with Tracker, or Rake if it's such a big issue."

He makes a scoffing noise.

"What's going on with you, Arrow?" I ask him straight out. "Is it because I told you I loved you? I didn't know that would freak you out so much."

He slams his bottle down, making me jump. "It's not because of that, Anna."

He doesn't say anything else.

Okaaayyyy then.

"Right," I say, grabbing a cereal box and pouring some into a bowl, then smothering it with milk.

Arrow stands, the stool scraping the floor as he slides it back. "I'll be home late tonight."

Of course you will.

He walks over to me and cups my face, his hands cold from the beer bottle. Lifting my chin, he kisses my lips. "I hope you like the car."

"I do, thank you. You shouldn't have though," I tell him, not wanting to sound ungrateful but wanting him to know that I don't expect anything like that from him or anyone else.

"Anything for my woman," he says, kissing me one last time before disappearing.

Anything but the one thing I want.

Him.

The weekend rolls in and the club is having a party. Faye is running around organizing things, and I'm doing a grocery run with Tracker.

We walk down the aisle, me pushing the cart and him acting like a kid in a candy store.

"We need these," he says, grabbing cartons of soft drinks. "And these."

He "needs" everything.

When we walk down the next aisle, I grab a jumbo box of condoms. "What you need is these."

I throw it into the cart.

He grins. "I'll need more than that. Good idea, maybe I'll get one of the women to walk around handing them out." He pauses. "Naked."

"You're a pig," I reply without any heat.

"Is Lana coming?" he asks, sounding a little unsure.

"No," I reply. "I'm not going to subject her to this. She doesn't trust men much as it is."

"She's a grown woman; stop babying her, Anna Bell."

"I don't baby her. She's a gentle woman. She doesn't need to know that you, who she likes, participates in orgies."

"She likes me?" he asks with a grin. Of course that's the only thing he heard.

I shrug, playing it off. "I told her you had a nice pierced cock and that's all it took."

He tugs on my ponytail. "Lana isn't like that."

"No, no, she isn't," I admit.

"We need those," he says, pointing to some other crap that we definitely do not need.

"Tracker, I don't think—"

He gives me his puppy-dog eyes.

"Fine."

He cheers.

Eh, what did I care? I wasn't paying for all this shit.

TWENTY-FIVE

THIS party wasn't like any I'd ever been to before. The place is filled with rough-looking men—some good-looking, some not—and lots of women.

None of them were shy.

I glance down at my tight black high-waisted jeans and black crop top. The expanse of my stomach is showing but I am still probably the most covered-up woman in the room. My hair is down and big, I'd teased it for extra volume, and I'd given my eyes a smoky look. Still, I am dressed for clubbing and the other women are dressed for . . .

Well, sex.

When I saw Allie in what appeared to be her lingerie, I never imagined everyone else would be dressed like that too.

I cup my drink, lifting it to my mouth and forcing myself to take a sip.

"You okay?" Arrow asks, drawing me down to sit on his lap.

"Yeah, just taking everything in," I tell him.

He kisses my nape. "You look beautiful, Anna, but if these

men don't stop staring at you like that, I think we're gonna have a problem."

I turn and smile at him. "You're the one who has me. Let them look."

"Do I?" he suddenly asks.

"Do you what?"

"Have you."

I frown. "You know you do, Arrow, what's this about?"

He licks his bottom lip. "Nothing. I need a drink. You want a refill?"

He's already drunk, and I don't think he needs another, but I don't say anything. I haven't seen him drink this much since we first met. I didn't miss the worried look Rake sent me when he saw Arrow earlier either. Everyone knows something's up with him, but we don't know what. He won't talk, and no one wants to push him, but something has to give.

He stands up with his hands on my waist. "Don't move from here, okay? I'll be right back."

I nod and take his seat as he goes to the kitchen.

"Hey," Faye says, dropping into the next seat. "Arrow said you needed some company. I feel so old; I'm seriously ready to go to sleep."

"Who's looking after Clover?" I ask, smiling.

"Dex's mother," she replies, wrinkling her nose.

"You don't like her?"

She shrugs. "More like she doesn't like me. I used to date Dex's younger brother."

My eyes flare. "That sounds like quite a story. The longer version, please."

She laughs. "How long do you have?"

I look around. "Apparently all night."

She smiles and tells me everything that happened—it *was* quite a story. We talk for another half an hour and then Faye leaves in search of Dex.

When Arrow still hasn't returned, I'm about to go and find him when a man walks up to me. I look around for a familiar face but see no one. The man takes the seat next to me, eyes roaming my body, his mouth curved in a wicked grin.

"What's a classy woman like you doing here?" he asks.

I don't know what to say to that. The man is wearing a cut, so he's obviously a member.

I sip my drink. "Just enjoying the party, waiting for my man to get back."

He smirks. "If I was your man I wouldn't leave you sitting alone at a party like this."

I force a smile. "I was just going to find him actually, but nice to meet you."

Lie, Anna.

He puts his hand on my back. "If you don't find him, I'm sure I can show you a good time."

I practically run to the kitchen.

When I'm passing the game room I bump into someone.

Janet.

I can't seem to catch a break.

"Still here?" she sneers.

"Apparently so," I muse. "Now get the fuck out of my way."

She smirks. "It's cute that you trust Arrow so much. If it were me, I wouldn't even let him out of my sight."

"Well, good thing I'm not you then."

I don't like the smug look on her face.

"You know, even with how much Arrow loved Mary, he wasn't faithful to her. At all. He fucked other women all the time. So what chance do you have?"

Janet walks off, leaving me wide-eyed in shock.

Arrow wasn't faithful to Mary, the woman he claims to have loved so much?

I don't know how to process that right now.

I continue to the kitchen, where I find Arrow sitting there alone. He's staring down into his drink like it holds all life's answers. Then suddenly he lifts the glass and throws it across the room.

I jump.

"Arrow?" I say, stepping into the room. "What's wrong?"

He expels a deep sigh, leaning forward and rubbing the back of his head in frustration. I stand in front of him and tilt his head back, framing his face with my hands. My thumbs gently caress his jaw as I speak. "You can talk to me, you know. About anything. I won't judge you."

"As soon as something good happens in my life, I somehow fuck it up, even if it was just a cruel twist of fuckin' fate."

I freeze. "What does that even mean?"

He pushes my hands away from his face and stands, looking hollow. "Go back into the room and lock the door, Anna."

"What?" I ask, my face scrunching in confusion. "What are you going to do?"

"Just have a talk with the brothers, then come to bed. I just need a minute."

"Okay," I say, hesitantly leaving the kitchen, and retreating to our bedroom.

However, when he's not back in the room after an hour, I start to worry. I didn't like that look on his face, especially when I didn't know why it was there. So I go in search of him. When I step back into the game room, I see him there, talking to Tracker and Rake.

The conversation looks intense.

A second later, a woman walks over to him and sits down on his lap. Like a spell is broken by her presence, the men all stop talking, looking lost in their own thoughts.

Arrow doesn't push the woman off him. He just sits there drinking, looking extremely unhappy, and maybe even a little guilty.

Why would he feel guilt?

I know he felt guilt over Mary, but he'd been dealing with it. In my imagination I thought that maybe I'd been helping him deal with it somehow.

She kisses his neck.

He still doesn't push her away.

My chest burns.

I guess a lot has changed in the last hour while I was sitting in the room like a good little girl waiting for Arrow to return.

Rake notices the woman kissing Arrow's neck, his expression turning deadly.

"You gonna let some bitch touch you when you have my sister waiting for you?" he asks loudly, his fists clenching.

Tracker looks confused and a little pissed off. "Arrow? What the fuck, man?"

"What the fuck are you doing, Arrow?" Rake asks. "After everything? I will fuckin' beat the shit out of you!"

"Don't fuck up and lose her," Tracker says. "You will regret it."

Arrow laughs without humor. "I've already lost her, so what's the point?"

Rake and Tracker exchange glances. "What the fuck are you talking about?"

"What do you mean you've already lost her? You need to explain now, before I lose my shit," Rake growls.

I step forward, revealing myself. "Yes, Arrow, what do you mean?"

Arrow glances up at me, guilt etched all over his face.

I look at the woman on his lap. "Get out of here."

She looks to Arrow, who looks at her as if he's only just realizing she's there. Without a word, he pushes her off him.

Bit fucking late for that, isn't it?

"What the fuck, Arrow?" I ask, my hands shaking with anger.

And pain.

And fucking confusion.

He doesn't say anything, so I leave. I don't want anyone to see how much this is affecting me.

I hear the men yelling at him. He calls my name, but too fucking bad. I don't get him! He was fine before, even though I know something has been bothering him, then I find him with some woman sitting on his lap? Why didn't he push her off? What the hell is going through his mind?

He's hiding something.

I don't need this shit.

I don't need a man who isn't sure of his feelings. He knows I love him. He *knows*.

Apparently it's not enough.

I'm not enough.

Fine, then. I can't stay here tonight—I pack a bag and head to Lana's house.

I step out into the cool air and take in the scene, a shitload of motorcycles and a few men standing around and talking. I frown when I see no other than Slice, Talon's friend. What is he doing here? I walk straight up to him, smirking at the almost nervous look that passes in his expression. He's dressed in all black, no cut. Sneaking in maybe? What is he up to?

"You're a little close to enemy headquarters, don't you think?" I ask quietly so only he can hear.

His eyes narrow. "What do you want?"

"What are you doing here?" I ask him. "You better not plan to hurt anyone."

His lips tighten. "What do you want?"

"I want a ride. I need to get out of here. You owe me, and don't even think of taking me anywhere else other than where I want to go."

I left my car keys in my room and I sure as hell wasn't going back into the clubhouse.

He calls Talon.

Talon tells him to do it.

"Let me speak to Talon first, so I know you're not going to murder me or something," I say.

He hands me the phone. "Hey, Talon."

"You okay, Anna?" he asks, sounding concerned.

"I need a quick escape. What is Slice doing here, anyway?" I ask him.

"Never mind about that. You can trust him. I trust Slice with my life."

"And what does that mean to me?"

I hear him sigh. "You and I both know we need to talk. Why don't you let Slice bring you here?"

We do need to talk. I need answers.

"All right," I tell him, then hang up the phone and give it back to Slice.

"Take me to Talon, please."

He grits his teeth. "Get the fuck on my bike, princess."

He says *princess* in such a mocking way I want to punch him. But I don't, because I need him right now.

I get on his bike.

I could feel my heart breaking the whole way home.

I don't like Slice.

He takes me straight back to their clubhouse. On the ride over I had time to think, to go over what happened and to try to figure out the puzzle that is Arrow's recent behavior.

I realize that recently two things happened.

One was when Arrow spoke to Talon, and two was my telling him that I loved him.

I thought it had to do with the former, and hoped it wasn't the latter.

Talon was somehow the key in all of this, and I was glad to be at his clubhouse, so I could demand some answers.

I needed them badly.

I slide off the back of Slice's bike, eager to get away from him. Handing him his helmet, I mumble a thank-you. He nods his head to the door. "Talon is through there."

He walks to the door and I follow behind him.

"Where is everyone?" I ask him, looking around the empty place.

"Out," he replies, stopping at a door and knocking twice.

"Come in," I hear Talon call. Slice opens the door, but only I walk in. Talon looks up, his white-blond hair falling across his forehead. He pushes it out of his face and flashes me a small smile.

"Nice to see you, Anna," he says quietly. "Take a seat."

I lower myself into the seat and stare at him expectantly.

He smirks. "Nothing to say? No kidnapping accusations?"

"Not this time. I have a feeling that you know things, and right now I want some answers," I tell him in a strong, even voice.

He laughs without humor. "I knew Arrow wouldn't tell you."

"Tell me what?" I demand. "I'm sick of all this. Just tell me what's going on!"

He sobers. "I never wanted to hurt you, Anna, I hope you believe that."

I don't like the sound of this.

"What did you say to Arrow that day?" I ask.

Talon expels a heavy sigh. "It's more what I showed him."

He reaches into a drawer and pulls out a piece of paper. He stares at it once before sliding it across the table. I pick it up with trembling hands and read it from top to bottom.

"Who is Samuel Pierce?" I ask him, my bottom lip trembling.

Talon suddenly looks unsure. "My stepfather."

I swallow hard. "What? I don't—"

I was looking at a birth certificate.

My birth certificate.

I didn't even know I had one. I just assumed my mother had lost it.

It said that my father's name was Samuel Pierce.

All I felt was confusion.

"My mother married your father. I was a baby at the time, and your dad raised me like I was his own," he says gently. "This is what I showed Arrow. I knew it would break him—and he fuckin' deserved it after what he did."

I swallow hard after hearing the name of my father for the very first time in my life.

"I can't believe this," I murmur.

"Why did you tell Arrow and not me or Rake?" I blurt out.

He cringes. "I wanted to kill Arrow. But I didn't, because of you. So I guess it was my fucked-up way of revenge."

"How is this revenge?" I ask him, brows scrunching in confusion.

Talon takes a deep breath then. "Anna, you know how my dad died, right?"

"You call him your dad?" I ask, not knowing how to feel about that.

He nods. "I do."

I was Samuel's daughter, but I didn't know him; neither did Rake. Yet Talon, who wasn't of his blood, got to be raised by him and call him Dad.

Talon's dad was the president of the Wild Men MC, I remember being told that.

My mind races trying to figure everything out, but then it hits me.

The Wild Men MC killed Mary. Faye told me they broke in one night when all the men had gone on a run, leaving only women and prospects in the clubhouse.

Arrow got his revenge . . .

By killing their president.

My father.

I cover my face with my hands, struggling to breathe. My chest burned, the pain so strong I'm surprised I wasn't in flames.

I'd never met my father, and now I'd never get the chance. A feeling of loss overwhelms me. Losing something I never actually had in the first place.

I don't know how to process this. I am confused; I am hurt. I still want Arrow. Why didn't he tell me? This should have come from him. He knew everything this whole time and kept it to himself. Instead, he slowly pushed me away, knowing the second the truth surfaced he may lose me. I shake off my thoughts of Arrow and decide to ask the other questions that I need answers for.

"How long have you known?" I almost whisper.

"That you and Rake were his children? Dad told me a few months before he died, actually," he says, his hand rubbing his chest.

I bite my lip, gathering courage to ask the next question. "Why didn't he want us?"

Talon grimaces, then looks down at the table. "As far as I know, Dad was married to my mom when he was with your mother. My mom was his old lady, and yours was . . ."

"His whore," I supply in a hollow tone.

He sighs. "Anna, it wasn't—"

"Why didn't he ever come and see us?" I demand. "What, did he just fuck Mother and run when Rake was born? Then come back to get her pregnant with me and leave again?"

He's silent for a moment.

"I don't know exactly what happened. I know that Dad saw

Rake when he was a baby. Then my mother found out and she told him if he ever saw your mother she would leave him and never come back."

My jaw clenches. "So your 'father' decided to stay and look after you, his wife's kid, and ignored Rake and me, his own blood."

Talon looks ashamed, his face falling. "I didn't say it was right, Anna, I'm just telling you what happened."

"And how was I born then?" I ask.

"Dad kept seeing your mother, now and again," he says with a shrug. "His weak moments, he would say."

I was born because of a "weak moment"?

Just great.

"So he knew we were out there, with a druggie for a mother, but never bothered to do anything about it. Wow, he sounds like a real winner."

Talon stays silent.

"Is your mother still alive?" I ask him.

He nods. "Is yours?"

I shake my head. "Drug overdose."

Lost in my own thoughts, I have no idea how long I've been silent for.

Talon clears his throat. "Say something."

"So you knew I was your stepsister and you still kidnapped me?"

"You weren't hurt, and Ranger got the shit beaten out of him for hurting you," he says. "And to be honest, I wanted to see what you were like."

I run a hand down my face. "You're fuckin' insane."

"And you, Anna, blew me away. You were brave, smart, and

beautiful. Trust me, it was Dad who missed out on you, not the other way around."

A small smile plays on my lips. "I think you're right about that one."

"You have his eyes, you know," he says quietly.

"Yeah, my mother had brown eyes," I say, staring down at my plate. "I always knew I got them from my father, whoever he was."

"Your mother never told you?" he asks.

"Nope, she always said she didn't know who he was."

He scowls. "I'm sorry, Anna."

"Don't be," I tell him. "It wasn't your fault."

I feel tired.

Exhausted and empty.

Hollow.

"Talon, could you please take me to Lana's house?" I ask him.

He swallows, standing and walking over to me. "I'm sorry, Anna. Come on, of course I'll take you there."

I try to smile, but I think it comes out as more of a grimace.

How did everything get so messed up?

TWENTY-SIX

WHEN I'm safe at Lana's, tucked into the guest room bed, I check my phone. Fifty-two missed calls and twelve messages. Not wanting anyone to worry, I send out a message to Rake.

> With Lana. I'm safe.

He replies instantly.

> Thank fuck! I was worried, Anna.

Another message.

> I'll come and get you.

Yeah, that isn't happening.

> No, I'll come back tomorrow, I reply.

> Fine, love you. We need to talk.

Love you too, bro.

I don't read Arrow's text messages, or check my voice mail.

I also don't sleep.

Lana sticks her head through the doorway. "Morning!"

"Morning," my voice thick with fatigue.

She frowns, opening her mouth, then shaking her head. "Did you know that Arrow is sitting on my front porch?"

I sit up. "What?"

How did he even know where Lana lived?

"Yeah, no idea how long he's been there. Mother saw him when she was on her way to work and sent me a text."

I blink slowly a few times. "Did he scare her?"

Lana smirks. "No. Apparently she was worried about him because he looks like hell."

Typical.

Lana's mother was a saint—and she definitely passed on her kind and gentle nature to her daughter.

With a frustrated puff of breath, I get out of bed and walk to the front door. When I open it, I see Arrow sitting there, back against the wall, his head lowered. He looks defeated, and I hate it. He looks up when I clear my throat.

"What are you doing here, Arrow?"

He wets his lips. "You wouldn't return my calls."

"And for good reason," I snap. "I didn't want to talk to you. How did you even get here? You better not have ridden, because you were drunk as hell!"

He winces, and I wonder if he's still a little drunk.

"Tracker dropped me off," he says, running his hand through his hair. "Can we talk?"

I look around. "Why didn't you push that woman off your lap?"

He swallows. "She just came and sat there. I was so busy feeling fuckin' sorry for myself that I didn't even think. She was just sitting there, Anna, it's not like we were fucking. You know I'd never be unfaithful to you."

"And how do I know that? You weren't even faithful to Mary, and you loved her."

His expression is etched in pain and guilt. "Who told you that?"

"Is it true?" I ask him.

"Not exactly."

"What's that supposed to mean?"

"Mary knew I wasn't exclusive with her," he says, pushing himself off the ground and coming to stand in front of me. "When she died, I knew I'd screwed up. I should have treated her better. But I also learned my lesson, to never take someone for granted. Which is why I would never do that to you."

"Janet told me," I say. "And then I walked in and saw that woman get comfortable in your fuckin' lap while you just sat there, like it was a daily occurrence that someone else's ass was pressed against your crotch!"

Arrow curses and lifts his hand to my cheek. "I'm sorry, I don't want to hurt you, Anna. I never did."

"Don't be sorry, just tell me why you didn't think that I deserved to know about my father. Or that Talon is my stepbrother, or that . . ."

I trail off.

"Or that I murdered your father?" he says in a broken voice. "Fuck. I wanted to tell you, Anna. I was going to tell you."

His voice breaks. "But how the fuck do you tell someone that? Especially someone you love?"

He loves me?

"I don't know, Arrow, but I know that I wish you'd told me," I reply, looking away from him. I sit down on the porch steps, defeated.

"I didn't want to lose you, Anna. I can't lose you. I need you to know that if I knew . . . if I knew, I wouldn't have done it. Fuck, Anna. I didn't know. I didn't even know you then . . ."

"Fuck," he mutters, going to his knees before me. "I do love you, Anna; do you know that?"

My heart grips on to his every word.

"I wanted to say it back to you when you said it to me, I wanted to . . ."

"Why didn't you?" I ask.

Why now? I want to ask. Is he just telling me because he thinks he's going to lose me?

"Because I knew I didn't deserve to say those words, and I don't deserve to say them now, but I'm selfish when it comes to you."

Arrow hugs me, wrapping his arms around me tightly and telling me how sorry he is, how he never knew, how if he could change it he would.

I believe him.

"You didn't know, Arrow," I tell him. "But I need some time alone, okay? I just need to work through all this."

He looks like his heart is breaking, but I need to fix me now. I can't fix anyone else when I'm feeling so broken.

"Anna, don't ask me to leave you alone. I fuckin' can't."

"Just give me a few days, Arrow," I tell him. "Please."

"Okay," he whispers, kissing my forehead, then swooping down and kissing my lips once.

The gentle kiss feels final.

Like he's saying good-bye.

I can feel the want, the need for me, pulsating off him.

I want to tell him everything is going to be okay—but I can't right now.

I'm too confused.

Blade picks Arrow up, and I get back into bed.

I roll over and bury my face into the pillow, crying for the father I'd lost but never had in the first place, and for the man I loved but didn't know if I could forgive.

The next morning, a large bouquet of flowers and a huge plush tortoise arrive at Lana's front door.

I know they have flowers for every occasion, but I didn't think there was one for finding out the man you love murdered a father you'd never met. Orange tulips, however, were beautiful and my favorite.

The note reads:

Don't give up on me. I love you. —Arrow.

TWENTY-SEVEN

T HE next day, Rake enters my temporary room at Lana's, coming to sit next to me and pulling me into his arms. "How you feeling?"

I shrug. "I don't really know, to be honest. Numb, I guess. You?"

He sighs. "I never knew him, Anna, and he obviously didn't care about getting to know us. He left us with our bitch of a mother, and he had to have known she was drug-fucked. Arrow, on the other hand, has always had my back, is my brother, and will always be there for me."

"Do you not care that Dad is dead because he was president of an enemy MC?" I ask him, frowning. It was obvious the club meant more to him than a father we never knew. How come I am having a harder time looking at it that way?

"Sometimes you got to make your own family, Anna," he says, smiling sadly.

It is a sad truth. I don't want to think about Arrow having killed my father, but I'd never even known the man. I love Arrow, and he's always been good to me.

"When did Arrow tell you?" I ask him.

"After the two of you spoke. He's devastated, Anna," he says, looking upset.

"What are you going to do about Talon?" I ask him. I couldn't think about Arrow right now.

His eyes harden slightly. "Nothing. He kidnapped you, Anna, and he knew you were his stepsister. That speaks louder than any words could. He's not even blood related to us anyway—just because that bastard raised him doesn't mean shit. And it's his mother's fault we never had a father in the first place."

"That's not true. It was our dad's fault he wasn't there for us, not Talon's mother. Although she sounds like a bitch too. Wow, our dad had really bad taste in women," I say with a bitter laugh, then continue. "I wish Talon had just told me the truth instead of putting everything on Arrow's shoulders."

No matter how wide and broad they are.

"I think he wanted to put it on Arrow, revenge for killing his father. He laughed in Arrow's face and told him that now he was going to lose someone he loved."

I lift my head off his bicep. "He said that to Arrow?"

"Yeah. Arrow feels like shit, Anna—I've never seen him like this in his life. Not even when Mary was killed."

I don't know what to say to that.

He killed my father. Shouldn't I want nothing to do with him? But I don't feel that way. I can't imagine my life without Arrow.

"I'm so confused right now," I tell Rake. "I don't know what to do, or how to feel."

"Do you love Arrow?" he asks.

"Is it that simple?" I ask, sniffling. "Of course I love him."

Rake smiles kindly. "I think it is."

"Love isn't always enough."

Rake nods. "I suppose so. But think about this—our father never bothered to see us, to check on us, to see if we were alive or dead. What has Arrow done for you?"

"Taken care of me, always."

Rake kisses my cheek. "I'm not telling you what to do. I love you no matter what, you know that."

"You're taking this a lot better than I am."

Rake chuckles. "My man didn't kill our father."

I slap his arm. "No, but your brother did."

"Arrow is my family, Anna, not this Samuel guy. Nothing will change that," he says, standing up. "Do you want me to get anything for you?"

"No, I'm okay, I just want to be alone for a while."

Rake's jaw clenches, but he nods once before leaving the room.

Two questions play in my mind.

Can I live with the fact that Arrow killed Samuel?

And can I forgive him completely? He doesn't deserve to have me throw it in his face whenever I am angry or upset.

It's all or nothing.

I don't sleep a wink that night, my mind filled with Arrow.

SEVEN DAYS LATER

"Get out of bed, Anna," Lana says, pulling the sheets off me.

"Why?" I ask, still half asleep.

"Because you can't sleep all day; get your lazy ass up!"

I open one eye. "Did you just yell at me?"

She grins. "I did, so now you know I'm not messing around."

I force myself to sit up and throw Lana a dirty look.

She just smiles.

"So I got a phone call from Faye today, about starting as Clover's nanny."

"Are you considering it?" I ask her. "It's good money."

"I know," she replies. "Really good money, but there's one problem."

I sit up straighter. "What?"

"I'm going to have to be around Tracker and Allie. I don't know if I can handle that, to be honest," she whispers, looking down at her feet. "The thing is, I could really use the money and I could help Mother out with some of the bills too, so I want to take it."

When I'd suggested Lana to Faye, I didn't even think about Tracker.

Crap.

"You don't have to do it—"

Lana sighs. "He's just a man, right? Maybe someone new will catch my eye."

I didn't want to tell her that if she felt for Tracker anything like what I felt for Arrow . . . well, I doubted those feelings would be going away any time soon.

"It's your call, Lana. I could ask Reid if he needs someone else," I suggest, but I can see in her eyes that she's already decided to take this job.

She nods. "The money is . . . wow, for part-time work, and the times she needs me fit in with my class schedule."

"I have to get to class, but we can talk more when I get back."

She kisses me on my cheek. "Go take a shower."

"I will."

She leaves and I hop into the shower, wondering if I made the right choice bringing Lana closer to the club.

And closer to Tracker.

I'm more than surprised about an hour later when Tracker pulls into Lana's driveway. I watch as he steps out of the car with a determined look on his face. Arrow has called me every day for the last week but has otherwise respected my wishes to be alone. We'd talk for a few minutes, he'd ask if he could bring me anything, if I needed anything. He was being so sweet and understanding. He'd ask me to come back to the clubhouse, but I told him I still needed a little space.

Everyone else has respected my wishes too—but it looks like that's about to change.

I open the door for him.

"Hey, Tracker."

"Anna Bell," he says, smiling faintly and kissing my cheek. "Where's Lana?"

"She's at school. What can I do for you?" I ask him as he glances around the house, taking in every little detail.

"Pack your shit; enough pouting. You're getting your ass home where you belong," he says, his tone brokering no argument.

I purse my lips together. "I don't know, Tracker, I—"

He rudely cuts me off. "Do you love Arrow?"

"Of course I do," I reply instantly.

There is no question about it. I adore the man. Head over heels.

"He's fuckin' hurting, Anna. Don't do this to him. Go and put him out of his misery," he says, frowning a little. "It's hurting all of us, seeing him like this. And don't tell him I told you any of this."

I open my mouth, then close it.

He's right.

He's right and I've known it for the last week. Why have I been wasting time? I don't need space, I need Arrow.

I either love him and want him, or I don't.

There is no in-between.

And I want him badly.

What the fuck am I doing?

"I see you're beginning to understand," he muses with a smirk. "I've seen him turn down every woman who's looked his way—trust me, Anna, you've done a number on the poor man."

"What women?" I ask, trying to keep the bite out of my tone.

He shrugs, but I can't help but see the grin he tries to hide from me. "Come on, grab your shit."

My "shit," as he so eloquently put it, isn't much. I'd gone shopping for everything I was using and it all fit into one bag.

He helps me into the car, then pauses. "Good to have you back, Anna Bell."

I smile. "Thanks for bringing me back."

I think we'll have a silent drive home, but Tracker decides to be chatty.

"You should go and fuck the shit out of him. Oh, and give him head, lots of head."

I blink a few times. "Thank you for that advice, Tracker."

"You're welcome. Do you know what else we men really like? We like it when you—"

I pinch his shoulder.

"Ouch," he grumbles.

"Please, shut up," I beg of him.

"Should I stop for condoms?" he asks cheerfully. "What size is Arrow? Or maybe water balloons might do?"

I laugh at that. "Arrow's dick is huge; don't insult it in my presence."

"Whoa, touchy."

"What have I missed?" I ask him.

"Rake's angry you've been gone; Arrow's been moping around. It's pathetic really. I think twice he walked out the door to come get you, but then he turned around. He wanted to respect your wishes, no matter how much it almost killed him."

Fuck, my Arrow.

I should have returned sooner.

My mind was messed up, so I guess I did need that time to myself, but I didn't want to hurt anyone else in the process, and I knew I did hurt Arrow, and Rake as well.

I was only thinking of myself at the time, trying to work through my own issues.

I sigh and stare out the window. "I didn't know how to deal. Everyone kept things from me, but now I see that it really wouldn't have changed anything. Arrow didn't want to lose or hurt me, and I can see where he was coming from. It was a difficult situation."

"I know, Anna, and no one blames you. You did what you had to do, it was just a few days' break; Arrow is going on like he's lost you forever," he grumbles.

"He probably thought I wouldn't come back."

"Well, he was wrong," he replies. "And trust me, if you weren't back in a few days he would have gone and gotten you. He was about to break, even I could see that. He wasn't going to live without you."

Tracker parks the car and we walk into the clubhouse side by side.

Rake grins and runs to me, lifting me in his arms. "Thank fuck you're back, sis!"

"Good to be back," I murmur, my eyes searching the room for Arrow.

"He's in his room," he tells me, kissing my cheek. I smile and walk to the room, only to find it locked. I knock a few times.

No answer.

I knock harder.

"Fuck off!" he yells, his voice hoarse, causing me to grimace.

"Arrow?" I call out.

The door flies open in seconds.

I study him.

Dark circles under his eyes, a bruised cheek, his hair a tangled mess.

"Can I come in?" I ask softly.

He blinks. "You're here."

I smile at that, walking into the room and turning to face him. He closes the door behind him and closes the space between us in a few steps. "I've missed you, Anna."

I stare at him in silence, until he continues.

"When I killed for Mary, to avenge her, I never once thought I'd be losing the only woman I could ever see myself making my old lady. Fuckin' marrying. I never even thought I'd ever get married in my life until I met you."

He could see himself marrying me? I wanted that. More than I'd ever wanted anything.

"I missed you too, Arrow. I was just hurt. I needed to come to terms with the fact that I'd never meet my father, and that he'd never wanted me in the first place. My mind was everywhere, and I needed time to work through it all. I was mostly feeling sorry for myself, which was stupid. I didn't mean to hurt you in the process, or to push you away. I forgive you, Arrow. You didn't know who he was at the time; you didn't even know me then. When I fell for you, I knew the man you are. I know what you're capable of. I also know you would never hurt me."

"Anna—"

"Nothing else matters, Arrow, except this," I say, going up on my tiptoes and kissing his cheek. "This, what we have, I could never turn my back on it. I love you, Arrow."

"You really forgive me?" he asks in a hope-filled tone.

I nod. "I knew that when I came to you, I'd have to have forgiven you fully, or this won't work between us. But I have, Arrow."

"So sweet," he murmurs. "I was so fuckin' scared you weren't going to come back to me. I was giving you a few more days before I came to Lana's house."

"What were you going to do?" I ask him.

His eyes smile down at me. "Anything I had to, Anna, anything. I wasn't going to live without you. You gave me a taste of what it was like to live again, to actually live. Before I met you I wasn't living, I was just not dying. I couldn't go back to that. I'm so fuckin' crazy about you I should be embarrassed."

A bubble of laughter escapes me at that.

He lowers his head and kisses me, leaning my body back and cupping my face with his strong hands. He tastes like strawberry candy, which I know he practically lives on and shares with Clover when no one is looking. When he pulls away, he smiles down at me. "I love you too, Anna. I'm sorry I fucked up."

I lick my lips. "You could always kiss me again."

He grins. "Fuck, I love you."

He throws me down onto the bed, his mouth devouring mine.

"Don't ever leave me again, Anna," he commands in a deep tone. "Do you hear me?"

"I won't," I mumble against his mouth. "Don't give me a reason to again."

He lifts my top off.

"I won't, darlin', never again," he grits out before his mouth is on my body, taunting, teasing, showing me what I've missed out on. "You're mine, Anna, don't fuckin' forget that again."

"I never forgot that, Arrow," I whisper, tugging at his T-shirt, silently begging him to take it off. He gives in to me, pulling his white T-shirt over his head and throwing it somewhere around the room. I gasp when I see my name sprawled on his ribs in scripted font.

"When did you get this done?" I ask, running my fingers over the beautiful ink.

"The day you left," he says as he pushes me back on the bed. "Need to taste you."

My lower belly clenches at that thought.

He lifts my skirt, pulls down my panties, and puts his lips on me.

I stare at his dark head of hair, before I close my eyes and let the pleasure consume me.

Fuck, it feels so damn good.

I force myself to open my eyes, wanting to watch him as he pleasures me, lifting my hips up to his mouth.

Gripping my hips, he pins my body down to the bed so I can't move, then continues to lick me through my folds. When he runs his tongue over my clit, my back arches involuntarily.

"Arrow," I moan out, reaching my hands down and threading my fingers through his hair.

He pulls back. "You wanna come in my mouth or on my cock?"

"Both," I reply back to him.

His mouth tugs up in the corners, before he lowers his head and continues licking me. When he sucks on my clit, my orgasm hits out of nowhere.

"Fuck, fuck, fuck," I grit out, between clenched teeth, breathing heavily.

So. Fucking. Good.

When my body finally goes limp, he moves his mouth away and wipes it with the back of his hand. Feeling sated, I crook my finger to him.

"What do you want, Anna?" he asks as he pulls his pants off.

"I want you in my mouth," I tell him boldly, sitting up on my knees and waiting.

He curses and steps closer to me, so his hard arousal is in front of my face.

"Open your mouth, darlin'," he croons, touching the side of my jaw with his hand. I instantly open for him, sucking his length into my mouth as far as I can take it. He groans, staring down at me with brown eyes filled with such passion it causes my heart to race. He lets me lick him a few times before he pulls away. "Need to be inside you, Anna, now."

"How do you want me?" I ask, spreading my thighs apart in invitation.

He curses again. "Lay back down, I need to see your face."

I lie down on the bed and he braces himself over me, then slides himself in with one long thrust.

"So fuckin' good, Anna," he whispers. "I missed you so much."

"Missed you too," I reply, pulling his face down and kissing his mouth. He continues to pump himself inside me, and reaches down to play with my clit until I come again, this orgasm more powerful than the last. I call out his name as I finish, and he soon joins me, his strong thighs trembling as he comes inside me. Afterward, he lays back and pulls me into the crook of his arm, placing a gentle kiss on the top of my head.

"Never letting you go," he murmurs.

"I never want you to," I whisper back.

His hands tighten around me.

Rubbing the sleep out of my eyes, I wander into the kitchen to see Arrow standing there, butt naked, cooking breakfast.

Buns of fucking steel.

"Morning," I rumble, my voice thick with sleep as I admire the view. "What is it with you and cooking naked?"

He turns and grins widely. "Mornin', beautiful."

"What are you making?" I ask, placing a kiss on his waiting lips before peering into the frying pan.

My hand gropes one of his ass cheeks.

Arrow turns off the stove and then turns to me. His cock is hard, pressing into my stomach.

"You're not the only one who just woke up," he murmurs, glancing down at himself and smirking.

I look down too and smack my lips together. "And what are you going to do about it?"

Arrow licks his bottom lip, then lifts me in the air, a squeak escaping my mouth.

"Gonna eat you, then I'm gonna fuck you, then I'm gonna feed you."

His lips are on mine.

Then he does exactly what he said he would.

THREE MONTHS LATER

I call the number I was given, sitting up in bed. He answers on the fourth ring.

"Yes."

"Talon," I say. "It's me, Anna."

He's silent for a few seconds. "Hey, Anna, to what do I owe the pleasure?"

"Can you meet me somewhere? I thought we could hang out."

"When?" he asks instantly.

"In half an hour. How about that café you dropped by last time?"

"All right," he says. "I'll see you then."

I get dressed in my favorite pair of worn, ripped jeans and a plain black tank top. I don't bother with any makeup, and leave my hair down, letting it dry by itself. As I leave the bedroom, I notice the clubhouse is quiet. Talon has left me a few messages over the last month, and I got the impression that he wanted to spend some time with me. I think that even though we aren't blood related, he still sees me as family. I know he loved my dad, and sees me as a connection to him. He isn't a bad guy, so after a month of his reaching out I decided why not, I could have Talon in my life. It didn't cost me anything, and we were connected in a weird way.

I see Arrow and Rake having a drink together and try to walk by unnoticed.

"Whoa, where do you think you're going?" Rake calls out, making me stop in my tracks.

"I'm going to have a coffee with Talon," I tell him.

Arrow's face flashes with worry, before he's able to mask it. He turns away from me and concentrates on his drink instead. "You're not fuckin' going alone, Anna. I'll come with you."

My eyes narrow. "You can't come with me, Arrow. He's not going to hurt me. Besides, I'm going to a public place, that same café where I saw him last time."

Today is the anniversary of Mary's death.

Arrow has been broody all day, and I know he wants to be alone. When I'd asked him if he wanted to talk about it, he said no. When I followed him to the bar, he didn't say a word to me. He's stuck in his head, and he needs time to work through it. Time that I will give him. Whatever he needs. I decided I'd make myself absent, and since Talon had contacted me again just the other day, I thought why not. My brother wasn't any happier about it, but I was curious about why Talon wanted to reach out to me so badly. Maybe he was just feeling alone and wanted to talk to someone. Since Damien now avoids me like the plague, I could always use another friend.

Rake's jaw sets stubbornly. "Blade is taking you and that's final."

I point a finger at him, then drop it. There's no point arguing with him. "Tell Blade we're leaving now."

Rake nods and leaves the room.

I stare at Arrow's back. I can't just leave him like this. I know he doesn't want me to see Talon but it's something that I want to do, and he can't be controlling my every move. I walk over to him and touch his shoulder. "I'll be back, okay? Nothing has changed, Arrow."

He turns his head and smiles sadly. "I love you, Anna," he says. "Just remember that. Don't let that fucker mess with your head."

Did Arrow think that I am going to change my mind? That suddenly I am going to hate him for what happened with my father? Because I'm not. I meant what I said, and forgiveness is forgiveness. I wasn't bringing up what happened again unless one of us wanted to talk about it, never in anger or using it as a weapon against him. I'd never do that to him.

"I love you too, Arrow, and I know you love me," I whisper, kissing him on his cheek. "He's my stepbrother, and he wants to talk. It has nothing to do with how I feel about you; my feelings for you won't change. I know today is a hard day for you, so I want you to have your space. If you want me to come to the cemetery with you later, let me know. Or if you want to go alone, or with Faye, that's okay too. If you need me, just call me, okay?"

I run my hand down his back, then leave the clubhouse without another word.

For the first time ever, Talon is without his usual smirk. He sits there, in the exact same seat he occupied last time, looking a little unsure. I pull the chair out next to him, the sound of it scraping the floor making him glance up.

"Hey," he says, pulling the chair out a little more for me to sit.

"Hey," I say, sitting down. "Did you order something to eat?"

"No," he says, shaking his head. "I was waiting for you."

We both order a burger and some fries, then stare at each other as soon as the waitress leaves.

When our meals come, he opens his mouth to say something but then shakes his head and eats a fry instead.

"You and Rake ever going to talk?" I ask.

Talon smiles sadly. "I doubt it. He doesn't feel any connection to me. I'm surprised he let you come."

I point outside. "There's a prospect keeping an eye on me from the car. And what do you mean 'let me come'? I am my own woman, you know."

Talon laughs then, a deep, musical sound. "You're precious cargo, that's why."

"I love him," I add slowly.

"Rake?"

"Well, of course I love Rake, but I meant Arrow."

His lips tighten. "He killed our—"

"He killed *your* father. And if he knew, he wouldn't have done it," I add.

"You're defending a murderer? Who killed someone of your own blood?" he asks, brows furrowing.

"He did it because your men killed Mary, someone who was important to him. Besides, are you telling me you haven't killed anyone?"

He shakes his head no.

"Beaten anyone? Threatened anyone?"

"Of course I've done those things, I'm not innocent, but I've never taken a life," he says.

"Yet," I add.

He tightens his lips at that and says nothing. What is there to say?

"Are they going to let you see me again?" Talon asks, pushing his plate away.

"They don't have a choice, and of course I want to see you again," I say. "Maybe we could see each other once a month or something."

He smiles widely, running a hand through his white-blond hair. "I'd like that."

"Good," I reply. "But I need you to understand that I love Arrow and I won't ever leave him."

"Anna," he adds, jaw suddenly tight, "I won't ever approve of you being with Arrow."

"I wasn't asking for your approval," I say firmly. "You don't have to like Arrow, but around me you won't disrespect him."

His lip twitches. "Noted."

"So, tell me about you. Everything I've missed out on," I say, lightening the mood.

"Well," he starts. "I remember sliding down a tunnel, and then there was a light—"

He laughs when I pinch him.

He tells me a little about his childhood, but I feel like he's leaving things out on purpose.

"I'm not very close with my mother," he says. "I was close with my—with our dad though."

I nod my head and smile sadly. "Hey, at least he was there for you."

He frowns. "I'm sorry, I didn't mean to . . ."

"It's fine, Talon," I say. "I've made my peace with anything to do with my dad. I honestly feel like he was your dad, not mine. Can I ask you something?"

"Sure."

"Why did you keep contacting me?"

He sighs. "Honestly, Anna, I feel like you're family. I want you in my life. It's not guilt, although I do wish that Dad had been there for you. Okay, maybe there is a little guilt. I kind of feel like I took something that wasn't meant for me. But that isn't why I want to be in your life from now on."

I nod, accepting his answer. "I think I understand. Maybe you could tell me some cool stories about him sometime."

"I'd like that," he says, looking hopeful.

A comfortable silence appears between us.

"Are you going to be president of the Wild Men one day?" I ask.

He nods, eyeing me closely. "I am. Is that going to be an issue?"

"Not if we don't let it."

"I don't want to come between you and Rake. I know he's

been there for you your entire life while I'm only just entering your life."

"Rake and I will be fine, we always are. You know, you both share something in common. He didn't want me to be with Arrow either," I admit to him.

"Really? Why?" Talon asks, frowning. "One of his own brothers? That should be a good thing, keeping you close."

"He said he wanted better for me," I tell him. "Maybe a man in a suit. A professional. Someone who comes home at six every night and doesn't live dangerously."

"But you didn't want that?" he asks.

I lift my shoulders in a shrug. "I just want Arrow. I didn't go looking for a biker. I didn't go looking for anyone, really. I just saw him and I wanted him."

"And so you took him," he replies, lip twitching. "Trust me, Anna, you suit this lifestyle. You're strong and tough but with a sweetness inside that no one will be able to destroy. Arrow should be on his fuckin' knees, grateful that he has someone like you."

My mind flashes to Arrow on his knees, telling me how sorry he was.

"He's not perfect, but he's mine," I reply. "He's good to me."

"He better be," he grates, tone menacing.

"So, do you have a woman in your life?" I ask him, changing the subject. "Anyone I need to threaten?"

He chuckles. "No one special."

I roll my eyes. "Is that code for just club whores?"

His expression turns innocent. "Where did you learn such a word Anna? I have no idea what you're talking about. I'm not sure how the Wind Dragons run their club, but—"

I smirk at him. "Save it, Talon."

"I think we should get some dessert; how about you, sis?" he says, flashing me a boyish grin.

"I think you read my mind."

We both share a smile.

When I get back to the clubhouse later that day, Arrow is waiting for me.

"Will you come to the cemetery with me?" he asks. "Everyone is going."

"Of course I will," I tell him. "Should we pick up some flowers on the way?"

He nods, a grateful expression on his face. "You know, Anna, when I think of Mary, all I feel is guilt. A good woman I didn't do right by, a woman who died paying the price of this lifestyle. A woman I couldn't even commit to."

He sighs and takes my hand in his. "I've never loved anyone the way I love you, Anna. Never. I just want you to know that."

I lift his hand to my lips and kiss his fingers. "I get you, Arrow, I know."

I know that he doesn't want me to worry about him being upset on the anniversary of Mary's death. The truth is, I'm not. He has loved before me, and that's okay, because I have him now and that's all that matters to me.

"How was your lunch with Talon?" he asks.

"It was good; I told him we could try and do it every month," I tell him, reaching up to do a missed button on his shirt. I ignore his frown and smile up at him. "Come on, let's go."

In the living room, Faye is waiting for us, along with the rest of the MC. She runs to Arrow, who hugs her tightly. I watch them embrace and feel lucky that Arrow has her in his life, and that she's now in my life. Faye is a great friend, and I feel like an idiot over how I first felt when I met her. I know the two of them were closest to Mary, and I let them have their moment.

I'm more than surprised when Sin wraps his arm around me. "You're a good woman, Anna, and you make a hell of an old lady."

I smirk. "Thank you, Sin. I never knew you liked me."

He grins. "I didn't like that Rake and Arrow were fighting over you, but I can see you're a worthy woman. Arrow did well for himself."

"I'm glad you approve," I mutter, but then turn to him with a smile. "You're not so bad yourself."

He laughs then, and, damn, he really is a good-looking man.

Vinnie wraps an arm around me from behind. "Everyone ready to go?"

"Yes."

Irish opens the car door for me, and I slide in. "Thanks, Irish."

"Welcome, Anna," he replies in his sexy accent.

Arrow and Faye come out of the clubhouse last, Arrow's eyes immediately searching for me.

"She's in the car, calm down," Sin says to him, shaking his head.

Arrow opens the door. "I want to ride."

He lifts me out of the car and carries me to his bike, placing me on it. He puts a helmet on me but doesn't bother with one for himself. "Hold on tight, darlin'."

I smile. "I always do."

And I always will.

When we get there, we all stand at her gravestone, everyone a few steps back except for Faye and Arrow. Tears spill from my eyes as I feel the pain radiating off them.

Faye places flowers at her headstone and speaks quietly.

Arrow says a few words, then stands.

We all touch the gravestone and then leave.

ARROW

"I hope you're happy, Mary, wherever you are," I say to the gravestone. "I know you gave me everything you had, and I didn't appreciate you enough, and I'm sorry. I know if you met Anna, you would love her. Just as much as I love her. I will never take her for granted, Mary. I'm sorry you lost your life, and I will carry that burden with me forever."

I take a deep breath. "I killed her father. I fuckin' killed her father, and if I could go back and change it I would. I wouldn't have killed him in revenge for your death. It nearly made me lose Anna."

There is nothing I wouldn't do for Anna. To think that I almost lost her . . .

Fuck.

"I hope you're happy, Mary, wherever you are," I whisper, then turn away.

I step away from the stone and look at her.

My Anna.

The love of my life. If I believed in all that shit, I'd say she was my soul mate.

Here she stands with tears in her eyes, crying for a woman from my past.

There's no jealousy in her eyes, no hurt.

Only understanding.

How the fuck did I get so lucky?

Me, a fuckin' sinner.

A tainted man.

A guilty man.

How was I given such an angel?

A beauty, a fuckin' scientist.

The sweetest woman who ever lived.

I take her into my arms and kiss the top of her head.

I guess God really does believe in forgiveness.

Acknowledgments

THIS book was written during a hard time in my life, and I think it's turned out to be one of my favorites. I hope it will be for you, too.

First of all, I'd like to thank my agent, Kimberly Brower, for being amazing and going above and beyond. I'm so thankful to have you!

Abby Zidle and Gallery Books, you have been so wonderful to work with, thank you for everything!

My sister, Tenielle, as always, for helping me with anything I need. Words can't express how much I love you. You keep me grounded, you keep me sane.

My beta readers for always making time for me, and for the encouragement they give! I appreciate each and every one of you more than you know.

Thank you to Rose, Nina, Lisa, and all the other bloggers who support me on a daily basis. Love you lots!

The biggest thank-you goes to my readers. I've received so many messages and comments from people who adore this series, and I really hope you love Arrow as much as I do.

When you want something, you have to take it. You have to fight for it. And Tracker is more than worth the fight.

Will Lana be able to get through Tracker's tough exterior to the good man she knows is inside? Find out in the third book in this sexy series from bestselling author Chantal Fernando!

TRACKER'S END

Coming summer 2015 from Gallery Books

LANA

"ANNA, who is this?" a blond god calls out.

I step closer to my best friend. When Anna moved back into town, I'd never have guessed I'd be thrust into a world of motorcycle clubs and insanely hot, yet dangerous bikers. Nothing was going to be boring around here from now on—that was for sure. The man who approaches us is probably the most handsome guy I've ever seen in my life, and I'm not even exaggerating. Playful green eyes, angular features with a strong jaw covered in stubble, I can see tattoos peeking out from his white T-shirt. I can also see a muscled arm that I imagine wrapped around me.

Yeah, maybe I will start hanging around here more often.

Like, every day.

"Tracker, this is Lana." Anna introduces us, explaining, "This is one of Rake's friends."

I'm still getting used to calling Anna's brother, Adam, by his MC name. I've known Adam—I mean, Rake—since I was a young girl. He wasn't in an MC while he was in high school, but he still caused trouble wherever he went. At heart, though, he's a good guy and cares about his younger sister.

"Nice to meet you, Tracker," I say quietly, glancing shyly at him.

He smiles slowly. "Pleasure is all mine."

I have to remind myself to breathe.

"So you're Anna's partner in crime?" he asks, moving closer.

I glance at Anna, then back at him. "No. I'm usually the one trying to keep her out of trouble."

He laughs, rubbing his chest absently. My eyes follow the movement, unable to stop staring at the way his shirt clings to him. "I can see that. Only known her for a while, but I can already see how she starts trouble."

Anna gives him the finger.

Tracker gives me a look that clearly says *See what I mean?*

A small smile forms on my lips. "It's usually her mouth that gets her in trouble."

"Traitor," Anna fires back good-naturedly.

"Or because she thinks I need protecting."

Tracker studies me. "You are kind of small and cute. It's hot."

I duck my head shyly.

"Don't embarrass her," Anna chastises, then pauses. "And don't flirt with her. You have a woman, remember?"

I'm surprised by my disappointment at hearing he's taken, but I brush it aside. This is not the kind of guy I can trust, clearly. His flirty, friendly demeanor is definitely a well-practiced act—it's probably worked on countless women in the past. It won't work on me, though. Nope.

I try to keep my expression impassive as Tracker studies me for a moment, a thoughtful expression on his face. As if coming to a conclusion, he nods and moves his gaze away from me. "Just being friendly."

"Well, don't," Anna replies. "Come on, Lana. I'll introduce you to everyone else."

"Okay," I murmur, following behind her.

I can't help myself. I turn around to look back at him.

But he's not looking at me.

He's staring at the ground, lost in thought. He almost looks confused, his eyebrows drawn together, as though he doesn't understand whatever is on his mind.

I wonder what he's thinking about. I wonder if he's thinking about me. Not that it matters. He isn't available.

And I'm probably not his type anyway.

My thought is proven correct when a beautiful woman walks up to him.

His beautiful woman, I realize as she puts her hand against his chest with a seductive look on her face.

She's everything I'm not. Tall, slim, and dressed in tight leather pants, a black top showing off her toned flesh, and shiny red high heels. She's the epitome of a biker chick.

I look down at my worn jeans, graphic T-shirt, and flip-flops, and I keep walking. I may not be oozing sex appeal like that woman, but that's just not me. Sometimes you have to know who you are *and* who you're not.

ONE YEAR LATER

TRACKER

SEE her.

As usual, she's standing a little behind Anna, almost hiding. Fuck, she's shy. It's cute as hell. Women are usually forward with me, the same way I am with them. But Lana? Her gaze avoids mine as much as it can. I know she wants me. I know lust when I see it; but with her, there's something more there. She wants more than a fuck. She *deserves* more. For the last year I've tried to stay away from her. I didn't think I was good for her—oh, and I wasn't really single, either.

I'm still not good for her.

But wanting her—that has stayed constant since the moment I met her.

She's dressed in a blue top that hugs her petite frame and jeans that cup her juicy ass. That ass could bring a man to his knees. Feeling myself harden, I shift uncomfortably and force myself to remove my gaze from her. I scan the room, my gaze landing on Allie.

Fuck.

The situation between me and Allie is a huge clusterfuck. A whole fuckin' mess that I went along with because it was easy. She was here; she wanted me. She knew the lifestyle. Easy.

Allie is the daughter of a fallen member of the Wind Dragons Motorcycle Club. Because of this, we let her stay in our clubhouse, and we look after her. She's hooked up with a few of the other members, I know, but when her claws landed on me, the bitch dug deep. She wanted to be my old lady, and I let her play the part for a while without giving her the official title. Looking back, I know I didn't treat her how I would treat my old lady, how I would treat Lana if she was mine. The feelings just weren't there—and they still aren't. I was looking for something in Allie that I didn't find, but I held on anyway. I led her on more than I meant to. Staying with her was me being a selfish fuck, because I should have let her go when our relationship first started going south. Which was right after it fuckin' began. I have the feeling she knows it won't work, but is hopeful anyway. Whatever it is, it's a fucked up situation that needs to be over with.

Allie is jealous, mouthy and has a vindictive streak in

her that people shouldn't underestimate. She hates Lana with a passion and is jealous as hell of her. I mean, she'd been a bitch towards Faye and Anna as well, with her snide comments and general cattiness, but with Lana it's different. Faye and Anna can put Allie in her place, but Lana is more quiet and unaware. I've seen the scheming looks Allie gives Lana, almost like she's planning something. Maybe she sensed the connection I feel with Lana. I always tried to protect Lana from her, because I know Allie can be vicious. Whenever Lana was around, I gave Allie a little more attention, just to curb her jealousy. But by trying to save Lana from Allie, it pushed Lana away from me a little bit more each time. It had to be done, but now I want Allie and me to be completely done, and I want to close that distance with Lana.

Allie does have a sweet side, a vulnerable side, which she always tries to hide. It just wasn't enough for me to overlook the bad. Overall she was a hard bitch who was born to be on the back of a bike, just not mine.

But Lana . . .

I wanted her while I was with Allie, even though I pretended that I didn't. I tried to make sure she thought I only wanted her as a friend, but I'm not sure what message I really sent. Mixed fuckin' signals for sure.

My head turns, my attention on her once more.

She's beautiful. Sweet. Not a mean bone in her little body . . . and yet . . . she belongs on the back of my bike. The loyalty I've seen her show Anna when she and Arrow got together made me realize just how strong she is. She's so much tougher than I'd initially thought.

This one is *mine*. I wanted her then. And I want her now.

There is no more fighting it: Pretending I don't want her.

Trying to ignore her. Giving her the impression we don't have a chance in hell. All the games are coming to an end.

I'm going to soak all that sweetness up.

Consume her.

And no one is going to stand in my way—not even her.

She's my end.

LANA

CAN feel his gaze on me, but I pretend to ignore him. Instead, I concentrate on the beautiful little girl in front of me. Clover is the Wind Dragons Motorcycle Club princess. Daughter of the President, Sin, and his kick-ass wife, Faye, Clover is protected by all and loved by many. With jet black hair, hazel eyes, and the cutest smile, the five year old is a force to be reckoned with.

And I'm her nanny.

Today is only the second time I'm watching her, but honestly, she is a treat. It's extremely amusing to see how this little girl has all the rough men of the MC wrapped around her little finger. Hell, I can probably learn a thing or two from her. She's currently sitting on Arrow's knee, waiting impatiently as Arrow pulls a piece of strawberry candy from his pocket, unwraps it, and pops it into her mouth.

Did he carry around that candy for her?

The girl is good.

"Don't tell your mother," I hear Arrow tell her quietly, in that gravelly voice of his.

"I won't," Clover replies, grinning.

I shake my head at her, amused. Arrow is Anna's man, and the club's vice president. I happen to think that they're great for each other. As long as Anna is happy, then so am I, and it's clear that she's over-the-moon about Arrow. Feisty and strong as she is, Anna is like a happy cat when he's around, and he's the same. He adores her and would kill anyone who tried to hurt her. I wish I had that.

Anna's brother, Rake, is also a club member, which is how she met Arrow and I guess how I ended up here.

The men in the Wind Dragons MC are intimidating, but they've only ever been nice to me, albeit a little overbearing. I know that they love Anna, and as her best friend, they also look out for me. I like to think of myself as extended family.

Anna suggested to Faye that I would be a great nanny, and more importantly, that I could be trusted. She thinks I need the money, so when Faye asked me, I accepted. Really, I just couldn't think of a reason to refuse. But then, the more I thought about it, the more I wanted to do it. Faye needed someone, and I liked her and wanted to help. It also gave me more time with Anna. Before I was Clover's nanny, I usually only saw her once a week or so. So now I can see her more often, while getting paid to be here. Win-win.

And then there was Tracker. As much as I wanted to deny it, I was looking forward to seeing more of him, even if only from a distance.

Arrow stands, putting Clover down on the couch. "Gotta go, princess."

Clover pouts. "So soon? Why?"

"Hey, I'm still here," Tracker calls out, mock hurt in his tone.

Clover turns to Tracker. "I know, Uncle Tracker, but you don't have candy."

The two men both laugh, and I join in.

"I have to go and meet Anna," he says, patting her on the head. "I'll see you tomorrow."

Arrow's brown eyes then turn to me. "You okay, Lana?"

I nod. "I'm fine."

Why wouldn't I be? Okay, so I look out of place here. I *am* out of place here. My black hair is up in a messy bun, and I have on my reading glasses, no make-up, jeans, and a loose black tank top. Truth be told, I usually look better than this on a day-to-day basis, but I'm proving to myself that I do not care if Tracker finds me attractive or not.

Nope. I do not care.

Not one bit.

And neither does he.

"Call me if you need anything," Arrow murmurs, eyes darting between Tracker and me before leaving.

"I'm here if she needs anything," I hear Tracker say to him in a hard voice.

I'm pretty sure I hear Arrow mutter, "That's what I'm afraid of," as he walks out the door. With Arrow gone, Clover runs to sit next to Tracker, taking his hand in hers. Standing there awkwardly, I shift on my feet, no idea what to do with myself. With no option but to look at him, I let my eyes take him in.

Today his shoulder length blond hair is tied up in a bun, a *much* nicer bun than the one I am sporting, and it looks sexy on him. But then again, he always looks sexy. He has a certain appeal to him that I just can't escape. And I know I'm not the only one. His green eyes are steady on me and slightly narrowed. I wish I didn't find the stubble on his face so attractive, but I do. The man belongs on a magazine cover and is well aware of his charm. He's also a badass, dangerous biker—and the contradiction is extremely appealing.

"Clover," Tracker says. "Why don't you go get some coloring books and crayons?"

"Can I use one of the new ones you got me?" she asks in excitement.

"Uh, yeah!" he says, trying to match her excitement. She whoops, jumping off the couch and rushing off in search of her things.

Tracker turns to me. "Sit down, Lana," he commands quietly.

I look around the room before I sit down on the couch opposite him. "Okay."

"I'm not gonna bite," he says, flashing his sharp white teeth at me in a wolfish grin.

I think he does bite. And I want him to bite me.

Shit, I'm so screwed.

"What was that thought?" he asks, amusement written all over his too-handsome-for-his-own-good face.

"Nothing," I say with a casual shrug. I need to stop being so expressive. "Are you going to be here all day?"

Maybe I'll take Clover out somewhere. No point sitting here and being teased with something I'll never have.

"Yeah," he replies, tilting his head to the side and studying me. "I live here."

"Right," I reply, shifting on my seat.

"How is school going?" he asks, leaning back on the couch. I'm still getting my business degree. After high school, I'd worked and helped my mom instead of jumping straight into college. Because of this, I'm twenty four and still in school. I don't mind, though; I'm just happy to be studying something now.

"I'm on break now," I say. "Just started."

He nods, eyes widening. "Right. Anna told me that. I forgot." He flicks his tongue over his bottom lip, and I can't help but stare at it.

"So you're going to be here every day watching Clover?"

I shake my head. "Not every day. Four days a week. While I'm on break anyway."

I honestly don't know why Faye wants me to look after Clover here. There are always people going in and out. Anna told me that during the day, while Clover is here, the clubhouse is a family environment and everyone is well behaved, but when night falls, all bets are off. It doesn't explain why Faye doesn't have me watch Clover at her house. It would be safer and quieter, in my opinion—but Faye's the boss. I worry that maybe she doesn't fully trust me yet and wants there to be other people around just in case.

Visiting the clubhouse does have some perks, obviously. I can stare at Tracker when he isn't looking, sad as it sounds, and so far I find myself doing it at every opportunity. Anna is also here more often than not, so I'm looking forward to spending more time with her.

"That works," Tracker replies. I don't miss the way his gaze lowers to my chest, then lower, over the curve of my thighs. The tension in the room suddenly spikes. I quickly look away and am relieved when Clover comes back into the room, books and case in hand. She sits next to me and shows me all the different coloring books Tracker has bought her. I can feel Tracker's eyes on me, but I stay focused on her. Or try to, at least.

"I want to play a game," Clover says after fifteen or so minutes of coloring silently.

"What a great idea!" I blurt out. Tracker smirks, clearly aware of how tense I am around him.

"How about hide and seek?" he replies, glancing down at the little girl. "You go hide and I'll come find you."

Clover grins, then darts off the couch and into the hallway. I look back at Tracker to see his gaze steady on me. "I want to ask you something."

"What?" I ask, pushing my glasses up on the bridge of my nose.

I shift in my seat again as he lazily peruses my body from head to toe once more, his lips kicking up at the corner. "You free after you finish up here?"

Was I free? I open my mouth, then close it. "Why?"

"I want to take you for a ride," he says, licking his lower lip.

"A ride?" I repeat slowly. My mind jumps to dirty things.

He nods, eyes flashing with amusement. "Yes. I want to take you out on the back of my bike."

His intense stare lets me know that this means something important. I don't understand much about his MC lifestyle, except bits and pieces I've seen for myself or what Anna has told me. Excitement flutters in my stomach at the thought of my arms wrapped around him, my hair blowing in the wind. But then I think about Allie, and the butterflies exit, my stomach plummeting. This is always the issue with Tracker.

He isn't single. Even when he says he is, he isn't. She is always there. Sometimes on the sidelines, sometimes in the forefront, but nevertheless, *there*.

Why does it have to be her? Anyone but her. I am not about to share him, or any man. I want a man that only has eyes for me. A simple enough request, I'd think, but proving hard to find. The fact that I have a hard time trusting men doesn't help, either. I am one of those suffer-in-silence, keep everything to themselves type of people. I hardly ever put myself out there, which is probably why I'm still single.

"What about Allie?" I ask, curious as to what his answer will be.

Anna told me he's on- and off-again with her, and it's been

this way for years. To me, it sounds messy. A complication I don't need or want, no matter how drawn to him I am.

I want him, badly. But Tracker is bad news. I think about him. I dream about him. I fantasize about him. But I keep my distance. Why? Because I'm smart enough to know that we have no future. My head tells me one thing—stay away—but farther south says something else—invite him in. I get wet just at the thought of him. He has that much control over me. The wanting, will it ever end? I sure as fuck hope so.

The reality is that he probably has that effect on most women. Including Allie—that's why I do what I can to discourage his flirting and persistence, which is getting more and more frequent and which I'm having a harder time refusing.

Tracker scowls, a look of displeasure entering his dreamy eyes. "Allie and I are over. I'm not seeing anyone right now."

But for how long? I didn't want to be caught in the crossfire of their relationship. While he may insist that it's over with them, it's clear she doesn't think that, which suggests he's leading her on. Why would I want a guy like that? I am worth more than that.

I am at war with myself. I can only hope and pray that my mind wins over my body.

"Okay," I say slowly. "Ummm . . ."

I don't know what to say. The rejection is hard to form on my lips. The sounds didn't want to come out, my body betraying me once more.

His eyes and mouth soften, as if he senses my inner turmoil. "I thought maybe you and I could . . ."

Could what? Have sex?

Did he think I was a sure thing?

I mean, he had to know I was attracted to him, right? I can't stop the excitement I feel at the thought of being with him.

Just thinking about his touch makes me blush and makes my sensuality come alive. I want to explore that side of me, with him.

Then something occurs to me. Does he want me to be his rebound girl? The thought of that hurts. As lame as it sounds, I don't want to be his rebound. I want to be his forever girl. His wife. His old lady, as I've heard Faye be called.

Yeah, I'm living in a dream world. And if Tracker knew my thoughts he would run to the other side of the country. I don't even know if he does commitment. From what I've heard, he wasn't always faithful to Allie, another strike against him. Cheating is unforgivable to me. William was the first and only cheating scum I will have anything to do with. If Tracker's okay with sleeping around on a girl who cares about him—even if she is a massive bitch—then he's not someone I want to waste time on.

"I don't think so, Tracker," I reply before he can finish his sentence, looking down as I speak. The words hurt coming out, because really all I want to do is scream *Yes*! My resolve hardens, and I push those thoughts away.

"Why not?" he asks quietly. "I've seen how you look at me."

Yep, he knows. Of course he knows.

No wonder he thinks I'd get on the back of his bike just like that.

He knows.

And I can't believe he just said that. Red-cheeked, I choose to ignore his comment and point towards the hallway. "Go and find her."

He stands, but then crouches in front of me, his hands resting on both of my thighs. "We would be so fuckin' good together, you know that, right?"

I know. We would be. While it lasted anyway.

Then I'd be left to deal with the ramifications of giving in to him.

A broken heart.

"Yeah, but for how long?" I reply, forcing a smile that doesn't reach my eyes. "I don't want to be just another woman to you, Tracker."

He studies me, eyes flashing. "I don't think I'd put in this much effort for a one-night stand, Lana."

I think about that. What am I to him? Just a game? I don't know. I wish I could know what was going on in his head, but there's no way I'm ready to risk my heart with this man. I need someone I could trust, someone who I know will be faithful and loyal to me. When I stay silent, he sighs.

"Luckily, I'm a patient man," he murmurs, sliding a finger down my cheek with a gentleness that surprises me. He stands and calls out, "You better have found a good spot, Clover, because I'm coming."

I try and hide my grin as I watch him roam the clubhouse, looking for Clover. She must have hidden in the kitchen, because I hear laughter, his low chuckle and her high-pitched squeals, coming from there. For a second, I imagine that this is *our* house, and he is playing with *our* daughter.

Aaaand that's why I'm a good writer. I have a huge imagination.

Shit.